Romeo Stalker

Irene Woodbury

Publishing Coordinator – Sharon Kizziah-Holmes

Paperback-Press
an imprint of A & S Publishing
A & S Holmes, Inc.

ISBN -13: 978-1-951772-58-1

PART ONE

Jenny and Zane

CHAPTER 1

"Hey beautiful, what's up?" Zane purred softly, the back of his hand stroking Jen's long blond hair ever so lightly.

"Zane! Oh my God, what are you doing here?"

"Just wanted to check in with my baby," he said. "I've been trying to call since I got back, but you don't pick up. So I thought I'd swing by, and this is even better. I get to see you by moonlight."

Jen smiled and shook her head.

Zane looked in her eyes, searching for that familiar sweetness and love. There was an instant connection. The chemistry was still there. Her heart leapt and then fell. She was excited, scared, and confused all at the same time.

They gazed at each other for a few seconds, then six-foot Zane opened his well-muscled arms and enveloped the slender, five-foot-six blonde. Jen snuggled close, with her head resting on his shoulder. They stood like that for a few minutes, holding each other and savoring the thrill of being back in each other's arms.

Kissing lightly, then more deeply, Zane

murmured in Jen's ear, "Where's your mother?"

A pang of excitement went through her.

"At work," she said softly, panting lightly.

"Well then, let's go inside."

"Zane, no, we can't," she whispered, backing up and staring into his glistening, dark eyes. "A lot has happened since you left for prison. I need to talk to you. Can't we go someplace for a drink?"

It was one AM on a weeknight, but in Las Vegas that meant nothing, of course. There were all kinds of small, quiet bars they could run to and hide in a corner and have drinks and talk. Taking Jen by the hand, Zane walked her to his shiny black SUV. After helping her into the plush, leather passenger seat, he slipped in the driver's side, and off they sped to the Sandstorm, a dark, intimate cave of a watering hole a few blocks from Jen's house.

Ducking into a cozy corner booth, they ordered drinks. Jen looked sultry and alluring in a short black halter-dress with sequin trim and four-inch stiletto heels.

Zane stared at her pale blond hair, luminous green eyes, and full, lush breasts. She was checking him out, too. He had never looked better. Prison life had obviously agreed with Zane. He seemed healthier, like he had been eating and sleeping regularly. He was dressed in jeans, a blue silk shirt, and leather boots. His light, caramel-tone skin was smooth and clear, his longish black hair cut in sexy, blunt layers. A playful sparkle, intelligent and mischievous, danced in his dark-brown eyes. And his body had filled out nicely. Zane had been lifting weights in the big house and sported heftier biceps in his arms and shoulders. The whole package was very hot and sexy.

They couldn't take their eyes off each other, but when they began to talk, it got tense and stormy.

"Babe, I've missed you so much," Zane murmured with a tenderness and intensity that took Jen's breath away. "Two years in that hellhole, I hated every minute. But now I'm out and I want to change my life. I thought about you every second, you must know that. I wondered what you were doing, who you were with. I wrote you letters, but you never answered. Did you get them?"

"Um, no, I guess I didn't," she answered, gazing down and shaking her head.

"Your mother must have thrown them out," he muttered, annoyed. "Protecting you from a horrible, violent criminal. What the hell was she thinking?"

"I don't know," Jen sighed. "I guess she thought she was doing what's best for me."

"Well, she was wrong," Zane said defiantly. "I'm what's best for you, Jenny. I've always loved you, you know that. Yeah, I had some big time problems and got in trouble with the law, but it never meant I didn't love you. I thought of you every minute I was locked up. I wanted you every single day and night. That's the only thing that kept me going, knowing I was coming back to you."

He paused for a second, hoping for some response. But Jen remained silent.

"You look so beautiful, sweet and innocent," he went on, lifting her chin. "I hope nothing has changed between us. You were the first person I wanted to talk to, the first person I wanted to see.

But you ignored my calls for two weeks. Why did I have to sit in a parked car in front of your house for days, hoping to catch you coming home? That's not much of a welcome."

"I'm sorry," Jen murmured, "my mom again. She was worried about me seeing you. She's scared about the drugs and you getting in trouble again. She knows you're out, and made me promise to stay away from you. That's why I didn't take your calls. I didn't want to upset her and I was too scared of what you wanted from me."

"Sweetheart, you never need to be afraid of anything about me," Zane replied, reaching for her hand. "I'm a changed man. I want to go straight and be the guy you always wanted. I want a normal, happy life with you and my kids, and maybe one or two of our own someday. I want us all to be together as a family. What I really want is you."

Jen stared ahead blankly and said nothing.

"Zane, I'm sorry," she finally uttered, looking him in the eye. "Things can't be the way they were. They just can't. My life has changed. I've changed."

"Why do you say that? What's changed?" he demanded. "Is there someone else? Tell me! Are you with someone else?"

Jen couldn't bear to answer him. Gripping her vodka and tonic, she took a sip.

"Yes, it's true," she finally admitted after a tense pause. "There is someone else. A guy from San Jose I met at work. He flies in for weekends and we do fun stuff together. He's been really good to me. We're not seeing other people, so I can't be with you. Please understand what I'm saying."

"Understand what you're saying?" Zane asked, angry and flustered. "Yeah, I do, I just don't accept it. What happened between us was good, the best I've ever had. I learned a lot in the slammer and I don't ever want to go back. You're what kept me sane in that hellhole and now you want me to understand that you're with another guy? Well, I don't!"

He gripped Jen's wrist while he talked. A wave of fear coursed through her.

"Zane, I'm sorry, so sorry," she stammered. "But you have a whole new life ahead of you. You'll get a good job and lots of women will be interested in you."

"Well, I don't want them, I want you," he shot back.

"I'm sorry, that's just not going to happen. I can't be with you."

Her reply was stark and uncompromising. And her words, delivered in a clipped, staccato tone, carried an air of finality that left Zane speechless. Taking a deep breath, he leaned back in his chair and shook his head.

Somehow they moved past the strained dialogue and rambled on for another hour, at first about people and places they both knew, then round and round in circles about Jen's new boyfriend. Zane couldn't get the guy out of his head. He seemed obsessed. At three AM, they finally left the Sandstorm and Zane drove Jen home.

In her driveway, he gave it another try.

"Jenny, I know I screwed up big time. I've made

a lot of stupid mistakes. But I'm a new man now, and you're the main reason. Won't you give me another chance?"

Jen looked at the ground and shook her head gently. Kissing Zane on the cheek, she repeated softly, "Things have changed. You've got to accept that. I want to be straight with you."

Zane walked her to her door and they kissed lightly.

"This doesn't feel like the end, does it, Jen?" he asked plaintively, his nose nestled in her sweet-smelling hair. "Please tell me! I love you more than I've ever loved anyone. Promise me you'll think about this some more."

Jen wouldn't respond to his pleas. She felt too sorry for him and too weak. She just stood there for a long moment, hunched over sadly, searching for a graceful exit. After kissing him again, she turned suddenly and darted inside.

On the other side of the door, Jen felt queasy, sweaty, and faint. The heat was intense that August night in 2016, and Jen's mom, Brandi, had left the air conditioner off. The house was sweltering. Jen hit the button, collapsed on the living-room couch, and burst into tears. She couldn't stop. She realized she still had feelings for this guy and she couldn't shake them.

Exhausted, confused, and crying, Jen lay there motionless for long minutes, contemplating her fate. She didn't know what she would do. She couldn't go back to Zane. She felt intimidated by him, and yet she was touched by the emotion he showed that night. He was sober, straight, and ready to be the man she'd wanted him to be during the four years they were together.

But now she didn't really want him anymore. She wanted Colton, the guy she had been dating for nine months. The tech whiz from Silicon Valley gave her a feeling of safety, security, and stability. He was also cute, sexy, and romantic. With Zane there was always fun and thrills, but chaos, craziness, and a touch of danger, too. That stuff seemed old and dated now. Excitement, yes, but not the right kind.

Jen had outgrown her need for nonstop drama and amusement-park thrills. Her childhood with Brandi had also been a roller-coaster ride through life's uncertainties and insecurities. And then there was the baggage that went with it: the loneliness, money problems, lack of family and a steady father figure. All this was pushing Jen towards Colton. She had never met his wealthy family back in San Francisco, but she hoped that would happen soon. At least she knew she could count on him. Colton was always there for her, sincere in his feelings, and that was the important thing.

Lying on the couch that night, through her tears and runny mascara, Jen weighed her options. She wondered how she and Colton would end up. Would they marry someday? How would his family feel about her job as a pop-out girl, and her drama-queen childhood as the daughter of a thrice-divorced cocktail waitress in Vegas? There was so much heat and passion between her and Colton now, but would their relationship stand the test of time?

CHAPTER 2

When Jen woke up at nine, Brandi was asleep in her room. After a quick shower, Jen threw on a lavender terry-cloth robe and ambled to the kitchen to start the coffee. She was glad Brandi wouldn't be up for a while. It gave her time to sort through the confusion and decide whether to tell her about seeing Zane. Maybe she should hide it from her because it would upset her too much? No, Jen thought, that would just get her into more trouble down the road. She would have to level with her mom.

Camped at the kitchen table that hot morning with the sunlight streaming in, Jen sipped her coffee and thought back on her long, troubled history with Zane. Meeting him was the most exciting thing that had ever happened to her, but also the worst.

It had all started back in 2010, when she was a perky high school senior known to all as Jenny Conover. She hadn't dated much, which pleased her mom, who wanted to protect her daughter from the opposite sex for as long as possible.

Jenny was a pleasant, upbeat girl who was too

busy with school work, friends, and singing and dancing lessons to pay much attention to boys. But at age 17, all that changed when she landed her first job in a coffee shop at the Venetian and met Zane Hollister.

Almost overnight, Brandi, who'd been a cocktail waitress at the same casino for over 20 years, became an anxious, worrying, fretful parent.

Her fears were justified. Zane was no mere boy. Far from it. He was every inch a man, or looked to be. Tall and rugged, with taut muscles and six-pack abs, he came across as powerful and sexy.

He usually hung out in nudie clubs on Industrial Road, making drug deals, or huddled in smoky poker rooms with undesirable types. But one day he and a couple of his cohorts slithered into the Venetian coffee shop, and the spark was lit.

Zane started showing up there a few times a week, and often left Jenny huge tips for coffee and a doughnut. God only knows where those $100-bills came from, or any of the other money he threw around so casually.

Jenny was impressed and flattered. Every time Zane walked in the door, she was breathless with excitement.

He was 25 years old, with a rap-sheep a mile long. A smooth-talking, manipulative father of two, with suave good looks and a dark, tangled past. Trouble with a capital T, in Brandi's book.

Jenny, on the other hand, was an innocent, underage virgin. Right away, Zane started asking her to go out with him to clubs with fake IDs, to Reno for high-roller weekends, or to spend nights with him in his ranch-style house on Cinder Rock Drive, right near the Conovers' place in Summerlin.

Zane was a real ladies' man, with countless ex-girlfriends, an endless parade of big-breasted blond or raven-haired molls and bitch-waifs, with major drug habits and the poor self-esteem to go with them.

Brandi found out all about him because, at the time, she was dating Nick Tatro, a fiftyish, craggy-faced security guard at the Venetian who worked part-time for Vegas Metro. When Jenny started talking up Zane, Brandi's maternal instincts kicked in and she went straight to Nick for the lowdown.

From what the private eye could find, Zane was bad news, dealing cocaine, meth, and heroin, and probably an addict himself. Jenny was too young and naive to see any of this. She was totally dazzled by the suave bad-boy from east Las Vegas.

And why wouldn't she be? He showered her with presents of pretty clothes and jewelry, wheeled her around town in a shiny black SUV, and spent money like there was an endless supply. Dressed in expensive silk shirts, designer jeans, and leather jackets, Zane treated Jenny to show openings, five-star restaurants, and fancy clubs.

Reveling in the constant stream of money and attention, the pretty high school senior quickly grew spoiled. The geeky-faced boys at Cimarron Memorial High never stood a chance.

A couple of months after they met, Zane got Jenny together with his bright-eyed, high-wire kids, Danny and Dakota. The foursome were soon kicking back for fun outings at the Adventuredome in Circus Circus, Lion Habitat at MGM Grand, and Dolphin Habitat at Mirage. Jenny fell hook, line and sinker for those kids, and their smoking-hot, smooth-talking daddy.

Much too soon, a love affair blossomed. It was Jenny's first, and Brandi, a mother herself at age 18, was terrified her daughter would get pregnant. She made sure she went on the pill, but also told Jenny flat out, "This guy is not for you. He's a disaster waiting to happen. Stop seeing him, or you'll end up pregnant, on drugs, in jail, or dead."

But Jenny wouldn't listen.

"Mom, you're being over-protective," she would respond. "Zane told me all that police-record stuff is bogus. I don't know what he does in his spare time, and I don't care. I just know that when we're together, he treats me like gold."

Brandi threatened to restrict Jenny's free time on the Strip. But at the end of the day, what more could she do? Jenny had a good job that she loved. She made ample tips, and they needed the money.

And so the love affair throttled on. Zane was the most glamorous, exciting guy Jenny had ever met, and the sexual chemistry was off the charts. Their love-making was tender, passionate, and intense, something she remembered in detail to this day.

Brandi never let up on her crusade to get Zane out of Jenny's life. To appease her, Jenny would sometimes agree to stop seeing him. But she never actually did. The lying and duplicity rumbled on for a couple of years. All along, Brandi remained nervous and on edge.

To her great relief, Zane met his downfall in the

wee, small hours one Sunday morning in January 2014 at the Rio casino. State narcotics' agents put the bite on him for selling heroin and meth to an undercover DEA (Drug Enforcement Agency) agent.

For the first time the cops, who knew Zane had ties to a west coast drug cartel, were able to catch him in the act. It was a crushing blow for the young tough. He was convicted and sentenced to two years in the Northern Nevada Correctional Center (NNCC), a medium-security prison in Carson City.

Brandi was overjoyed. She felt like she could finally breathe again. Jenny was shocked and sad, but not for long. She was level-headed enough to know Zane was trouble, and domineering, too. And thanks to her mom's urgings, she was well aware that she needed to focus more on her own life.

After Zane went to prison, Jenny left the coffee shop and briefly got a job as a background dancer in the Legends in Concert show at the Imperial Palace Casino. It was fun and she gained lots of exposure, but the paychecks were meager.

In the spring of 2014, a few months after she turned 21, Jenny, who now went by the sleeker, more grown-up Jen, landed a gig at a thriving Vegas start-up called Stripper Grams. Her specialty would be popping out of six-foot layer cakes at parties and special events.

Whatever the occasion, Jen adored doing pop-outs. It was creative and challenging and made people smile and enjoy themselves. She was entertaining them, and using her singing and dancing talents to rake in huge tips. Of course she was also stripping, and that didn't please Brandi. But she was clad in a lace bikini at the end of her act, so it wasn't like she was totally nude.

Jen was having a blast doing the cake follies, and the customers were wild for her. She was a classic American beauty, with a combination of Marilyn Monroe's pale, sultry-baby sexiness, and Grace Kelly's finely-chiseled wholesomeness. Who could resist that?

And then there were the pop-out cakes, also irresistible. The girls would emerge from a tall, plastic cylinder hidden in the center of the towering confections and do their acts. The six-foot cakes, usually in alternating layers of chocolate and yellow, would then be sliced and devoured by the boisterous conventioneers. Luscious pop-out girls, followed by mouth-watering cake. What a win-win!

The only downside to all this lusciousness: Jen was often pursued by turned-on customers at the events she worked. She soon learned to avoid contact with most of these strange and smarmy characters. But in October 2015, with Zane still locked away in Carson City, she met someone she actually liked and everything changed.

CHAPTER 3

When he saw a scantily clad Jen emerge from his boss's birthday cake in a massive ballroom at Caesar's, Colton Barnes, a hotshot systems analyst from Silicon Valley, was dazzled. At the raucous party afterwards, he walked up to the gorgeous blonde and introduced himself. Both were smitten from the get-go, and ended up going for drinks at a swank club after the event.

It didn't end there.

They spent that night in Colton's suite at Caesar's. The besotted twosome barely had time to tear each others' clothes off, the attraction was so electric. The sex was sweet, intense, and powerful. It was real, and blew them both away. One of those perfect nights you sometimes have in life.

The next morning, while Jen slept, Colton slipped downstairs to a boutique and bought her a turquoise-blue silk dress with a lapis necklace and bracelet set to match. When Jen woke up, she was surprised and delighted to see white boxes tied with pink ribbons lying at the foot of the king-size bed.

Colton kissed her passionately, and the boxes tumbled to the floor as they fell back into bed for a rousing start to the day.

An hour later, Jen was still in afterglow when there was a knock at the door. Colton opened it and an elegant room-service cart with a vase of red roses in its center was wheeled in. While gazing at comped newspapers, they savored a tasty, romantic breakfast in bed. Then Jen wriggled into her new blue dress, and off they traipsed for a day of fun on the Strip.

Colton flew back to San Jose on Monday morning. But he couldn't stop thinking about the beautiful blonde he had met over the weekend. How sweet and charming she was, so different from all the girls he'd known at Stanford and beyond. Compared to her, they were all either silly and immature, or brittle and hard-edged. Yes, Jen was the gorgeous girl next door who'd popped out of Matt's birthday cake, but she was also an intelligent, vulnerable, interesting person.

It might seem strange that a 30-year-old Silicon Valley super-geek, who was a straight-A student from first grade through college, would fall so hard for a pop-out girl from the other side of the tracks. But when you looked more closely at the whole picture, it made perfect sense.

Colton was tired of the girls he'd met at Stanford and in Silicon Valley. After his latest break-up, he'd made up his mind: no more girl-geeks who ate, drank, and slept technology. Most of these women didn't know an STD from a computer virus. As far as they were concerned, it was the same thing.

Colton wanted someone softer, more down to earth and real, someone like Jen who just wanted to have fun and love him for who he was, not for what he could do for her career. She also wasn't one of those rich Nob Hill debs he met at his parents' dinner parties who lived to impress, and be impressed. Who name-dropped every five seconds and casually dropped gauche hints about daddy's net worth. These women were just as competitive and hard-edged, in their own way, as the tech types. Ballbreakers in Tori Burch dresses and Jimmy Choo shoes. No, Colton was fed up with both geek girls and debutantes. He wanted a real relationship with someone he could trust and relax with.

Gorgeous Jen totally fit the bill. She and Colton were crazy about each other from day one. But the idea of a relationship seemed impractical: she lived in Vegas, he in San Jose. That wasn't about to stop Colton. He'd never dated a girl in Sin City before, and was anxious to get to know the town better. And besides, he loved racking up frequent flyer points. So, starting that month (October 2015), he became a regular on Southwest #4132.

On Friday afternoons, barring any delays, he'd make it to Vegas in time for Happy Hour on the Ghost Bar deck with Jen. Afterwards, they'd dine at someplace chic but casual like The Palm, or Rendezvous at Caesar's. Now and then, they also hit drop-dead romantic spots, like the Top of the World at Stratosphere, or Jen's favorite, Eiffel Tower restaurant in Paris. Money was not a concern, which gave them endless options.

Afterwards, the hot couple would strut their

stuff at a show like Love at Mirage, or Celine Dion at Caesar's. Then it was time to hit the casino for some blackjack, craps, or video poker. If they were winning, they'd play on. If not, they'd saunter to another club, like Cleopatra's Barge, or Pure, for music and dancing. Whatever was left of the night, and all of the next morning, was spent blissfully tucked away in each others' arms in Colton's suite at Caesar's.

Jen usually worked one day each weekend, but on her day off the couple would savor fun little adventures that Colton would research and book from his office in San Jose. One weekend they went tandem skydiving in Mesquite, which was a blast. They also tried downhill skiing on Mount Charleston, blasted through the Valley of Fire in pink jeeps, relished hot-air ballooning over the Vegas valley, and rode through the Toiyabe National Forest on Harleys.

Sunday nights were always sad for the couple because they both knew Colton would be flying home the next morning. By Monday afternoon, he'd be back in his office and hard at work. During the week, he and Jen called each other at least once a day to check in. They missed each other and were always anxious for Friday to roll around again.

By the time Zane was released from prison in July 2016, the couple had been dating in the lap of Vegas luxury for nine blissful months.

As Jen sat at the kitchen table that hot Wednesday morning while Brandi slept, she couldn't help wondering, what now?

CHAPTER 4

After changing into shorts and a tee, a confused, agitated Jen drove to the gym to work off some nervous energy before facing her mom later. By two pm, she and Brandi were both awake, at home, and in the kitchen eating grilled-cheese sandwiches.

Jen knew that the mere mention of Zane's name would rile Brandi, but, still, she felt uncomfortable keeping her encounter with him a secret.

"Mom," she began hesitantly, setting her sandwich down, "Zane was waiting for me when I got home last night. He walked up to me in the driveway and..."

"No, damn it, no," Brandi cried, leaping from her chair. "You need to stay the hell away from that lowlife-scum. He's no good for you!"

Jen was startled but hardly deterred by her mom's outburst. As calmly as possible, she went on to explain how the ex-lovers couldn't tear apart and ended up having drinks at the Sandstorm.

"After two years in prison," she said, "he seems different, you know, more serious and mature. I think he was totally sober and straight last night, no drugs. He said he wants me, his kids, and him to be together as a family, and he'll take care of us all. He wants me to come back."

"Oh, no, no, never!" Brandi retorted, waving her arms wildly. "Of course he wants you to come back. You're the best thing that ever happened to him. No, absolutely not. I'm telling you, cut it off right now!"

"Mom, please, don't you think you're overreacting a bit?"

"No, I don't," Brandi shot back. "When it comes to Zane, there's no such thing as overreacting." Then, with her face taut and darkening, she asked, "So, what did you say? How did you react to Zane's tender declaration of love in our driveway?"

"I, uh, told him we can't be together again, that there's someone else I'm happy with," Jen replied. "I felt really sad turning him down. I could see how hurt and disappointed he was.

"He said he thought of me constantly while he was gone," Jen continued, "and that he wrote me lots of letters. But I never got them. Mom, what happened? How many were there, and what did you do with them?"

Sitting back down, Brandi shook her head and clenched her arms tightly.

"Okay, okay," she finally admitted, "Guilty as charged. But you're my daughter, my baby. Since I was 18 years old, you've been my sun, my moon, my stars, the center of my universe. And Zane Hollister's a smooth-talking criminal with a record a mile long. Why would I want my baby mixed up with someone like that? Why wouldn't I do all I could to keep those letters from you, so you could meet someone else and have a chance for a happy, normal life?"

"Mom, I get all that. I know you did what you did out of love. But I wish you had at least let me read them and make up my own mind. So, how many were there, and what happened to them?"

"A couple dozen, maybe," Brandi said sheepishly. "They're in a shoe box upstairs. I'll let you have them, but don't get all dreamy-eyed and romantic and think that just because that slimy criminal wrote to you from prison, you owe him something. You don't. You're better off with Colton.

"There's more security and stability," she went on. "He's been good for you, Jen. I haven't met him yet, but from what you've told me, he's a nice, normal guy who's polite, well educated, and from a wealthy family. Not a bad way to go, sweetie."

"Yeah, mom, I know," Jen nodded, "but I've never even met his folks. At least with Zane, I know I'm accepted. I'm not so sure about Colton's parents. His father's a big-deal plastic surgeon to all these rich society women. Colton's mom gets her hair done three times a week and throws fancy dinner parties that everyone in town wants to attend. She's a major fund-raiser for children's charities and the homeless. And his sister's studying at UCLA to become a pediatrician.

"They're all well-educated and high class. What would they think of my job?"

"Don't worry about that, honey," Brandi said

firmly, patting Jen's arm. "You can always make a career change if you need to. I'll bet you're a whole lot smarter, prettier, and nicer than anyone in Colton's family. But even if things don't work out with him, Zane Hollister is not the answer."

Then, with an air of resignation, Brandi added, "I'll give you the letters. But don't get all love-struck and carried away. Remember, if things don't work out with Colton, there are plenty of other fish in the sea."

Jen nodded and seemed to agree as she finished her grilled cheese.

That afternoon, stretched out on the couch, she read Zane's letters. They were beautiful little essays, laced with drama and poetry, and filled with love, remorse, promises, and endless compliments. As Jen read them, she was touched by Zane's sincerity and persistence.

But she was also alarmed. He was dead serious, which made her suddenly realize she needed to stop this whole thing before it got out of hand.

Two days later, Colton jetted into Vegas, as usual, on Friday night. He and Jen, dazzling in a pale-blue silk halter-dress trimmed in lace, had drinks at Hyde in Bellagio. Later, over dinner at Rendezvous, a French place they both loved at Caesar's, Colton remarked that Jen seemed a bit sad and distracted. Was there something on her mind, he wanted to know.

Between bites of Sole Meuniere and sips of chardonnay, she launched into the whole wrenching Zane saga.

"He was 25 when we met," she recalled softly. "A good-looking, cocky, confident guy who grew up in the rough part of town. His father was a con artist drug dealer, in and out of prison, and his mom was addicted to drugs, too.

"When Zane was 13, his father died trying to escape from a prison chain gang. That was the turning point, I guess," Jen said somberly, shaking her head. "After that he avoided school and got into drinking and drugs. By the time he was 21, he had a rap sheet a mile long. Mostly drug-possession and petty burglary offenses."

As Jen spun the narrative, Colton's face darkened. His hand tightened around his wine glass. He seemed upended and almost startled by what he was hearing.

"Jen, you're such a straight arrow, how could you get involved with a sleazy character like that?" he finally asked, shaking his head in bewilderment. "This sounds so far removed from what you're about."

"It is, Colton," Jen assured him, "but I was young, and I knew nothing about the drug or criminal worlds. I was too caught up in the excitement and glamour, I guess. I thought Zane was fun, a little dangerous, and really hot. By the time we met, he'd had two kids by two drug divas who were both long gone. His mom took care of them from the day they were born, and then while he was in prison."

Looking down awkwardly, Colton nodded.

"Speaking of mothers," he remarked after a brief pause, "where was yours when all this was going on? She must have been pretty upset that you were dating this shady dude."

"She was," Jen replied. "Mom has this friend named Nick, a security guard at the Venetian. She asked him to check out Zane's background, and he turned up all this shocking stuff about his family and police record.

"Mom confronted me with it and told me point blank to stop seeing him. But I was young and in love for the first time. I wasn't about to give up the most exciting part of my life.

"From then on, I lied to her about where I was going and what I was doing, and went right on seeing Zane. We ended up being together for four years.

"The only thing that could separate us was prison," she recalled. "He got busted in a DEA raid at Rio in early 2014 and was sentenced to two years at a prison in Carson City.

"The reason I'm telling you all this," Jen continued, after steadying herself with another sip of wine, "is that Zane just got released a few weeks ago, and he's been trying to call me, nonstop. I've managed to avoid him, but a couple of nights ago, he showed up in my driveway at 2 AM, and we ended up going for drinks and talking. I told him about you. He was upset, and kept saying he wanted us to get back together."

Clearing his throat nervously, Colton shuffled in his chair. Jen's revelations had hit him hard and he couldn't seem to speak. He was shocked and concerned for Jen. And no doubt a tad worried about himself, too. He asked Jen what she wanted.

"I don't want to get back together with him," she replied in a firm, clear tone. "Believe me, it's over. Back then I didn't know anything about the drug world. It was creepy. There were always strange people lurking around, delivering packages or collecting money. Some of them had guns. But by the time I had a clue what was going on, I was too in love to be able to leave. I couldn't just walk away, and Zane wouldn't have let me anyway.

"Towards the end, right before he went to prison, It was like I was walking a tightrope, waiting for some disaster to happen. I could never deal with that kind of tension again. But I don't want to reject him, you know, in a way that makes him go back to using. I couldn't live with myself if that happened. Somehow, I've got to convince him he's better off without me, and that he needs to move on with his life and find someone else."

Looking down and shaking his head, Colton asked, "Better off without you? I don't think he's going to buy that. What will you do if he refuses to accept that? I don't think he'll go quietly."

Taking another sip of wine, Jen stared at Colton.

"Well, he'll have to," she insisted, "he'll just have to. He can't have a relationship with someone who won't see him or take his calls, can he? He'll have to realize it's over and move on."

As they nibbled chocolate-mousse cake and ordered more wine, Colton glanced over at Jen with doubts in his eyes. She was glad she had bared her soul about her ex, but she couldn't help noticing that Colton seemed shocked and disappointed in her for having this dark chapter in her past.

A pop-out girl with an ex-convict-ex. Not exactly the ideal profile for the glamorous babe that he loved and was currently sleeping with. It seemed to sadden him and make him think twice about her. He also found himself wondering if Jen had other dark secrets that were just as shocking and distasteful.

Though Friday night's dinner was awkward, Colton and Jen went on to have a pleasant-enough weekend. She stayed with him, as usual, in his suite at Caesar's. When she woke up in his arms on Saturday morning, she felt safe and secure, a million miles from the ugly, scary world of drug addiction.

That weekend, they enjoyed an Eagles concert at the MGM Garden Arena, took a jeep tour of scenic Red Rock Canyon, and stuffed themselves with shrimp pizza at Il Pastore. Jen had only one pop-out gig, a Saturday-afternoon event for pediatric dentists at Mirage, so that was manageable.

On Sunday morning, over brunch at Bouchon in Venetian, the couple talked more about the future. While carefully dodging the Zane issue, Colton pledged his love for Jen, a mild surprise for both of them, and hinted that maybe someday he would relocate to Vegas, where the two of them could live together as a "preliminary step towards something more permanent."

He was learning to appreciate the many sides and charms of Sin City, he said, and felt there was strong potential to launch a tech start-up there, or perhaps an offshoot of the company he worked for, QuInternet Electronics.

All this took Jen by surprise. Though it was a bit vague and hypothetical, it reassured her at a time when she really needed a boost. She was happy and at peace. But not for long.

CHAPTER 5

The following week, Jen picked up the phone without looking at the caller ID. Mistake, big time. It was Zane. After a quick spurt of small talk, he asked her to go to a Santana concert at Hard Rock Casino with him. An agitated, uncomfortable Jen begged off, claiming she was busy with work. Zane was disappointed, but let it go. Then, two days later, he called again with another plea. He let her know his two kids, ages 7 and 9, missed her like mad and were dying to reconnect. Could she join the three of them for dinner at the Rainforest Café in MGM Grand?

Jen adored Zane's kids, and couldn't resist. As she trekked through the casino on her way to the restaurant, two raven-haired little scamps suddenly accosted her, shrieking "Jenny! Jenny!" When Jen, dressed in an animal-print sundress and sexy sandals, leaned down to greet Danny and Dakota, she was engulfed in sticky little hugs. Standing nearby in a bank of slots was Zane, grinning ear to ear.

The kids were overjoyed to see Jen, and it lifted

her spirits, too. But that's all it was, an innocent, early dinner for four. Of course, Zane wanted more, and started peppering Jen with questions about the time she spent with Colton. She managed to put him off, but the evening ended on a sour note when she insisted on leaving, before dessert, to meet friends at Bellagio.

For the next month, Colton and Jen's weekends were fun and normal. Zane continued to pester her for dates, but Jen would find ways to decline. Undaunted, he kept trying. He wasn't taking the hint. He was hoping she'd change her mind; she was hoping he'd back off.

Zane's calls finally became so incessant that they started to drive Jen crazy. "Somebody please save me from this guy!" she wailed one morning after listening to a recording of Zane's kids greeting her on her voice-mail. Furious and frustrated, she finally decided to unplug her phone and shut the world out.

She was busy with work, and taking singing and dancing lessons again, so it was fairly easy. But the effect on Zane was dramatic: he became more agitated and desperate. At some point, the stream of rejections became so upsetting and infuriating that he began drifting back to drugs.

Unscrupulous doctors would routinely write him prescriptions for uppers and downers, even though they knew he was addicted. These pills made Zane mean and unpredictable. One day when Jen picked up the phone by accident and got into a brief conversation with him, she heard the familiar slurring in his voice and realized he was back on drugs. Her heart sank. She knew Zane was now a loose cannon, a disaster waiting to happen.

Soon, bizarre, scary incidents started to occur on Jen's weekends with Colton. At first, these were mere subtle intrusions. They would be asleep in Colton's suite at Caesar's and the phone would ring at three AM. Colton would answer, but the caller would abruptly hang up. This happened again and again. After the calls, Jen and Colton would lie awake for hours, trying to convince themselves it wasn't Zane. But they both knew it was. Finally, Colton started unplugging the phone every night.

Then Zane started showing up on their dates, or following them around. One night they were playing blackjack at Bellagio when he suddenly appeared and parked himself at their table. It rattled the couple and made them uncomfortable, but what could they do? After saying hi to Jen, Zane kissed her in a tender, intimate way that suggested they had once been lovers. She couldn't hide it, neither could he, and Colton took it all in.

Sometimes they would be eating dinner, and Zane would saunter by with a flashy, trampy-looking girl, or a few of his raunchy pals. This happened at Mesa Grill and at a Mexican place in MGM called Diego's.

One morning at the Carnegie Deli in Mirage, Colton and Jen were having eggs and hash browns, when Zane suddenly appeared in head-to-toe black leather with another creepy-looking dude.

He didn't do a thing. Just got a plate of food, parked himself at a nearby table with his ominous-looking cohort, and glared. The message was clear:

he was there, and watching. Colton's blood was boiling, and he started to get up. Jen begged him not to, but he ignored her and marched over to Zane's table. Moving within inches of his face, Colton demanded, "What are you doing here? Get out and leave us alone. Jen wants to be with me."

Staring back at him in a cold, menacing way, Zane replied, "I don't owe you any explanations for what I do. The last time I looked, eating breakfast at Carnegie Deli wasn't illegal. Now crawl back to your table, geek-dude, and leave me the hell alone. My eggs are getting cold."

CHAPTER 6

With every passing month, Colton and Jen's weekends became more strained and tense. Zane was now on their trail, full steam, stalking and taunting them. He seemed to be showing up everywhere. He had an eerie sense of where they were going to be, like riding the High Roller, a towering, ferris-wheel-like monstrosity on the center Strip. One afternoon, Jen caught him peering at her from an adjoining gondola. And then there was the time at Shake Shack in New York New York, when they glanced up from their burgers and saw him glaring at them from a counter stool.

Zane-sightings at some of the couple's favorite haunts were becoming more scary and intrusive. But what could they do? Tell the police he was stalking them? How could they prove it? The cops wanted specific acts and incidents. Zane was showing up at the same places, but he wasn't actually doing anything. Staring at them wasn't a crime.

The whole situation was becoming totally unnerving. In his own twisted way, Zane was reminding them he was still out there, lurking in the shadows, waiting for Jen to come back to him.

Jen thought of calling him and pleading with him to stop, but decided against it. The thought of talking to him directly repulsed her. Besides, wasn't that just what he wanted? It would only reinforce his warped, sicko behavior.

Her anxieties were further stoked by her belief that Zane was doing drugs again, big time, and probably dealing them as well. Both she and Colton were at wit's end, praying for a return to normalcy. But Zane's constant presence made that impossible.

And then, in November 2016, events began to escalate in an even more dangerous, desperate way. Zane gave up calling Jen and asking her out. He stopped showing up as often on her dates with Colton. Instead, he dropped behind the scenes and began scheming to inflict physical harm.

The first attack came the day after Thanksgiving 2016. Jen had performed pop-outs at a pair of sports-themed parties on the holiday, and was now craving a fun adventure. Colton and she planned a thrilling outing with Jen's best-friend and pop-out-girl pal, Amber Dean, and her boyfriend, Dave Perkins, a lighting technician for the Fantasy show at Luxor.

Their goal was to conquer SlotZilla, a monster zip line that glides high above Fremont Street in downtown's tourist district. From cables dangling 10 stories high, riders are propelled through the air, over and along a four-block route. They are affixed to wires solely by steel clamps as they sway and bobble through a neon maze of casino lights. The

Cyclops-like contraption leaves riders giddy but grateful to survive the threat of a 114-foot free-fall.

Colton and Jen had conquered the beast before, but Amber and Dave were SlotZilla virgins and psyched to take their first ride.

The weather was chilly that late fall day and all of them were bundled in jeans and leather jackets. The carefree couples began by feasting on greasy burgers and fries at the Heart Attack Café, an eatery for the overly indulgent that dares corpulent diners to weigh in on a scale at the door. Jen and Amber could barely finish their Coronary Dogs with Flatliner Fries, and the guys were put to the test with Triple-Bypass Burgers, all of it served up by waitresses in nurse uniforms.

With their bellies near bursting, they ambled up an iron stairway to the SlotZilla ticket cage, where they flung caution aside and plunked down $80 for four tickets.

After being strapped into sturdy harnesses, the foursome rode an elevator further up to the lift-off platform. There, before anyone could ask too many questions or chicken out, they were clamped to SlotZilla's thin wires and thrust off into the great unknown. Suddenly, they were soaring like mighty eagles down Fremont Street.

It was an overcast afternoon, and downtown Vegas was its usual chaotic, moveable feast of jugglers, semi-nude stragglers, panhandlers, and glammed-up showgirls. Brightly colored, retro casinos lined both sides of Fremont Street Mall, which was jammed with stalls hawking popcorn, paintings, and jewelry. Both couples shrieked in ecstasy as they tumbled through the air, hugging their cables for dear life.

At 35 miles per hour, they zoomed down the lively boulevard, past the nouveau-riche D Casino, quirky Four Queens, classic Golden Nugget, and grungy Mermaid's Casino. And then suddenly, Vegas Vic, a towering neon cowboy that rides herd over downtown, was in their faces.

They were howling with delight as the ride drew to a close, still four stories above the street that was teeming with tourists, souvenir shops, and showgirls.

"This is amazing," Colton hollered, waving at Jen, who looked back at him.

"Awesome, isn't it?" she yelled in response.

"Oh my God!" he screamed suddenly, even louder, his eyes wide.

Jen turned back again and saw Colton's head suddenly jerk upwards as he grabbed the main strap that connected his harness to the line. Following where he looked, Jen cried, "Oh, no!" as she noticed his strap had frayed and was barely holding him.

"Help!" she wailed over and over. But nothing could be done. In horror and powerless to do anything, she watched as the last fibers broke, severing Colton from the cable and plunging him towards the street below.

"Colton!" she shrieked as she watched the love of her life hurtling downwards to certain death.

A freak turn of luck saved him at the last moment. His terrifying dive was cushioned by a giant wooden bin of tee shirts and jackets parked on the pavement in front of Mermaid's Casino. Crashing into the container with a wallup, Colton bounced upward trampoline-like a dozen feet, then plopped back down on the dense, soft mound of cotton and fleece. The impact was hard and dizzying enough to leave him bruised and in shock.

As soon as Jen and the others finished their ride, they hurried down two flights of stairs, leapt out of their harnesses, and raced one long block to where Colton was lying.

Frenzy had enveloped Fremont Street. A pair of Metro cops rushed up to caution the semi-conscious Colton not to move until an ambulance arrived.

Surging to the front of the crowd, Jen told security officers she was his girlfriend. The minute she saw that he had survived the fall, she burst into tears. She knew he could easily have broken his back, or been killed by the impact.

When the paramedics arrived, they gently placed Colton on a stretcher, loaded it into an ambulance, and rushed him to Las Vegas General. Dave and Amber stayed behind, while Jen rode with him.

"You're going to be okay, babe," she whispered over and over as they raced to the emergency room. There doctors x-rayed Colton and gave him flexibility and motor skills' tests. Jen was assured that his injuries weren't serious, just minor cuts and bruises and some swelling on his ribs and legs. The nurses assured her he would be released the following day.

As Jen paced in the hospital corridor, she wondered how this ghastly accident could have happened. Her mind suddenly zeroed in on Zane.

Could he have somehow damaged the straps? But how would he have known when and where to strike? Did he have an accomplice?

Jen later decided that the idea was probably too preposterous to consider seriously, and Metro agreed. Their preliminary investigation found no evidence of foul play. They concluded the whole incident was a bizarre mishap caused by a faulty harness strap.

Suspicions still lingered in Jen's mind. She told the cops that Zane had been stalking them for months. But without hard evidence, they could only list him as a person of interest, and nothing more.

And so the freakish SlotZilla incident gradually faded into the background, and life somehow trundled on.

CHAPTER 7

As Christmas 2016 approached, Jen was busy popping out of festively decorated cakes at a plethora of conventions and holiday parties. She and Colton planned to celebrate the big day with their respective families. Colton and his clan were inviting a slew of relatives for a traditional turkey dinner in their elegant San Francisco townhome. Between pop-outs, Jen planned to spend a cozy Christmas with her mom and grandmother, who was flying in from Houston.

In mid-December, Jen and Colton spent a final, pre-holiday weekend together. There was a romantic dinner at Eiffel Tower restaurant and a holiday concert at Paris. Then they returned to his suite at Caesar's and concluded the evening with a long, thrilling romp on the king-size bed. It was a sweet, blissful night. For a brief period, the young lovers were able to forget their troubles and totally focus on each other.

Life seemed calm and carefree that lovely December weekend. All was quiet on the Zane front. Jen hadn't heard from him in weeks. No phone calls, no showing up unannounced on her doorstep, no late-night stake-outs. Maybe he had settled down and found someone else. Maybe it was all going to be okay. Or maybe not.

Just as Jen lulled herself into a false sense of security, the craziness began again, and this time it was even darker and more sinister.

On a crisp December afternoon, the couple had gone Christmas shopping at an outlet mall just off the south end of the Strip. Both of them had an army of friends and family to buy for. Colton had rented a silver Lexus SUV, top of the line, for the weekend. The mall parking lot was jam-packed, but they managed to snag a quiet space in a corner, well distant from the main entrance.

It was a cool, breezy Saturday with a trace of warm sun, just the mild winter weather that draws planeloads of east coasters and Europeans. Despite the flood of shoppers, Colton and Jen were able to briskly work through their lists. Names were crossed off, left and right. Twice, they lugged shopping bags back to the car, until the rear section was almost bulging.

Of course, they made time for a quick lunch in the food court, where they chowed down on Chinese and sipped hot chocolate while listening to Christmas carols.

Weary but relieved after their retail marathon, the couple collapsed in the SUV to chill for a few minutes before heading back to the Strip.

Around seven PM, they hit the road, and that's when the trouble began. It was a drizzly evening, with a touch of fog, which made the roadway known as Las Vegas Boulevard all the more daunting. All six lanes, it seemed, were chock full, abuzz with big trucks, SUVs, and impatient drivers.

The couple were on the road just a few minutes when they neared the busy intersection serving the private executive terminal for McCarran International Airport.

"Maybe I should've gotten Mom the pink sweater instead of the black one," Jen was musing to Colton. "She loves pink, but the black one is so classic and will go with everything."

"Well, if you want," Colton told her, "we can go back tomorrow and get the pink one, too."

"They probably won't have her size by then," Jen said, shaking her head. "There was only one small left in the pink, and the store was so crowded."

As they chatted, they were picking up speed without realizing it.

"Colt, there's a light ahead, please ease up," Jen advised, gazing at the cars on the road. Colton, who was going almost 50, tried to slow for the light. But when he hit the brake pedal, to his horror, nothing happened.

Barreling down the middle lane, he frantically pumped the pedal again and again, but the SUV kept charging ahead. Jen screamed as their big rig hurtled into the intersection, with Colton desperately pounding the horn to warn other drivers who were darting across lanes to safety. But he couldn't avoid an old red pick-up turning left directly in front of him. As he twisted the wheel sharply, his SUV smacked the truck's rear bumper.

The pick-up was barely fazed and kept rolling through the crossing, but the sudden impact propelled their own vehicle into the right lane and off the road, with Colton and Jen twisting and thrashing in their seats. Plowing dead ahead onto the sidewalk, the hulking SUV knocked over a row of newspaper boxes before smashing through the airport's chain-link fence. Jen was still screaming as the car churned, bulldozer-like, onto the tarmac and throttled forward till it smacked the nose cone of a parked Piper Cherokee.

The powerful collision blasted their own windshield into a thousand tiny pieces. In a shower of shattered glass, Jen gasped and groaned as a horrible pain ripped through her back. The smash-up had sent her bucking full force against her seat belt, but the strap had held tight. Colton wasn't so lucky. Wrenched violently out of his harness, his head collided with the steering wheel and dashboard.

When the dust finally settled, Jen struggled to turn her neck to look at him. His head was tilted down, his eyes closed. He was out cold, with blood oozing from his mouth. Jen was panicky and barely conscious herself.

A small clutch of pilots and ground crew ran to the SUV, now a huge, smoldering tangle of crunched metal, glass, and plastic. The plane was still intact, despite the smoking nose cone and a twisted propeller.

Ambulances and police cars with lights and sirens ablaze sped to the scene. Jen tried to tell the medics what happened, but they urged her not to speak. She was carefully lifted from the wreckage, laid on a stretcher, and loaded into an ambulance. Ditto for Colton, who was far worse off.

As a small crowd gathered outside the flattened fence, the pair were rushed to Las Vegas General. Through the haze of tangled events, Jen's mind focused again on a single name: Zane Hollister. Although her mental abilities were dulled, she was certain he was responsible for this horrible mess. Who or what else could it be?

On the way to the hospital, the medics took their vital signs. At the emergency room, they found that Colton had suffered a severe whiplash, two fractured vertebrae, chest trauma, and cuts and bruises. Jen also had whiplash and numerous cuts, but no broken bones. As the doctors treated them, hospital staffers tried to reach Brandi, but couldn't, so they left a message on her cell. They were, however, able to contact Colton's parents, who were frantic with worry and tried to take command, barraging them with questions.

Dr. Barnes immediately concluded his son was well enough to be flown by private helicopter back to San Francisco. He wanted this done early the next morning. He knew the staff doctors at Golden Gate Hospital, where he wanted Colton air-lifted.

Within hours, Colton was carefully removed from his bed, carried to a helicopter pad on the roof of the hospital, and flown to Golden Gate, where he spent two weeks recovering. His parents then had him brought home, where a private nurse took charge.

Brandi's legs nearly buckled when she called the

Vegas hospital to check on her daughter. Rushing there, she found Jen lying stiffly in bed with a giant, bulky bandage around her neck. But aside from cuts and bruises on her face and arms, she appeared okay.

As Jen tried to explain how the accident happened, she burst into tears and asked how Colton was. She was surprised to learn that he had been air-lifted out, but, from what she knew of his parents, it was par for the course.

The next morning, Brandi took Jen home. Because of her injuries, and fears that Zane would strike again, Jen took a couple of weeks off from Stripper Grams.

As soon as she could, Jen phoned Colton in San Francisco. With feverish intensity, they whispered greetings, talked about their injuries, and exchanged snippets of passion and intimacy. With that same closeness, they spoke again every day as they recovered. But they had neither the strength nor the energy to confront the real issue at hand. It was Zane, of course. Was he behind the crash? And if he was, where would he strike next?

For Colton, the crash was a painful reminder that the weird accidents had to stop before they worsened and someone ended up seriously hurt or dead.

Over and over, he thought back on his year-long affair with Jen, and tried to make sense of the string of misfortunes that had befallen them recently. But he couldn't. They defied logic.

Nobody had any answers, including the cops. But they determined that the brakes of the rental car, and also its air bags, had been tampered with, heightening suspicions that Zane was involved. When Jen heard this, a wave of despair washed over her. How were they ever going to stop him?

The Metro police added a chilling footnote: a surveillance camera in the mall parking lot had been disabled by parties unknown a few hours before the accident. All the other parking lot cameras were operating.

Now constantly haunted by harrowing flashbacks, Jen was convinced Zane was behind both the zip line mishap and car crash. Was he so enraged by her dating Colton that he was now trying to kill him, or both of them?

Her fears were intensified by her belief that Zane was back on drugs. His slurred voice the last time they talked was a dead giveaway that he was on prescription pills, heroin, or God knows what else.

CHAPTER 8

W eeks passed, and Jen continued to live in a state of high anxiety and fear. For Colton, the pressure was just as intense. The couple avoided direct mention of their alleged stalker, but he clearly intruded on their everyday thoughts and actions.

Fearful of another attack, they took to subterfuge and deceptive tactics. On the phone, they talked in vague, clipped phrases. On the road, they resorted to awkward, and sometimes even dangerous, ploys to elude or out-maneuver what appeared to be suspicious drivers following them.

Jen had nightmares and would burst into tears in the middle of the day for no apparent reason. When she told her mom what she suspected about Zane, and how it was affecting her, Brandi went straight to Nick, her security guard friend. He relayed word to Metro, and Zane was brought in for questioning. They threw a lot at him, but no charges were filed.

That's because Zane produced an airtight alibi, swearing he had been in Virginia City the week of the crash, and that he had relatives there who could prove it. He ended up walking. Without any hard evidence, there was no way he could be taken into custody.

Nick felt angry and frustrated that Jen and Brandi were being victimized by a "two-bit, ex-con thug." Through him, Jen managed to get a Temporary Protective Order against Zane. By law, he would be required to stay away from her and cease his "offending behavior" for 45 days.

"What happens after 45 days?" Jen inquired one day while Nick and Brandi were having coffee at the kitchen table.

"The order can be extended to a year by the Justice Court," Nick replied, "but you would need to attend a formal court proceeding, with Zane present as the offending party. I don't think you want to do that, do you?"

"Um, no, I guess not," Jen said softly, shaking her head.

"The next step would be a restraining order," Nick went on, "and that would require a court appearance, too."

"Oh," Jen sighed, gazing somberly at Nick and her mom. "Do either one of you actually think things like protective orders or restraining orders mean anything to Zane? He's too cocky and delusional to care."

"Honey, please don't be negative," Brandi urged. "Nick is trying to help. Just take it one day at a time and do the best you can."

"Until Zane strikes again?" Jen lashed out, "with some other horrible accident or dirty trick?"

"Sweetie, don't be upset with me," Brandi shot

back. "You're the one who wouldn't stop seeing him when you worked at the coffee shop. You're the one who snuck around for four years. I tried to stop you, but you wouldn't listen."

"Mom, shut up!" Jen cried. "The last thing I need right now is a lecture from you, okay?"

With that curt response, she rose from her chair and stalked off, leaving Brandi and Nick to finish their coffee in an atmosphere of heavy gloom.

Each of Zane's malicious stunts exacted a huge toll on the couple emotionally, but, for Colton, there were financial repercussions as well. Because the crash had been the result of foul play, the car rental agency's insurance covered only a portion of the damages to the airport fence, plane, and rental car. Colton had some coverage of his own, but the accident was such an oddity that nobody knew how to classify it. So Colton and his parents ended up paying a large portion of the damages themselves.

It was a very messy, expensive, complicated case that left Colton and his parents with a rather dark, distasteful perception of Jen.

Two weeks after the crash, she went back to work. Before reporting to her first event, Jen pleaded with her supervisor, a slick, 40-something badass-ex-showgirl named Destiny Pellegrini, to let her work events that wouldn't keep her out late at night. With Zane lurking about, it was just too risky.

At this point, Jen was feeling fragile and vulnerable. The prospect of popping out of a six-foot, multi-tiered cake in a tight, red-silk bustier didn't exactly thrill her. But she needed the money, and the distraction would help.

The pop-out gigs kept Jen sane, but with Colton recovering at home in San Francisco, her weekends were lonely and bleak. She spent long hours lying on the sofa, dazed and huddled in a blanket, or meandering forlornly through the streets of Summerlin in a work-out suit, baseball cap, and sunglasses, always looking over her shoulder. Her life was becoming one long anxiety attack.

As bad as things were, Jen hesitated to confide her worries to Colton. He had his hands full recovering, and there was nothing he could do anyway. He was stewing with indecision himself, wondering if the time had come for him to re-evaluate his fairy-tale relationship with Jen. Had Zane's desperate, deranged antics now brought the lovers to the breaking point?

CHAPTER 9

N ever did two people need a little Christmas more than Brandi and Jen that angst-ridden year of 2016. With Brandi's mom flying in from Houston for a three-day visit, excitement was in the air. But Grandma Paulina's Sin City stay turned out to be far more contentious than celebratory. Although there were a couple of nice dinners and some joyous slot outings at Caesar's, the bitter arguments between Paulina and Brandi took center stage.

Both of them played the blame game to the max. During a heated confrontation one morning over breakfast, Brandi blamed Paulina for her alcoholic-father's death in a homeless shelter. A livid Paulina refused to accept responsibility for Earl Putnam's dreary, destitute death, despite the fact she was married to him for 22 years and they had three kids.

The next day, when Paulina found out Zane was stalking and terrorizing Jen, she attacked Brandi over her three failed marriages. Paulina felt strongly that Jen's turbulent childhood had set the stage for her involvement with a slick con artist like Zane.

Brandi was furious with this assessment, and let Paulina know it, loud and clear.

Poor Jen was caught in the middle of all the shouting. It was a difficult, tense time. Thank God Jen had her daily phone calls with Colton to look forward to. He was still recovering from the SUV pile-up, but able to make it to his parents' San Francisco townhome for Christmas dinner. His family continued to be bewildered by the strange accident that had laid up their precious boy. They were beginning to wonder if perhaps his new Vegas girlfriend had brought some of the town's darker vibes with her.

By mid-January, Jen was working full-time again at Stripper Grams. She loved doing birthday parties, but her lush talents also rocked at retirement bashes and conventions. Nowhere was this more apparent than at the March 2017 Consumer Electronics Expo in Vegas. With Colton proudly looking on among a crowd of 2,000 one Tuesday night, Jen's pop-out act was totally killer.

Afterwards, behind heavy velvet curtains backstage, the shapely blonde wriggled out of her black-lace bikini and into a purple silk mini-dress. Then she strolled out of the mammoth Las Vegas Convention Center with Colton and his handsome boss, Matt.

Climbing into Matt's sleek, black BMW, the trio drove a few blocks to Piero's, a cushy old mob joint down on Paradise Road. After a five-course pasta feed with plenty of red wine, they were all in high spirits. Just past eleven that tranquil evening, they breezed out of Piero's heavy oak double-doors.

It was a balmy spring night in Vegas, the kind when even the crapshooters slow down. Reaching their rental car in the parking lot, they paused for a moment while Matt checked his phone. Suddenly, the desert stillness was shattered by a deafening series of rapid pops, like firecrackers gone wild. Colton's head jerked backwards, towards Matt. He was horrified by what he saw. His boss had been shot multiple times. There was a gaping wound near his shoulder, and two others lower down. He was lying on the ground writhing in pain, with blood spurting from his upper body and mid-section forming tiny rivulets in the asphalt.

Looking down at him, Jen screamed. Colton grabbed her arm and pulled her to the other side of the car, where they both crouched down. With their heads craning towards Paradise Road, they saw a dark car speeding away towards the Strip.

A moment later, an eerie quiet returned, so they ran to Matt. Kneeling beside him, Colton tried to stanch the blood.

"Go inside and tell them to call 911. He's losing a lot of blood!" he yelled at Jen.

She was gripped with fear for this guy she barely knew, and for Colton and herself, too, that there would be more gunfire. But somehow she got her feet in motion and raced inside.

"Someone's been shot!" Jen shrieked at the hostess. "Call 911. Please hurry!"

As the horrified woman picked up the phone, several people from the restaurant ran outside to lend a hand.

A small group had gathered by the time Jen

returned. She was crying and shaking uncontrollably as Colton pressed several white bar towels to Matt's shoulder and abdomen. He was semi-conscious, groaning, and still bleeding heavily. His light brown hair was wet with blood, his powder-blue shirt torn and drenched. Colton was imploring his best buddy over and over, "Hang on Matt, the ambulance is coming. We're going to get you help."

Within minutes, an emergency medical van with sirens blaring raced into the lot. Colton relayed scant details of the attack to the EMTs and said he knew nothing else. Giving them his name and Matt's, he said they were from San Jose and in town for the Electronics Expo. Jen, it was explained, was a local who lived in nearby Summerlin.

While one medic took Matt's vital signs, another wrapped bandages around his bloody shoulder and mid-section and gently placed him on a gurney. Then he was loaded into the ambulance, which sped off into the night.

While the crowd dispersed and someone from Piero's began the clean-up, Colton and Jen clung to each other for support. She was terrified. Who on earth could have done this senseless, violent act?

One name instantly came to mind: Zane Hollister, the smooth-talking druggie who had been making her life, and Colton's, hell since he left prison eight months earlier. Could Zane really have done this gruesome drive-by shooting?

Absolutely, Jen concluded, based on the agony she and Colton had endured over the months. First, there was the weird zip line accident, then the bizarre car crash. And now the dirty tricks had escalated to a dangerous new level; an innocent third party had been shot multiple times.

While Matt was rushed to the hospital, Colton and Jen were carted off to the police station for questioning. Jen was in tears as she recounted their recent ordeals with Zane. The officers were aware of most of them, but no one had ever been able to catch the perpetrator in the act.

The scene at the station-house was grim and chaotic. Jen and Colton were both groggy and nauseous, with Matt's dried blood caked on their clothes and shoes. Deeply shaken and in shock, they confided their worst fear to the officers: that Matt's shooting had been a tragic mistake, and Jen's toxically jealous ex had actually been aiming for Colton.

At one AM, Colton and Jen were finally let go. An officer drove them to Caesar's, where they were staying in a suite on the same gilt-edged floor as Matt's. After quickly changing clothes, they headed out to Las Vegas General to check on their friend.

Matt was still in surgery, so they settled themselves on black-vinyl chairs in a dreary visitors' lounge and drank what passed for coffee from an old vending machine. Jen was numb and dazed. She had recently gone back to work and was set to perform at a few more parties that week at the huge tech show. But now all that seemed uncertain.

While the stunned couple awaited word on Matt, the cops called his mother, Delia, in San Jose, and his sister, Megan, in Atlanta. Both were shocked and devastated, and said they'd fly in as soon as they could. Matt's ex-wife, the mother of his three sons back in San Jose, was also notified. She was every bit as upset and unhinged as his mother and sister.

As soon as Jen could muster the strength, she called her mom at home. Brandi nearly collapsed at the news.

"Honey, I'm worried about you and Colton," she blurted, upset and tense. "You're both in danger. Tell the security people at the hospital about Zane, in case he tries to attack you or someone else there.

"Why can't the cops find that goddamn bastard, lock him up, and throw away the key?" she ranted as she put the phone down.

After speaking to Jen, Brandi called the Venetian to let them know she'd be late for work. Jen had sounded anxious and scared at the hospital, and Brandi wanted to be there for her only child.

Matt came through the six-hour surgery as best he could, thanks to a team of excellent trauma surgeons. Somehow he managed to survive the three bullets, but he had lapsed into a coma from the loss of blood. A weary doctor told Jen and Colton it was touch and go. Matt was 43 and in good shape, so that would help, but the next few days would be crucial.

CHAPTER 10

Early on Wednesday, Colton began phoning QuInternet colleagues back in San Jose to deliver the grim news that Matt was in a coma. He also called staffers in Vegas for the Expo and gave them the latest.

Mid-morning, a pale, exhausted Brandi arrived at the hospital to see Jen. Mom and daughter were close, and had been since the day, 24 years earlier, when Jen had been born in this very hospital.

Brandi was only 18 at the time, a newlywed with a troubled past and an uncertain future. She'd never planned on getting pregnant and cried her eyes out when she found out she was. After a quickie Vegas wedding to her old buddy from San Jose, Lizard Moats, and a difficult pregnancy, she gave birth to a beautiful girl. From the first moment she laid eyes on baby Jenny, she cherished her more than anything in the world.

The now 42-year-old single mother was a former teenage beauty queen whose road to happiness in Sin City had been paved with family tragedy, discord, and deprivation. There had been one jarring crisis after another, as she juggled her cocktail-waitressing job and three failed marriages, to hold onto her sanity and her daughter.

Finally, she had carved out a new life and identity on the Strip that brought some semblance of stability. But now, once again, as the slim, attractive blonde walked through the double glass-doors of Nevada's main emergency hospital, doubts and fears consumed her. She was worried, not only about her daughter's safety, but also about what might happen to Colton Barnes, Jen's preppy, 30-year-old systems analyst boyfriend.

Brandi knew little about him beyond the basics: that he had grown up in a wealthy San Francisco family, graduated from Stanford, and now worked for a successful tech firm in Silicon Valley. Although she had never actually met him because of her late-night and weekend shifts, Brandi was relieved that her daughter had finally found a decent, upwardly mobile guy. As for Colton's boss, the man now fighting for his life, Brandi knew nothing except that he was in town for the expo.

Into the brightly lit, brown-carpeted hospital Brandi strode, wearing a long, black trench coat, burgundy jeans, and a pink sweater to ward off the mid-morning desert chill. In a low, nervous voice, she asked the admissions' clerk where Jen was, but they didn't have her name, or Colton's.

Brandi tried to call Jen on her cell, but there was no answer. So she told the clerk that an acquaintance of her daughter's had been shot the night before in the Piero's parking lot, but she didn't have his name.

Setting her coffee cup down, the clerk, a chatty, grey-haired woman with a Brooklyn accent, tapped a few keys on her computer.

"Oh, here it is, right in my face," she said, scanning the register of admissions. "The patient's name is Matt Quinby. He's out of surgery, but in critical condition. Your daughter and her boyfriend must be in the visitors' lounge up on four."

Reeling as if she'd been sucker-punched, Brandi stared hard at the clerk and asked her to repeat the name.

"Quinby," she said, "Matt Quinby. Fourth-floor visitors' lounge for your daughter and her boyfriend."

Brandi was stunned, absolutely rocked.

"Matt Quinby?" she gasped, repeating the name. The clerk nodded and Brandi turned away with the wind suddenly knocked out of her. Her face was white as a sheet.

"No, it can't be," she whispered to herself, shaking her head and edging forward to a lounge where she collapsed in a large, lumpy upholstered chair.

The name "Quinby" evoked a thousand anxious, conflicting memories and jolted every nerve-ending in Brandi's small, reed-thin body. That's because it was the name of her long-lost high-school boyfriend, her first love, and the guy who was the biological father of her daughter. Yes, Matt Quinby was Jen's father. But he had no idea, nor did Jen.

Brandi still couldn't believe what she'd just heard. Then she frantically started connecting the dots: Matt Quinby, San Jose, owner of a thriving

Internet company. She suddenly realized, amazingly, that it was true. This Matt was her Matt, the cute, lanky guy who used to stroll with her, hand-in-hand, down Lincoln Avenue in Willow Glen, the wealthy San Jose neighborhood where he grew up. The guy who took her on countless sailboat and roller coaster rides, to movies, baseball games, and the junior prom.

In short, Matt had been the love of her young life. They had been all set to marry in the summer of 1992 when she was 18-year-old Brandi Putnam, a fresh-faced beauty queen who had just graduated from San Jose High and was working at the local Jack In The Box. But after a racy scandal involving her mom and a married minister erupted, she had left town with Lizard Moats, a high school friend, four days before the wedding. A few weeks later, while stranded in Vegas with car trouble, Brandi learned she was pregnant. She was certain the baby was Matt's.

Now, 24 years later, her mind shifted into fast-forward as she imagined what this startling twist of fate might mean. If Matt survived, would Jen finally get to know her real father?

All through her childhood, Jen had assumed that Brandi's first husband, the long-haired, laid-back Lizard Moats, was her dad. But then she had grown up, gotten a job at Stripper Grams, and, unknowingly, bumped into her real father one day after popping out of his birthday cake at Caesar's. And now he had tragically been shot in a drive-by, presumably by her psycho-ex, in some ghastly mistake.

Brandi burst into tears at the thought of Matt's dying from his injuries. Oh God, she kept pleading and praying, that can't happen, it just can't. She still had deep and tender feelings for her former fiance. Those had never died. And now she desperately wanted Jen to get to know her real dad.

Brandi had no idea how much Matt knew about Jen's background, if anything, but she desperately wanted them to form some kind of relationship. Fate had kept the three apart all these years, but now the shooting had brought them together. It was meant to be.

Then and there, Brandi decided she would no longer keep this dark secret from Jen. Her daughter needed to know the shocking truth, and she needed to know it now. Brandi would tell her everything that very morning.

At 11 AM, she finally pulled herself out of the chair and rode the elevator to the fourth floor. In the visitors' lounge she spotted Jen, pale and wan in jeans and a black sweater, holding hands with an attractive, brown-haired, 30-something guy who was obviously Colton.

Jen got up and moved swiftly towards Brandi.

"Mom, you're here, thank God!"

After a long hug, Brandi anxiously asked, "How's Colton's boss?"

"Hanging in there," Jen replied, looking down sadly. "But it's touch and go right now. He's critical, in a coma. The doctors don't know if he'll make it."

"Oh my God," Brandi murmured, shaking her head.

Just then, Colton got up from a nearby sofa, and, with his hand outstretched, walked towards Brandi.

"It's good to finally meet you," he said in a polite but subdued tone.

"Nice to meet you, too. My daughter's told me so much about you," Brandi responded, nodding weakly and gazing into Colton's warm brown eyes. As the three of them stood awkwardly in the center of the drab lounge, Brandi wondered if there was any further news on Zane.

"No," Jen told her, taking a deep breath. "The cops are still on it. They've alerted police and state troopers all over the West, but so far, nothing."

"Don't worry, honey, they'll get him," Brandi said reassuringly, patting Jen's arm. "In the meantime, I hope they're going to give you some kind of protection. Zane is more crazed than ever from drugs. You guys need to be on constant guard. Every time he does something, it's worse. I shudder to think of what might be coming next."

"The cops are doing all they can," Colton interjected.

"Yeah, I know," Brandi remarked, sinking onto the sofa, "but it doesn't seem to be enough."

Then she looked up at Jen.

"Honey, I need to talk to you," she said with a hint of urgency. "It's a family matter, Colton. I don't mean to be rude, but would you mind, uh, leaving us alone for a few minutes?"

"Oh, sure," he replied, reaching for his cell on the coffee table and turning to head down the hall.

CHAPTER 11

Hunched together on a black vinyl sofa in the visitors' lounge, Brandi clutched her daughter's hand.

"Mom, what is it?" Jen asked, "you're scaring me."

Brandi took a deep breath. In a grave, soft voice, she began.

"Jen, I came to the hospital today not knowing the name of Colton's boss. When I asked the admissions' clerk, she told me, and I almost fainted. You see, Jen, Matt Quinby and I knew each other a long time ago. We were teenagers In love back in San Jose.

"Jen, he's your father. The man in that hospital bed," Brandi repeated, pointing vaguely down the hall, "is your biological father."

The words struck like a lightning bolt.

"What? But how can that possibly be?" a stunned Jen replied, blinking and staring hard at her mom. "That's crazy. I thought Lizard was my dad. You mean that's not true?"

"No, honey, it's not," Brandi replied. "Let me

explain. You know I grew up in San Jose. Matt's younger sister, Megan, was my best friend. We met at summer camp and I got to know Matt through her. Well, from early childhood, the two of us had a special connection, Matt and me. And it turned into love when we were teenagers.

"When I was 18, I was all set to marry him. But a week before the wedding, Megan told me that Matt's parents were dead-set against it because of Grandma Paulina's affair with minister Andrew, who was married, too. Andrew was going to perform our ceremony at St. Aubrey's, so it was a big, messy scandal.

"Matt's parents were shocked and appalled by what Mom had done, and they weren't too thrilled with Daddy either. He was an alcoholic, on welfare, who'd been fired from every job he'd ever had because of his drinking."

Jen's jaw was on the floor.

"Did you discuss all this with Matt and try to work it out?" she managed to ask, gaping at Brandi.

"No, honey, because I found out from Megan, who was 16 at the time, that Matt and his parents had had a huge blow-up about my family 10 days before the wedding was to take place. The Quinbys threatened to cut him off financially if he married me.

"Megan said Matt fought back. He wanted to go through with the wedding, even after they said they'd stop his tuition payments at Stanford. The Quinbys were in a panic, desperate to keep him from marrying into the Putnam family because they felt we were too low class and unstable."

"Oh, my God," Jen groaned, shaking her head in disbelief. "So that's why you left San Jose and came to Vegas with Lizard."

"Yes," Brandi nodded. "I loved Matt, but I didn't want to marry him after what Megan told me. I couldn't ruin his life like that. But I couldn't face him, because I knew he'd try to tell me everything was going to be alright, and that he loved me, and we would make it work, no matter what. But I was just as sure our marriage would be a disaster. I was terrified to go through with it.

"Four days before the wedding, I picked up and left town with Lizard. He was a school-friend from the neighborhood, and planning a trip to Chicago to visit relatives. I asked him if I could tag along, and he said yes.

"In June of '92 we set off in a battered old station wagon his parents had given him for graduation," Brandi went on. "But the car broke down in Vegas, and we ended up checking into a cheesy motel over by the sign. By the time the car was fixed, I was too sick to go anywhere. I didn't know it at the time, but I was pregnant with you, and Matt was the father. I was sure of it then, I'm sure of it now."

"What a strange, sad story," Jen said softly. Gripping her mom's arm, she whispered, "Matt Quinby is my father. Colton's boss is my dad. Oh my God, this is too much to make sense of. I'm in shock. How could you keep this from me all these years?"

"Honey, you and I went through three marriages and divorces by the time you were 17," Brandi explained. "I didn't want to bring any more chaos to our lives than there already was. And I didn't want to hurt you by telling you all about my past in San Jose, you know, my hot-mess mom and dad and all the mistakes they made, and how Matt's parents were so cruel and judgmental."

"This whole story is awful," Jen cried. "What kind of people do I come from? The Quinbys sound like rich, snobby monsters, and the Putnams sound like poor train wrecks. I wish I were a Moats. At least they're sane, decent people."

"Well, honey, in a way you are a Moats. Lizard considers you his daughter, and his parents think of you as their granddaughter."

"But it's not really true, is it?" Jen shot back. "None of what I grew up believing is really true, is it Mom? Maybe what you're telling me now is more lies to cover up all the other lies.

"How could you keep this from me all these years? If I had known Matt Quinby was my real dad, we could have had a relationship. He seems like a good man. He could have shown me a whole other way of life. I wouldn't have had to scrimp and save and worry about every penny. I could have gone to school, traveled, maybe become a veterinarian, like I always wanted. Instead, you suffered through three marriages that all fell apart and I got dragged along for the ride."

"Jen, I only told you this so you'd understand why I did what I did 24 years ago. It was all out of love for you. You were all I ever thought of, every step of the way."

"Yeah, sure, like Grandma Paulina was thinking

of you every step of the way when she ran off with the minister, right?"

"Jen, you take that back, right now," Brandi snapped, angry and hurt. "My situation and hers were totally different. She was a married woman with three kids. I was an innocent 18-year-old girl!"

"Okay, Mom, whatever," Jen said, rolling her eyes. "I know you did the best you could, but did you ever stop to think about how my not getting to know my real father would affect my life later on?

"And here we are, sitting in this strange, scary hospital all these years later, and Matt has been shot, probably by Zane. What's going to happen next? Will I ever get to know Matt? He doesn't even know I exist. I popped out of his birthday cake at Caesar's, but he doesn't know I'm his daughter!

"What kind of life are we living if it's all based on lies?" Jen went on. "What if Matt doesn't pull through? What if I lose him before I even get to know him?"

Looking down sadly, Brandi shook her head. She had no answers for her distraught daughter. As Jen burst into tears, Brandi tried to hold and comfort her, but Jen pulled away. A crushed Brandi began crying, too.

"Honey," she said, handing Jen some tissues, "please forgive me for what I did. I was 18 years old, scared, and confused. I thought I was doing what was best for both of us. You've got to believe me."

"Mom, don't try to sugarcoat this," Jen said with a dismissive flick of the wrist. "You ruined my childhood and my life. Who am I, a Putnam, a

Quinby, or a Moats?"

"You're all three, Jen, the best part of all of us. Please, please calm down. Yes, it's sad that we're sitting here in this hospital. But the bottom line is that Matt's been shot. Saving his life is all that matters now.

"I would love to see him, honey. Do you think I could, just for a few minutes? Which room is his?"

Jen sighed, nodded, and pointed vaguely towards 408B. Brandi got up and eased her way down the hall. At the doorway to Matt's room, she asked the nurse in a hushed, trembling voice, "Can I go in, just for a minute?"

"Yes, go ahead," she said. "He's in a coma and non-responsive, but you can see him, briefly."

Taking a deep breath to steel herself, Brandi edged forward and opened the door. Her heart was racing, and then it sank. There lay Matt, the handsome, buff young man she had loved and almost married 24 years before. He was now 43, pale, comatose, deathly silent, and attached to multiple machines. His upper torso was covered in layers of bandages. The mountain of gauze, tape, and toweling nearly submerged his thin frame.

In tears, Brandi sat down beside him and gently took his hand.

"Matt, darling" she whispered, her voice quivering. "It's me, Brandi, remember? We're here In a Las Vegas hospital and you've been hurt. You just had surgery, but you're going to be okay. You're going to come out of this. Please, Matt, we need you. Jen and I need you. Please come back."

Aside from his slow, labored breathing, Matt

didn't move a muscle. Brandi lingered for 20 minutes, crying so hard from the shock of seeing her old love like this that she couldn't muster the strength to get up and leave. The nurse finally came in, took her by the arm, and led her back to the visitors' lounge.

CHAPTER 12

J en just left to get coffee," Colton said to a dazed, distraught Brandi when she returned to the visitors' lounge. Nodding vaguely, she took a seat on the black vinyl couch.

From a nearby chair, Colton was staring at her. There seemed to be a lot going on behind his steely, dark eyes.

"Mrs. Conover," he began awkwardly, "Jen was stunned by what you told her about Matt. It seems so, um, improbable, and, uh, far-fetched. How could he possibly be her father?"

Brandi didn't like his tone.

"Why is it so unbelievable?" she bristled. "San Jose isn't that far from here. It's not like it's China or Outer Mongolia."

She then related the basic details of her teenage romance with Matt. This version was much shorter than the one she had told Jen, and lacked some of the darker, Romeo and Juliet undertones. But the bottom line was the same: a canceled wedding, an early-morning bolt from San Jose with another guy, and a surprise pregnancy in Vegas.

Colton was appalled.

"Jen could have grown up in San Jose with Matt and had all the benefits of wealth and privilege," he said, throwing his hands up. "Instead, you raised her here in a low-rent suburb and filled her head with lies about who her father was. Some guy you ran off with, who had a reptilian name. Forgive me, Mrs. Conover, but what kind of woman would do something like that to her own child?"

"How dare you!" Brandi lashed out. "I did the best I could and raised Jen in a good home. Lizard was a loving father to her, even though he was only with us a couple of years. And her other two stepfathers were wonderful to her, too."

"Oh, you mean the bigamist second-husband and the philandering third?" Colton sneered. "You exposed that poor girl to so much dysfunctional behavior. She never stood a chance. No wonder she took up with a lowlife thug when she was just 17 years old. I hold you responsible for Jen's relationship with Zane Hollister, and all the complications and traumas we're dealing with now."

"For the record, Colton," a furious Brandi interrupted, "Jen snuck around with Zane behind my back. I couldn't watch her 24/7. She was 17 years old and lying to me. I never knew what she was doing, or I would have stopped it. And about her stepfathers, they both loved her and she knew it. I did all I could. Jen was never deprived of anything."

"Except stability," Colton shot back. "You subjected her to a string of loser-husbands and she never got to know her real father. Now this horrible shooting has gone down and you're laying all this Matt-backstory on her. Again, what kind of mother would do something like that? Why didn't you simply tell Matt years ago that he had a daughter?"

"Because I feared the rich, powerful Quinbys would take her from me," Brandi answered, her voice getting louder and shriller.

"I was scared they'd sic their high-powered lawyers on me and I'd never see my daughter again. Jen was all I had. I wasn't about to risk losing her."

"Yeah, whatever," Colton said dismissively. "Jen is so confused and upset right now. The man you claim is her father has been shot because of her low-life ex. And I witnessed the whole thing.

"Matt is my boss and one of my best friends. He has three sons and an ex-wife who still loves him. He runs a cutting-edge tech firm with two thousand employees who need his leadership and expertise. And here we sit outside his hospital room, not knowing if or when he will ever wake up."

"Colton, you're tired and upset right now, and so am I," Brandi responded. "For Jen's sake, I'll try to forget most of what you just said because you don't know what the hell you're talking about.

"Let's try to be civil and make the next few days as peaceful as possible for Jen's sake. What's done is done, and Zane is still out there. That's what we need to focus on now. Keeping Jen safe, and you, too."

Colton nodded.

"I'm sorry if I came across as a bit harsh," he said, leaning forward and running his hands through his thick, dark-brown hair. "I love Matt like a brother, and last night I saw him gunned down in a parking lot. I'm just trying to cope."

"It's okay, Colton," Brandi said calmly, patting his arm. "Please take care of Jen. She's going through so much right now, with all this Zane stuff. Please hang in there with her."

Colton nodded, and both of them lapsed into silence. Taking a deep breath, Brandi put her head back and tried to relax.

A few minutes later, Jen returned to the visitors' lounge with a container holding three cups of coffee. The trio sipped and chatted about Matt's condition. It was polite but tense. There was a heaviness and sadness in the air because each one of them needed Matt so much. And they were all wondering if or when he would wake up.

That afternoon, Brandi reported to work at the Venetian, and Jen did a pop-out at a United Ironworkers' convention at Paris. The last thing she felt like doing was emerging from a cake in a skin-tight bustier to sing and wriggle before a packed house of 2,500 boozed-up welders and bridge-makers. But she needed the money, and there was no one who could sub for her, so she got herself over to Paris and did the gig.

She was sensational, as always, but unfortunately it was one of those jobs where the clients want the girl to stick around afterwards and party with them. Customers sometimes get too attached to a stripper, as if she's up there performing just for them, and it can be hard to shake them off. This was one of those times, with a posse of rabid party-animal conventioneers, each of them eager for some real-life skin in the game.

Jen didn't want to offend anyone or get into trouble with her snarky supervisor, but she was truly not in the mood to socialize. Finally, after enduring an hour of men gaping at her cleavage and trying to cop a feel while she made polite small talk, she managed to slip out with some bogus excuse about her sick mother. But it wasn't easy.

Colton, meanwhile, was anchored across the Strip at Caesar's in the deluxe suite he'd booked for the tech expo. Mostly, he was working the phones with clients and a handful of trusty lieutenants at QuInternet. But his heart was less on business than on the ongoing Matt-drama down the road at Las Vegas General, and the explosive showdown he'd had that morning with his girlfriend's quirky, quixotic mom.

Between business calls, he badgered the ICU nurses hourly for updates on Matt. Each time, he was told the same thing: there was no change in his condition and he would be contacted the minute there was.

CHAPTER 13

That night Jen and Colton had dinner at the rustically French Rendezvous in Caesar's. Beautiful, blond Jen wore a black-lace dinner-dress with four-inch heels, and Colton was decked out in a navy-blue suit.

Rendezvous had been the setting for many of their most romantic dinners. But on this night, almost 24 hours after Matt's shooting, the mood was especially tense. As they nibbled lettuce salads with apples and cranberries, they tried to be pleasant and polite, but the atmosphere was obviously strained.

Over glasses of Chardonnay, Colton revealed that he and Matt's mother would be managing daily operations at QuInternet.

"Delia is very upset over what happened to Matt. She would be here, but she's back in San Jose running QuInternet and helping out with his sons. Matt's ex-wife is with them, but she needs special care herself since a boating accident left her in a wheelchair a few years ago. Delia will be flying in next week."

"Oh," Jen said, nodding and taking a deep breath. "She sounds really nice. I'm looking forward to meeting her."

She was just being polite of course. The thought of meeting the powerful matriarch of the wealthy, patrician Quinby clan scared the hell out of her. Maybe it was because of what Brandi had told her about the past, and how the Quinbys had been dead-set against her marrying Matt. That didn't leave Jen with a very favorable impression of them.

"Matt's sister will be flying in from Atlanta in a day or two," Colton went on. "Your mom was best friends with her when they were growing up. Megan is in her late thirties now, and married to a pitcher for the Atlanta Braves. They just adopted twin five-year-old girls, so she has her hands full.

"She and her husband are at spring training in Florida, but she's flying in later this week. I'm not sure if he'll be with her or not. In the meantime, she's getting regular updates, just like the rest of us."

Again, Jen nodded. She was very curious, and also somewhat anxious, about the rich new relatives she had recently acquired.

While awaiting their main courses, Colton told Jen more about his phone conversation with Delia.

"Everyone is devastated about Matt," he said, looking down glumly and shaking his head. "I didn't want Delia to come here and endure what I went through today in that visitors' lounge, when you told me you were Matt's daughter. So I took the liberty of telling her the whole bizarre, tangled story, that I'm dating you, and that Brandi, a former

San Jose resident who was once engaged to Matt, is your mother.

"Of course she was floored. practically gagging on her coffee. Then I told her that Matt is actually your father, and she was even more flabbergasted. But the most shocking news of all was that we suspect your jealous ex-convict-ex committed the drive-by, and that he was probably aiming for me, based on what's been going on the past few months. She was stunned by the whole situation. It must sound like something out of True Detective to her."

"Oh," Jen gulped. "I'm sorry she was so shocked and upset, but I guess I understand," she said softly. "I want to meet her and get to know her. She is my grandmother, after all. Do you think she'll want to meet me when she comes to see Matt?"

"Yes, of course," Colton nodded, as their Duck A L'Orange and broccoli soufflé were being served. "But I don't know if she'll want to be anywhere near your mom. Just the mention of Brandi's name seemed to rattle her. She's never gotten over the fact that, four days before she was supposed to marry Matt in 1992, she skipped town with another guy. The reptile dude, what was his name?"

"Lizard," Jen answered. "Lizard Moats. He was mom's friend from San Jose High. They got married here in 1992 and I was born the following year. He was my dad those first two years, and has been ever since, even though he and his wife now live in Chicago with their kids."

"I'm sure he's a good guy and all that," Colton said, "but the mere mention of your mother's name got Delia's blood boiling. Jen, you better prepare yourself for when she and Megan roll into town. Don't get your hopes up for some warm and fuzzy family reunion. I wouldn't want to see you hurt."

"What are you saying?" Jen asked. "This is a very tough time for all of us, with Matt's shooting. Maybe we should forget the ancient history and pull together as a family, for his sake."

"Listen, Jen," Colton responded, leaning in. "Your mom just told us this morning that Matt is your father. We haven't had time to fully process that bombshell. But what if it's not even true? What if she had a relationship with another guy back in San Jose, or with someone here in Vegas, and that mystery dude is your real father, not Matt?"

"That's insulting to my mom," Jen lashed out, hurt and angry. Putting her fork down, she glared across the table at Colton. "If Mom says Matt's my dad, Matt's my dad. End of story!"

"Sorry," Colton said sheepishly.

"But what about the reptile-dude she ran off with?" he asked. "She married him. Maybe he's your real father."

"Mom says Matt's my dad, and that's good enough for me," Jen said. "Lizard was Mom's first husband. He's listed as my father on my birth certificate. I guess that was a lie, and Mom and Lizard both knew it.

"I'm going to have a talk with her when I get home tomorrow. Speaking of Mom," Jen went on. "She seemed upset when I came back to the visitors' lounge this morning with the coffee. What did you say to her while I was gone?"

"We talked about this whole strange situation,"

Colton replied. "I told her the truth, that I thought it was inexcusable that she kept you from your real father all these years. And on top of it, subjected you to her three loser-husbands.

"But again, Jen, maybe all this talk is premature because Matt isn't your real father. Try to keep an open mind. If you find out he's not your father, maybe your real dad is out there somewhere, healthy and whole, not shot up and lying in a hospital bed in a coma. How could your lunatic-ex do this to him?"

"Zane is a sick, deranged person on all kinds of drugs," Jen answered, looking down in shame and shaking her head. "The cops keep saying they don't have any hard evidence, so they can't arrest him. But they can't find him either.

"What are they doing, waiting for him to actually kill someone before they take action?" Jen asked, throwing her hands up. "What good are they, anyway? In the meantime, we're living in fear of what he'll do next, because you and I are still together, and that's something he'll never accept."

Colton frowned. With his lips clenched, he glanced downward in distaste. A look of disapproval and regret was on his face. It was like a knife to Jen's heart. Surely, he now regretted that he had ever met her after she popped out of Matt's birthday cake a year and a half before. A wave of terror washed over her when she saw the coldness in his eyes. Was she going to lose him now, too, on top of everything else?

Colton had finished most of his dinner, but Jen merely picked at hers. While the crème brulee' and coffee were being carted in, Colton dialed the nurses' station at Las Vegas General for another update on Matt.

"No change," they told him again. Colton relayed the information to Jen. She had tears in her eyes and he buried his head in his hands, right there at the table.

Needless to say, this tense dinner did not set the stage for a night of hot, steamy sex. Quite the contrary. After dinner, Jen wanted to run home to Brandi, but she was too exhausted from the shooting the night before to go anywhere. Plus there was the Zane factor. Maybe he was out there somewhere, lurking and waiting to strike again. What would it be this time? Another hideous accident or senseless shooting? Or perhaps a kidnapping or assault? Nobody knew where Zane was, or what he might do next. What an appalling, gut-wrenching way to live.

Back in Colton's suite, Jen and he gazed out on the Strip for a few minutes that warm spring night. It was a relaxing distraction from all the drama. The lights were glaring and flickering. Neon signs touting the myriad attractions of this five-mile-long international pleasure pit in the Mojave. Gourmet restaurants, razzle-dazzle shows, world-class shopping, spas, and slots. It was all there, but the atmosphere in Colton's suite was dreary and glum as he and Jen collapsed into bed.

An exhausted Colton fell asleep immediately. Jen, not so much. In the middle of the night, she tried to snuggle up to him, but he rolled over and moved to the other side of the bed. A chill went through her. Of course he was asleep, so he didn't do it intentionally, she told herself.

CHAPTER 14

A certain awkwardness was in the air. It had been only two days since Matt's shooting, and Jen was feeling sad and confused. She wished Colton could stick around for a few days to hold her hand and offer support. But that was out of the question. He had to fly back to San Jose that morning to conduct an emergency meeting with 2,000 anxious Quinternetters. The topic: how the elite tech firm would conduct business as usual while Matt was on a long-term medical leave.

After rushing through coffee and toast in their suite, a subdued Colton and Jen trekked through massive Caesar's to the parking garage. As Jen tried to keep up with her strapping, six-foot boyfriend while lugging her heavy overnight bag, he assured her he would return the following week to see both Matt and her.

Despite the kind words, Jen felt anxious and dejected. The night before had been the first time they'd slept together without making love, and it made her feel insecure and uncertain on many levels. As they parted ways at the entrance to the garage, there was a quick, polite kiss. With a heaviness in her heart, Jen trooped back through Caesar's and out to the Strip to flag a cab that would take her to Summerlin.

At noon, she shuffled into her house as if she had the weight of the world on her shoulders. Brandi had worked late and then come home and slept in. Now she was awake, dressed in a pink velour warm-up suit, and making a tuna-melt in the kitchen. Jen could smell the coffee and food the minute she got inside. Plopping her purse and bag on the hall table, she headed for the kitchen.

"Hi, honey, how are you?" Brandi asked, as her daughter walked in.

"Hanging in there," Jen sighed.

"I'll put a sandwich on for you," Brandi responded. "Relax, sweetheart, you look tired."

"I am tired, Mom. I haven't slept in two days because of Matt's shooting, and then all the drama afterwards with you at the hospital."

"I'm sorry, sweetie," Brandi said as she assembled Jen's tuna-melt and laid it in the skillet. "When I left San Jose 25 years ago, I never in a million years thought all this would happen. I'm still in shock from yesterday, too. How's Matt doing?"

"There's no change," Jen replied, shaking her head glumly. "Colton's been calling the hospital every hour. Matt's still in a coma and no one knows if or when he'll wake up."

Standing at the kitchen stove, Brandi touched her right temple and groaned, "Oh my God, Jen, he's got to make it. He's just got to." Jen nodded somberly, and the two hugged. Brandi then grabbed a spatula and began flipping the sandwiches. A few minutes later, after they were plated, with pickles, she and Jen sat at the table like they always did.

"Mom," Jen started, taking a sip of coffee. "I know you're upset about Matt, but there are some things I need to ask about your past with him. I hope you don't mind."

"Not at all, honey," Brandi replied with a tight little smile. "I'm your mother, he's your father, you have a right to ask whatever you want. Fire away."

Setting her sandwich on a plate and picking up her napkin, Jen hesitated for an instant. Having this conversation made her uncomfortable, but she had to forge ahead.

"You say that Matt is my dad and he was the love of your life when you were both teenagers. What kind of relationship did you have with his family in San Jose? Did you ever get along with them, even briefly?"

"Sweetheart, I knew the Quinbys since I was ten years old and Megan was eight," Brandi shot back. "We met at summer camp. I helped her clean up some glue she spilled while making a popsicle-stick raft, and we became best friends.

"The Quinbys were super nice to me from day one. They treated me like family. I was invited to parties, dinners, and sleepovers at their mansion. That's how I got to know Matt."

"So, why did they end up hating you?" Jen asked.

"Because Grandma Paulina got caught butt-naked in the greenhouse having sex with the minister who was going to marry Matt and me. That shocked and enraged the Quinbys. To them, it was a public disgrace. They no longer wanted me in their family."

"But up to that point, you and Matt were just two kids in love, doing all these fun date things, right?"

"Right," Brandi nodded. "In the summer, we went to Giants' games, in the winter, 49ers. We took hikes around Los Gatos Creek, saw movies, and hung out with other kids in the cool areas. Things like that. It was an easy, carefree time."

"So, when did you get engaged?" Jen asked.

"When he was 20 and a computer-sciences major at Stanford, and I was 18 and had just graduated from San Jose High. The proposal was dreamy and romantic. We were on his parents' boat, sailing around San Francisco Bay at sunset. Oh my God, Jen, it was perfect. We were so in love. Matt made me feel safe and secure in a way I never had in my life.

"I grew up on the poor side of town, in Meadowfair," Brandi went on, "with a family that never had enough money, and was always fighting and in turmoil. With the Quinbys, life was calm and easy. There was always enough. Enough money, enough food, enough time. More than enough, really. Matt and I were young and in love. We wanted to be together the rest of our lives."

"What was your engagement ring like? Do you still have it?" Jen asked.

"No. I wish," Brandi replied. "It was a two-carat, princess-cut diamond, set in platinum, custom-made at a jewelry store his family had an account with. It was gorgeous. I will never forget that night, or that ring. He totally swept me off my feet!"

"The ring sounds so pretty," Jen remarked. "What happened to it?"

"Would you believe I taped it to a letter I wrote Matt, telling him I couldn't go through with the wedding? On my way out of town with Lizard, I dropped it in a mailbox. He got it a day or two later. I have no idea what he did with the ring, or the letter."

"You were in Vegas with Lizard, by then, right?"

"Right, I had left town with him because of all the family drama. There were so many issues with my parents, and Matt's. I just couldn't cope. I couldn't go through with the wedding."

"But then you ended up marrying Lizard in Vegas. Why? Did you love him?" Jen wanted to know.

"Like a brother or a good friend," Brandi said softly, "but it was never a romantic thing. I was always in love with Matt. I think Lizard knew that from day one."

"So what was marriage to Lizard like? It must have been awkward at times."

"It was," Brandi nodded, "for the first six months, I was sick as a dog. My pregnancy was rough; I had morning sickness 24/7. Lizard was my knight in shining armor. He literally kept me alive by bringing me a Styrofoam container of food every night from his job at Excalibur. He also got me pre-natal vitamins from a free clinic on Sahara, and made sure I took them. My appetite was terrible. I didn't want anything but cherry pop and Twinkies.

Nutritionally speaking, it sucked.

"We got married for lots of reasons," Brandi went on, "the main one being he had good health insurance with his job, and I was desperate to give birth in a hospital.

"So I willingly walked down the aisle with Lizard, even though I wasn't in love with him. But I cared about him a lot, and I think he knew it.

"He always said he loved me, but then he ended up running off with a cocktail waitress from work. It killed me, but I had to accept it. On your birth certificate, he's listed as your father, and I will always be grateful for that."

"Lizard's a good guy," Jen agreed. "I will always love him, even though I know Matt is my real father. Lizard did so much for both of us."

"Are you going to tell him you know Matt is your biological father?" Brandi asked.

"Maybe, someday," Jen replied, "but not right now. Why should I? Matt's in a coma, and it would just upset Lizard to hear it after all these years. I think I'll leave things the way they are for now."

"Sounds like a wise decision, sweetheart."

"One more thing I wanted to ask you," Jen continued. "Um, does Grandma Paulina know Matt is my real father, or does she think it's Lizard?"

"I've always told Grandma Paulina that Lizard's your dad," Brandi answered, fidgeting slightly after a brief pause. "It was just easier. Grandma Paulina tends to overreact sometimes. I didn't want to tell her because I feared she'd take matters into her own hands and go after the Quinbys for money. I didn't want that because I thought they'd take you from me. So I said nothing to Grandma."

Jen took a deep breath.

"I guess I understand," she said. "I won't say anything, for now, either. Maybe in the future, if things work out, we can tell her Matt's my real dad."

"Okay, honey," Brandi said calmly, "we'll see. Grandma's kind of volatile and unpredictable. We'll have to figure that out in the future."

Jen nodded as she got up to pour refills of coffee at the stove. While she toted them back to the table, Brandi asked about her date with Colton.

"Oh, Mom," Jen sighed, stirring a teaspoon of sugar into her cup. "He's being such a bastard about this whole Matt-paternity thing. Over dinner, he told me to not get too used to the idea that Matt is my father, because he might not be. He said I need to consider the possibility that some other guy in San Jose, or Vegas, could be my dad. Could that be right, mom?"

"Absolutely not, Jen. You're a Quinby, through and through. I can promise you that. Matt was my first love, and my first lover. There was no one else. Don't listen to anyone who tries to tell you otherwise.

"Matt knows all this," Brandi went on, patting Jen's hand, "and when he comes out of the coma, he'll be thrilled to finally meet you. He'll tell Delia, Megan, Colton, and everyone else, that you're his daughter, and then you can finally get to know him."

"What about you, Mom? Are you hoping for a do-over with Matt?"

"It's a lovely daydream, honey. I'm open to it. But first things first. He has to come out of the coma and recover from his wounds. But enough about me and Matt. I want to hear more about your night with Colton."

Jen took a deep breath.

"It was kind of stormy," she said sadly. "He's been talking to Delia Quinby a lot since the shooting. The two of them are running Matt's company till he wakes up. She's coming here next week, and Megan is supposedly flying in tomorrow."

"Oh, wow, I wonder what it will be like to see her after all these years," Brandi said. "She's your aunt, Jen. That's pretty cool, isn't it?"

"Um, I don't know," Jen replied, shrugging.

"Well, she must know Colton, so that will work in your favor," Brandi said. "I just hope Matt's shooting and all this Zane stuff won't destroy things between you and Colton. I've got my fingers crossed for a happy ending with a big church wedding. Colton's a younger version of Matt. I missed out on my chance, honey. Don't blow yours."

"Oh, Mom, I think it may be blown already," Jen said, frowning. "He thinks we're both train wrecks. It hurt so much to look in his eyes last night and see how angry and full of doubts he is."

"Well, Jen, you should have listened to me seven years ago when you were 17 and started seeing Zane. I told you he was trouble. I begged, threatened, and ordered you to stop seeing him. You lied repeatedly and told me you would. But you were sneaking around behind my back.

"You were my daughter and I trusted you. What was I supposed to do? Hire a security guard to watch you 24/7? I had a job, too, and a social life of my own. I wanted to trust you, but I guess I was wrong.

"I guess it's my fault you were with Zane for four years before he finally got busted and sent to prison."

"Mom!" Jen said, plopping her sandwich on a plate, "I just lost my appetite. How many times do I have to tell you? Zane was good for me in so many ways. He brought glamour and sparkle to my humdrum life in Summerlin.

"I'd had these three stepfathers, and they all split. I guess I craved attention from a man who wouldn't leave me, and Zane was there for me in every way, including as a lover. No wonder I totally fell for him. Maybe our roller-coaster life with your three exes set me up for turning to someone like him."

"Jen, don't put this on me!" Brandi cried. "You better wake up and smell the coffee, girl. Stop blaming me for your mistakes!

"You need to focus on Colton now. You're going to lose him. He's going to slip through your fingers because of this Zane crap. And you can't blame him, can you? Who wants to look over their shoulder every day of their life, wondering if they're going to be shot, or in some horrible accident?"

"Just what I needed to hear right now. Thanks, Mom, for being so supportive!" Jen yelled as she got up, stalked off to her room, and slammed the door.

Brandi tried to get her to open up so they could talk, but Jen refused. Instead, she lay on her bed crying her eyes out and regretting everything about her life, before, during, and after Zane.

PART TWO

Treasure Island

CHAPTER 15

While Jen was locked in her room having a Zane meltdown, Brandi got a surprise phone call from Megan Quinby. She was absolutely rocked. The two hadn't spoken in 25 years. Given the circumstances, their call was an odd mixture of joy and awkwardness. After the requisite small talk, Megan explained In a soft, calm voice, "We're here in Florida for spring training. My husband's a pitcher for the Atlanta Braves. Everything was going well, and then the cops called with the terrible news that Matt got shot in a parking lot in Vegas. We were floored. I mean, who would want to hurt my brother? He's the nicest guy in the world."

"It's awful, I know," Brandi concurred. "Matt's been in a coma since the shooting. He's in intensive care at Las Vegas General. My daughter, Jen, and I saw him yesterday."

"Oh, thanks," Megan replied. "I'm sure it helped. Speaking of your daughter," she went on, her voice dropping a bit, "my mom gave me the most unbelievable news yesterday. She said there's an addition to the family since Jen, apparently, is Matt's daughter with you. If this is true, it's quite stunning. What a bombshell, Brandi! This even tops your wild bolt from San Jose four days before you were supposed to marry Matt back in '92."

"Ohhh," Brandi murmured, "those were hard times, Megan. I had a lot of problems with my mom and dad, and with your parents, too. I think you know what I mean."

"Yes, I guess I do," Megan admitted after a brief pause.

"I'm sure it's a lightning bolt to learn this now, of all times," Brandi continued, "but, yes, Jen is Matt's daughter. When I left San Jose all those years ago, I had no idea I was pregnant with her."

"Well, this is certainly a season for shocks and surprises," Megan responded. "But we can get into all that more when I come to town. I'm flying in tomorrow to see Matt and talk to his doctors. I'll be in Vegas a week or two. Maybe we could have lunch on Saturday? Jen's invited, too, of course. It'll be easier and more fun to meet her, and catch up with you, in a restaurant rather than a dreary hospital."

"Lunch would be great," Brandi replied, thrilled at the prospect of seeing her childhood bestie again. "Where will you be staying?"

"Bellagio. I was there years ago, for a wedding, and it was beautiful."

"I love it too," Brandi added. "It's like stepping into an Italian palace or villa. There's a great restaurant in the lower lobby called Cornucopia. Jen and I will meet you there at noon. I'll make a reservation for three. Call me if anything changes."

Two days later, Brandi was sitting in the dramatic, red-walled entryway of Cornucopia waiting for Megan. Jen had been excited about joining them, but at the last minute she got a pop-out gig and couldn't make it.

Brandi was nervous, but also keyed up. She was anxious to reconnect with her childhood best friend and find out a few things about Matt, too.

The five-star eatery looked elegant as always. Lavish paintings of food in all its glorious splendor were anchored to the walls of the bar, entryway, and large, sunny dining room.

From a huge picture window, Brandi was taking in Bellagio's iconic fountain show on serene, cobalt-blue Lake Como when she heard a familiar voice.

"Brandi, hi, is that you?" Megan asked when she finally arrived at 12:15.

Brandi got up and walked briskly towards her. After a warm hug, they were both grinning ear to ear.

"It's been a long time, you look wonderful," Megan said, taking a step back. "You haven't changed a bit!"

"Oh, thanks, I can't believe we're here. It's good to see you, too!" Brandi gushed..

"Sorry I'm late," Megan went on, a bit flustered. "I was tied up on business calls upstairs and couldn't get away."

"No worries," Brandi told her. "I'm sorry, too, that Jen couldn't make it. She's working today, but said she's looking forward to meeting you soon."

"Oh, that'll be lovely."

"So, are you all settled in?" Brandi asked. "How do you like Bellagio?"

"I love it," Megan replied. "That Murano glass-flower ceiling in the lobby is spectacular, and the conservatory is amazing. I just wish I were here under happier circumstances."

Nodding somberly, Brandi asked,

"Have you seen Matt yet? How's he doing?"

"Um, yes, I was at the hospital this morning, and there's not much to report," Megan sighed. "He's still in a coma, but stable."

Thin, blond, green-eyed Brandi may have looked the same as 25 years before, but Megan's appearance had changed a bit. She still had shoulder-length light-brown hair, and blue eyes like Matt's, but she was a tad plumper. In an attractive way, though. Brandi thought that if she had seen Megan out on the Strip, she would have looked familiar, but she might not have recognized her.

The two old friends were shown to a cozy corner table overlooking the lake. Brandi was clad in a chic black-and-white pants outfit; Megan wore a burgundy silk dress with tiny, multi-colored roses on it. Very Laura Ashley. It reminded Brandi of how her friend had dressed as a teenager.

While they checked out their menus, Megan chatted a bit about her job.

"I work for the biggest newspaper in Atlanta, writing a weekly column on all kinds of household stuff," she explained. "I also do segments on the local news sometimes. It's the same stuff over and over, but with a fresh spin. You know, how to make a killer peach pie, decorate a nursery on a budget, buy antiques like a pro. Things like that. It's a lot of fun. I love it."

"Oh, that's so cool!" Brandi said. "You're like a Martha Stewart, or Heloise, but younger and better looking, right?"

"Right," Megan said, chuckling. Brandi suddenly remembered the Megan she had known as a child, who loved baking cakes, rearranging her dollhouse furniture, and any kind of art or crafting project.

"You must be super busy," Brandi added. "Didn't you just adopt twins?"

"Yes!" Megan smiled. "I have two adorable, five-year-old girls running around my house, full-time. We had fertility issues for years and finally decided to adopt. It's been an amazing experience. The girls are doing great. They're at home right now with our housekeeper, but I check in a few times a day."

Megan looked happy while discussing her husband, career, and daughters. But when she moved on to Matt, her face darkened.

"My mom told me an ex-boyfriend of Jen's, who got out of prison recently, shot Matt," she said, tilting her head and staring at Brandi. "Is that true? Why would he do that?"

Brandi paused and took a deep breath. Clutching her wine glass, she took a sip and then attempted to explain the whole confusing, tragic tale of Matt's shooting, and how the crime had most likely been committed by Jen's jealous ex.

"The horrible truth," Brandi concluded, "is that Zane was probably aiming for Colton and shot Matt by mistake."

"Oh, my God," Megan gasped. "How could your daughter get involved with someone so sleazy and dangerous? Where is he now?"

"Who knows?" Brandi answered, tossing her hands up. "The cops can't find him. They questioned him once, after a weird car accident Jen thought he caused back in December. But he told them he was out of town at the time and had relatives who could prove it.

"That may be true, but somehow, some way, I'm sure he's behind all the scary stuff that's been happening to Colton and Jen over the past six months."

"This guy's a menace to society," Megan retorted. "He belongs back behind bars, and the sooner the better."

"Here, here," Brandi concurred, as she and Megan clinked glasses and sipped their Chablis.

After savoring tomato salads, followed by pasta-and-shrimp entrees, Brandi and Megan ordered slices of chocolate cake, which they nibbled while sipping coffee.

Their conversation had zigzagged from pleasant details of Megan's life in Atlanta to the disturbing subjects of Zane, and Matt's shooting, to Matt's life after Brandi left San Jose in 1992.

"Did you know he tried to find you after you left town?" Megan asked. "Mom told him not to, but Matt defied her, threw some things in a knapsack, jumped in his car, and took off for Chicago."

"Oh, my gosh," Brandi exclaimed. "I'm stunned. I had no idea."

"Yes, he was gone about a week," Megan went on. "What a trip. He hit a hellacious hail storm in Utah, then two girls from Texas stole his car. He reported it to the cops, rented another one, and finally made it to Chicago. But of course you weren't there, because you were here, right?"

"Right," Brandi nodded. "Lizard's old car broke down as we were entering Vegas. We got a cheap motel room near the welcome to Vegas sign. By the time the car was fixed, I was too sick to even think about leaving. You know, first pregnancies are often like that."

"So I've heard," Megan sighed.

"But enough about me," Brandi said. "Tell me more about Matt. When did he get married?"

"Oh, back In the spring of 2000, I think."

"What was her name?" Brandi wanted to know.

"Norris Blake. She's a few years younger than you, though you'd never know it by looking at her now. The last few years have been pretty rough. When she married Matt, she was a bright, beautiful, well-educated socialite from a wealthy San Jose family."

"Wow," Brandi said, impressed. "Someone told me she wrote a couple of novels. Is that true?"

"Yes," Megan nodded, sipping her coffee. "After her third baby, she'd had enough already of motherhood and went to work at QuInternet. Then she got bored with that, and started writing romance novels. There were two: one was a huge best-seller, the other totally flopped. I read them both. Real page-turners, interesting and dramatic, but a tad short on substance.

"I always got the feeling Norris wrote romance because it was so lacking in her own life. Her marriage to Matt was more about business and money than romance. A few years ago, they went to Lake Tahoe for a week to spend some time alone and get their marriage back on track. But they ended up having a terrible accident while aboard the family yacht.

"From what Matt told me later, they were having a nasty fight. Things spun out of control, and their boat was broadsided by another vessel. Both of them were thrown overboard. Matt came through okay, but Norris's leg was badly battered. At first, the doctors said she would recover. But after months of physical therapy and four agonizing surgeries, they realized the damage was permanent. She's been in a wheelchair ever since."

"How sad," Brandi said, frowning. "And now they're divorced, right?"

"Right," Megan answered. "They're co-parenting their sons who are now in their early teens. Mom helps out all she can, but the boys are pretty confused and upset after what happened to their dad.

"I think their lives were always turbulent because of the problems between Matt and Norris. I don't think he ever truly loved her."

"Oh, why do you say that?" Brandi asked, inserting her fork into a wedge of cake.

"Because Norris seemed so unhappy all the time. She got joy and fulfillment from her sons, work, and books, but never with Matt. I always sensed he was in love with someone else."

"Really," Brandi said, puzzled and curious. "Who?"

"You, of course," Megan shot back, looking her squarely in the eye. "I think he always wondered what would have happened if you two had gotten married in '92. There was no closure because you just disappeared one day. The two of you never actually broke up. So, in a way, the relationship just continued in his heart and mind."

Brandi was thunderstruck by Megan's comments. It was exactly how she had felt all through her own stormy marriages and divorces.

"You're definitely the one that got away," Megan added after a brief pause. "I think it broke Matt's heart when he found out you got married in Vegas. And then he heard you had a baby. He just assumed it was Lizard's."

"Well, yes, that's what I wanted him to think," Brandi said.

"But why, Brandi?" Megan asked leaning in. "Why wouldn't you want him to know you had his baby?"

"Because I feared your family would take her from me," Brandi replied. "The Quinby money and lawyers were always at the ready. I knew your parents would go into overdrive if they found out Matt and I had a daughter. They never would have allowed her to be raised in Vegas by a lowly cocktail waitress. They would have gotten their high-powered lawyers cranked up and taken her away. I couldn't risk that, so I did everything in my power to not let anyone know the father of my child was Matt."

Megan took a deep breath.

"Sounds like a sad and lonely existence," she observed.

"In a lot of ways, it was," Brandi admitted. "But at least Jen and I had each other. Nothing could change that."

Their long, intimate talk at Cornucopia had a therapeutic effect on both Megan and Brandi. After all these years, they could finally see the truth about each other, instead of the outlandish assumptions and half-baked truths they'd always taken as gospel.

Brandi was more than a willful, unstable runaway bride from the wrong side of the tracks. And Megan wasn't the spoiled, judgmental rich bitch Brandi had always dismissed her as.

After their long, lingering lunch, Megan returned to her suite to work on a column, and Brandi cabbed it to the Venetian where she was due to work an eight-hour shift.

Across the Strip at Paris, Jen was popping out of a six-foot cake at the huge National Association of Broadcasters convention. Later, she would troop next door to Bally's for a rousing, after-dinner performance for the International Engineers' Consortium.

It was a bustling Saturday in Vegas, and the living was definitely not easy for Brandi or Jen.

CHAPTER 16

I'm coming to Vegas this weekend," Colton announced to Jen on the phone one month after Matt's shooting. "I should stay here and work, but I miss you so much. Plus I want to see Matt and spend time with Delia. She's in Vegas. Have you met her?"

"Unfortunately, yes," Jen replied, rolling her eyes. "She blasted into the hospital last week to see Matt. We were never actually introduced, but when she saw Mom and me sitting in the visitors' lounge, she threw a fit. There was a nasty scene. Delia told Megan I was a security risk because of Zane, and that Mom and I shouldn't be allowed to visit Matt anymore."

"Oh, that's unfortunate," Colton said. "She's pretty traumatized over what happened to Matt. I guess some poor behavior is to be expected. I'm just sorry it was directed at you."

"Me too," Jen shot back. "And then she started ranting to Megan that she doesn't believe I'm Matt's daughter and that Mom and I are fortune-hunters, and I need a DNA test. It was horrible and humiliating. I didn't know if I could ever show my face at the hospital again. Thank God Megan spoke up for us."

"So things are going okay with her?" Colton wondered.

"Yes," Jen answered. "Megan seems really nice. She and Mom bonded over a long lunch at Cornucopia. It's easy to see how they were best friends as kids. They still get along great."

"Thank God you and Brandi have a friend in the Quinby family," Colton commented.

"Yes, Megan's cool, but Delia's a bitch on wheels. I never saw that woman before in my life, and she came charging into the hospital like a monster from the black lagoon. How can she be my grandmother?

"She practically threw us out, and tried to have us barred from visiting Matt again. It didn't work. Mom and I go every week, thanks to Megan. She lets us know when the coast will be clear."

"Good," Colton said, "Matt needs all the visitors he can get." And then he added, "Hang in there, babe. Things will ease up with Delia. Try to understand all she's dealing with, and cut her some slack, okay?"

"Yeah, whatever," Jen replied. "But she was pretty obnoxious to Mom and me."

Their call lasted for 20 minutes or so. Before hanging up, the couple agreed to meet on Friday night for dinner and drinks at their favorite Strip eatery.

Three days later, after performing two raucous pop-outs, a tired but excited Jen rushed home to shower and change. By 7 PM she was poised elegantly in the entryway of Rendezvous at Caesar's. In a low-cut, black silk cocktail dress, she discreetly powdered her nose while waiting for her man. At 7:15, her cell rang.

"Babe, I'm not going to make it to Vegas tonight," a rushed, hyper Colton declared, sounding upset but upbeat. "We had an important meeting with some tech guys from Dubai that lasted all day. We made a huge deal, but it took hours. Lots of give and take on this one, all around. Delia will be over the moon, but I won't get to Vegas till tomorrow.

"Will you forgive me? I've got our suite at Caesar's reserved, so that's all taken care of. It'll be just like the old days, only 24 hours later."

Jen was crushed.

"Oh, I uh, see," she stammered. "That's great news, about the deal. Congratulations. I'm at Rendezvous right now, waiting for you. They were just about to show me to our table."

"Sorry, sweetheart. Will you give me a rain check? We'll still have a great weekend, I promise. It'll just be delayed 24 hours," Colton said, trying to soothe her.

"I don't mean to rush this, babe, but I've got to go. We're heading out for sushi and sake to seal the deal. I'll talk to you tomorrow."

"Okay," Jen murmured. "I miss you. I'm, uh, disappointed…"

"Miss you too, babe, my cell's breaking up," Colton interrupted. "I'll call you when I get in tomorrow afternoon. Bye."

The line went dead.

Jen was hurt, but what could she do? It all worked out, sort of. She ended up having dinner that night with her best friend and co-worker at Stripper Grams, Amber Dean. They shared a shrimp pizza at Spago in Caesar's, where Amber had performed a pop-out at a huge vacuum dealers' trade show that afternoon.

They mostly talked about work things, but Amber always had plenty to dish about her boyfriend, Dave, and, ditto, Jen, on Colton.

The next day, Jen was psyched about seeing him. All morning she fantasized that he'd call her from the airport the minute his flight landed, and she'd rush to Caesar's to meet him for some afternoon delight in his suite before they sauntered off to Rendezvous.

It didn't happen.

Colton's flight landed late the next morning at McCarran. He quickly checked into a suite at Caesar's, then trotted next door to Bellagio, where Megan and Delia were staying in adjoining suites. After Megan booked a table for three at Biscuit, a hot bistro in Paris, the trio trekked across the Strip and savored a tasty lunch. While they ate, Colton told them all about the important deal he'd made with the Dubai contingent. Later, the three piled into his black Lexus SUV rental and sped off to the hospital to visit Matt.

In the car, Delia mentioned her nasty encounter with Brandi and Jen at the hospital.

"Those Putnam women were skulking around the visitors' lounge a week after the shooting," Delia recalled, rolling her eyes. "You'd better watch yourself with that daughter. There's a long line of unstable, troubled women in that family.

"Brandi's mother, Paulina, was a real piece of work. She was a waitress at the Waffle House, and ran off with the minister who was going to marry Matt and Brandi.

"A few weeks later, Brandi jilted Matt right before their wedding and blew out of town with another guy. Now she's a thrice-divorced, hot-mess cocktail waitress with a daughter whose father is unknown, although she claims it's Matt. And miss goldilocks-stripper Jen is on the road to big time trouble with her ex-convict ex, who's still on the loose.

"That's quite a load for anyone to carry, Colton," Delia went on. "I love you like family, so I'm giving you some motherly advice. Keep away from the pop-out girl. She may be easy on the eyes, but it's pretty poison."

Colton was jolted by the bluntness of Delia's words. Later at the hospital, the afternoon skidded from doom-and-gloom about Jen, to more doom-and-gloom about Matt, whose condition remained frustratingly unchanged.

It was a sad, sobering visit for Colton, Megan, and Delia. Afterwards, in an attempt to shift gears, the Quinby women took in a long-running show called Menopause the Musical at Harrah's. Delia was appalled by the raunchiness, but Megan found it hysterically funny.

Meanwhile, Colton and Jen met at Rendezvous for their Saturday night dinner date. Jen looked spectacular in a powder-blue satin cocktail dress that hugged her curves in all the right places. On her pretty, petite, size-six feet were matching four-inch heels. Totally killer. Colton couldn't take his eyes off her. And he looked pretty hot, too, in designer jeans, a dark cashmere sweater, and a black leather jacket. Silicon Valley swag all the way.

The dinner was lovely, but a tad somber. The couple hashed over current events at QuInternet, then moved on to Matt's condition, which made both their hearts heavy. As they dined on juicy lamb chops with a cognac-Dijon cream sauce and rich potatoes Dauphinoise, the conversation eventually wound its way to the topic of Delia.

"She was rude and hostile to Mom and me," Jen complained again to Colton.

"Babe, don't let it bother you," Colton replied with a dismissive flick of the wrist. "She's upset about Matt, and worried about his sons. Their mom has problems of her own. She's in a wheelchair, and hasn't been the same since the boating accident at Tahoe a few years ago. Delia has a lot on her plate right now. Give her a break."

"Stop telling me to give her a break," Jen shot back, "I'm not giving her anything! So much for family manners and kindness. She stopped just short of calling me a tramp, and then insisted that Matt isn't my father. Like Mom slept around with a bunch of guys before she got pregnant with me. That's just not true," Jen added, getting more upset by the minute.

"Mom isn't a whore now, and she wasn't back then either. If she says Matt is my dad, then he is. No ifs, ands, or buts. End of story."

"Of course, darling, of course," Colton said, patting her hand. "That was just crazy-talk from Delia. She lashes out sometimes and has no idea what she's saying."

Then he steered the conversation to Lizard Moats.

"What about the reptile-guy who was Brandi's husband when you were born? Does everyone think he's your father?"

"Yes," Jen replied. "Lizard's name is on my birth certificate. Mom told me she only married him so she would have health insurance when I was born. She said it was a brother-sister relationship, and they didn't even attempt to consummate their marriage for many months after I was born.

"They got divorced after a few years because Mom was still in love with Matt. Lizard could see that, and left her for someone else. Those are the facts, Colton. Matt's the only guy Mom was with before she left San Jose. I'm his daughter."

"That all makes sense, Jen, but Matt's a very wealthy man," Colton reminded her. "His company's one of the top firms in Silicon Valley. You can't blame Delia for being cautious and concerned."

"Obnoxious and insulting is more like it," Jen retorted.

"Well, she's been very generous and accommodating to me," Colton countered, leaning in.

"Babe, I love you," he added, "but I have to work with, and for, Delia till Matt's back at the helm. Please, would you give me a break on this? Can we all just get along, for Matt's sake?"

"Works for me," Jen said, tossing her hands up blithely. "So what is it about Delia Quinby? Why are you such a fan?"

"Oh, let me count the ways," Colton smiled. "First of all, she's a great lady, if you didn't know, kind, gracious, and generous to those less fortunate. She's involved in all kinds of charities that support children, abused women, and the poor.

"And of course, she's attractive and stylish. She knows how to throw an elegant dinner party with excellent food and interesting guests. Invitations to the Quinby mansion are coveted by the crème de la crème of San Francisco society.

"Then there's her business sense. I've been working closely with Delia since Matt's shooting, and I can tell you she's one sharp lady. Everyone always assumes Matt got his business smarts from his old man, Rand, who died 12 years ago. But my personal opinion is that his tech smarts and ability to deal with people came straight from Delia. She's got a great head on her shoulders; her opinions are always spot on."

Jen had heard enough. Turning away, she rolled her eyes and said sarcastically, "It's nice that you and Delia are so close. Too bad she hates my guts, especially since I'm her granddaughter. It really sucks."

"Babe, just try to be patient with her," Colton advised. "She's wary of strangers and used to people coming after her for money, jobs, or invitations. Give her the benefit of the doubt. She really is a smart, sensible, decent woman. She'll come around."

"Okay, Colton, whatever," Jen said. "Enough already about Delia. Let's get this conversation back to where it belongs: you and me and our paddleboat cruise on Lake Mead tomorrow. I'm so excited! The weather will be perfect and the scenery will be gorgeous. I'll have you all to myself out there.

"We're flying to the lake on a Maverick helicopter," she burbled on. "It's the top chopper company on the Strip. I've popped out of cakes at a few of their corporate events, and they're super nice.

"This will be a very cool experience. It'll get you away from the phone, the business stuff, and all the drama surrounding Mom and Matt. We'll be out on the lake on a Sunday afternoon in April, snuggling and cuddling. The focus will be totally on us!"

They both laughed. Jen could be so cute and charming when she wanted. Colton loved her warmth and vitality, not to mention her naivete. And her beauty, of course.

She was a gorgeous, blond babe, but also a strong-willed woman who knew how to get what she wanted. In soft, candlelit moments like these, Colton felt like one lucky dude. He could almost forget about her crazed ex, lurking out there somewhere in the dark with a loaded gun and an unsteady hand.

CHAPTER 17

There had been some tense moments during the Rendezvous dinner, but also some tender, romantic ones. By the time Colton and Jen got to his suite, it was game-on for a night of rocking sex.

Despite everything that had happened, from Zane's stalking, to the zip line and car accidents, and Matt's shooting, there was still a lot of passion percolating between these two. The lovemaking commenced, and nobody was disappointed. It was warm, sweet, uninhibited, and intense. What more could you ask of sex?

It was the first time they'd made love since Matt's shooting, and all the fears and anxieties of the past month melted away as Jen lay beside Colton in afterglow. He, of course, was sound asleep.

She finally lapsed into slumber, too, but not for long. Just as the clock struck three, the phone on the gilded nightstand rang. In a state of groggy confusion, Jen picked up.

"Hello," she said softly. But there was no

response. She repeated the word over and over, but the ominous silence persisted.

"Who is this? Who's calling?" she asked, annoyed and perplexed.

"Babe, it was probably a wrong number," Colton mumbled from somewhere in the middle of the bed. "Don't worry, go back to sleep."

Getting out of bed, Jen tried to pull the nightstand forward so she could unplug the phone. But it was too heavy. Plopping back into bed, she glanced at the clock. It was the precise hour Zane had called their room in the past. Could it be a coincidence? After Matt's shooting four weeks before, definitely not, Jen concluded. It had to be Zane.

The shaken beauty managed to tumble back to sleep, but it was fitful. And then, just 45 minutes after the first call, the phone rang again. Sitting bolt upright, Jen stared at it and froze.

A groggy, half-awake Colton asked, "Babe, aren't you going to get that?"

"No," she answered, "I think it's Zane."

The phone finally stopped ringing. Pulling a blue satin robe on, Jen dialed the Caesar's operator and asked if the two calls had been from inside or outside the hotel.

"Both were made from house phones," the operator replied.

Jen's heart sank.

"Where, exactly?" she followed up, "The casino? The hotel? The Forum Shops?"

"Sorry, ma'am, I don't have that information," was the response. As Jen hung up, a chill went through her. By then, she and Colton were wide awake.

"If Zane made those calls from inside Caesar's, where is he now?" a frazzled Jen asked, throwing her hands up. "Maybe he was here, right outside our suite?"

"I'll take a quick look," Colton said, jumping out of bed and throwing on a pair of black jogging pants.

He stared out the peep-hole, then opened the door and looked around warily. All was quiet and calm. As he re-entered the room, an exasperated Jen buried her head in her hands.

"What's he trying to do to us?" she wailed.

"Um, break us up," Colton replied, climbing back into bed. "This guy wants you back, and he's not going to stop till he gets you."

"Well, that's not going to happen!" Jen cried. "How does he even know we're here? There must be someone inside the hotel tipping him off when your name is on the guest list.

"Zane has connections all over town. He has friends and associates everywhere," she went on. "Look at the zip line accident. How did he cause that? Even the cops couldn't figure it out. He must have been following us that day, and he paid someone to tamper with the cables while we were waiting in line. What else could it be? There's never been an accident in the history of SlotZilla.

"And the car crash. The security cam was switched off in the mall parking lot where our car was, but nowhere else. I'm telling you, Zane has contacts everywhere. It's beyond anything the cops can figure out."

"Jen, is this a nightmare, or are we actually living this?" a bare-chested Colton asked, perched beside her. "We just had this great night, and now this. If what you're saying is true, we can't stay here again."

"Well, maybe it wasn't Zane," Jen said, backtracking a bit because she knew how much Colton loved Caesar's. "Maybe it was just some crazy coincidence. Some former guest calling from another hotel or city, to reach someone who already checked out."

"Jen, come on, we both know that's not what's happening here," Colton countered, looking at her. "Zane's driving us both crazy. We can't sleep. He shot Matt a month ago and left him in a coma. The guy's obsessed with you, and on top of that, he's a psychopath. How are we supposed to figure out what to do next?"

"Maybe I should get another protective order, or a restraining order?" Jen stammered.

"The one you got in December didn't help at all," Colton reminded her. "I don't think people like Zane give a damn about protective orders or restraining orders. Screw the police, and everyone else. They just want what they want, and the hell with everything else."

Since neither of them could sleep, they turned on the TV and watched a movie, Sleepless In Seattle, with Tom Hanks and Meg Ryan. It seemed so simple and sweet, almost quaint, compared to the drama and trauma they were actually living through.

A half-hour into the movie, Colton fell asleep,

but Jen remained wide awake. It was at moments like these that she felt closest to him, and yet so distant. She craved his love and approval. Colton was an impressive dude, with all the right credentials: college, pedigree, booming career, and wealth. A nice, sexy, successful guy she could see herself marrying someday and raising kids with.

Though she knew little about Mr. Wonderful beyond the obvious, that seemed enough. And Zane's deranged antics and criminal behavior had only served to point up Colton's attributes all the more. He was the perfect companion to stand by, and protect, her, to show the world that she had overcome adversity herself, and to inspire her to boost her own talents and chart a new course for herself. These were Jen's thoughts as she lay wide awake beside Colton those long, lonely, pre-dawn hours.

By the time the sun came up over the iconic Strip, both of them were awake. They had planned to take a Lake Mead cruise that day, but there was no way that was going to happen now. They were both too tired, too sad, and too scared. Maybe Zane would have them, and everyone else on board, capsized and drowned by day's end? From all they had seen and experienced, it seemed entirely possible.

Around seven AM, Colton called room service. Jen felt queasy and needed to eat something light to settle her stomach. Twenty minutes later, their coffee and toast arrived.

In jogging pants and a tee shirt, Colton opened the door. As the room-service cart trundled in, he glanced down at the floor. A white, business-size envelope was lying there. After signing the tab, he closed the door and picked up the envelope.

Jen had just ambled out of the bathroom, where she had taken a shower and washed her hair. She was standing in the center of the suite in a short, pink terry-cloth robe, drying her long, golden locks with a matching towel, when she saw Colton gripping the envelope.

"What's that, something from the hotel?" she asked.

"Um, I don't know. It was on the floor. I guess someone slid it under the door in the middle of the night."

"Well, open it," Jen said, crossing the room and standing nervously beside him as he extracted a piece of white paper from the envelope. On it was a multi-colored target. A crudely fashioned bulls-eye was in its center with a bullet hole and bright red blood gushing from it. Written across the page in bold, black letters that had been cut from newspapers and magazines and pasted on, was the word, C-O-L-T-O-N.

Jen's knees were suddenly weak. Dropping the towel she had been drying her hair with, she sank onto the bed.

"Oh, my God," she cried, "Zane was here, or he sent someone. He could have been right outside our door with a gun. What does this mean? Is he going to try to kill you, or me, or both of us? We need to call security. If we don't, we could end up like Matt, or worse."

Wide-eyed and alarmed, Colton stared at Jen.

His hand was shaking as he handed her a cup of coffee, and then poured one for himself.

Picking up the phone, he dialed security. Two officers came up right away and checked the hall camera on the 12th floor. The lens had been covered with a black cloth sometime during the night, preventing knowledge of whatever activity had taken place in the hall.

The situation was beyond the scope of normal activity for hotel security, so Vegas Metro was called.

While waiting for the cops, Jen slipped into the festive, red-and-white polka-dot frock she had planned to wear on the cruise that day, and Colton pulled on khaki pants and a long-sleeved polo shirt.

A half-hour later, brown-haired, blue-eyed, pudgy Metro cop Bart Nolan, dressed in a crisp, sand-colored uniform with holstered gun and silver badge, was listening attentively to Jen as she recapped all that had happened. Seated on a beige loveseat, with Colton perched beside her, she tearfully talked about the two bizarre phone calls made from somewhere inside Caesar's. Then she showed the cop the vile piece of paper with Colton's name scrawled across it.

"What can we do?" Colton asked, throwing his hands up. "Phone calls in the middle of the night, dangerous accidents no one can explain, following us around the Strip. How can this guy be allowed to stalk and harass us like this?"

"We've been trying to find Hollister since Matt Quinby's shooting," Nolan assured the couple. "But he has vanished into thin air. We've been in close contact with security at McCarran, and so far, nothing. Do you have any idea where he might go if he left town?" he asked Jen.

"Um, no, not really," she said softly. "He has relatives In Barstow and Virginia City, but I don't know if he'd go there."

"There's nothing we can do at the moment," Nolan informed them. "If we can find Hollister, we'll bring him in, as we've done before, for questioning. Last time, he slipped through our fingers with an airtight alibi."

With latex-gloved hands, he picked up the envelope holding the sheet with the bloody target on it.

"I'll take this back to the lab for fingerprint analysis. Anything on it will be checked against Hollister's prints, on file from his prison days.

"I'll get back to you with the results. In the meantime, watch your step at all times. These 'Romeo stalker' cases can turn on you just like that."

"Romeo stalker?" Colton asked. "What's that?"

"Someone who thinks they're pursuing a person out of love, but it's really a sick, violent obsession that often ends tragically," he explained.

"Oh," Jen gulped, staring at Nolan and nodding. "That sounds like what we're dealing with. What do we do now?" she asked. "What's next in this sick game?"

"I wish I knew," Nolan replied. "We can't predict how, when, or where Hollister will strike next, but from what happened last night, you're on his radar. He's getting ready to pull something again."

"Well, what can you do for us, aside from check fingerprints and pat us on the hand?" Colton asked. "Can you provide some kind of protection, like a full or part-time bodyguard, for Jen?"

"Unfortunately, that's not the way we work these cases," Nolan explained. "We simply don't have the manpower to provide round-the-clock security for every domestic relations case that needs it. We'd be overwhelmed.

"As I've explained, if the threat is real and there's credible evidence, we'll bring Hollister in. We need to wait and see where he strikes next. In the meantime, remain vigilant at all times, and don't go anywhere alone at night, when you would be most vulnerable."

Handing Jen and Colton his Metro business card, he added, "I'll get in touch with lab results. Call the station right away if you hear from him, or he makes any kind of move."

Clutching the cards, Jen and Colton sighed wearily, shook Nolan's hand, and walked him to the door of their suite.

CHAPTER 18

It was still relatively early when the cop left that Sunday morning. Dazed by the lack of sleep and rush of events, Jen was anxious and quivering with tension. Standing in the center of the suite, she and Colton clung to each other for support, dumbfounded and uncertain what to do next. Neither was up for the Lake Mead cruise, but they'd missed their pick-up anyway so it was no longer an option.

Colton was returning to San Jose that night, so the remaining hours were precious.

"Why don't we order some pancakes and eggs from room service," Jen suggested, "and have a nice, relaxing breakfast. Then we can watch a movie in bed and see where the day takes us. What do you say, babe?"

"Sounds cozy," Colton said, smiling. "First things first, I'll put the 'Do Not Disturb' sign on."

Jen was groggy and tired, but starting to feel better. Then the phone rang. "Should we answer it?" she asked.

"It could be someone from QuInternet, I better

pick up," Colton replied.

He was right, sort of. It was Megan Quinby, next door at Bellagio with Delia. They wanted Colton to join them for brunch at a fabulous French bakery-restaurant in the Venetian called Bouchon. Afterwards, the three would drive to Las Vegas General to visit Matt.

Colton glanced over at Jen, dressed jauntily in the polka-dot frock and nestled comfortably on a loveseat. They had been just about to call room service when the phone rang.

Somewhat awkwardly, he asked, "Can I bring a guest?"

"Jen?" Megan quickly responded.

"Yes," Colton said sheepishly. "And then she can come to the hospital with us. Even though Matt is still in a coma, he would love it. Believe me, he would feel her presence."

Putting Colton on hold, Megan spoke to her mother.

"Absolutely not," Delia replied tartly in the background. She knew Megan was letting Brandi and Jen visit Matt at the hospital, and it infuriated her. So, just to be spiteful, she clamped down now and refused Colton's request.

"Um," Megan sputtered, trying to be polite, "maybe we can do a rain check on brunch for four, and keep it at three today. Will that work for you, Colton? Mom would really prefer that Jen not be included."

"Oh," Colton said, disappointed, "that's unfortunate, but I, uh, understand. I'll meet you both at Bouchon at 11, then we'll go see Matt."

By the time the call ended, Jen was standing in front of Colton, furious, with her pretty face twisted into a snarl and her hands on her hips.

"You're going to have brunch with them?" she demanded.

"Yes," Colton answered. "Please try to understand, babe. I'm going back to San Jose tonight. I'll be at QuInternet first thing in the morning. Delia has some business things to discuss. It's not really a social call, it's more like a meeting. You would be so bored. Maybe some other time you'll be included. We'll do it, I promise."

"Why don't you call them back and tell them I'm more important than some goddamn business meeting, and you're going to spend the day with me," Jen bristled, staring at him. "We can go to a show this afternoon, or hit the casino before you leave."

"Jen, I can't, really, I can't," Colton told her, shaking his head. "Delia and I have accounting stuff to discuss on the Dubai deal. It's important for the company. Megan would have been happy to have you, but Delia bluntly told her you would not be welcome. It's petty, uncouth, and grossly rude, I know, but trying to force the issue will just cause more problems.

"I hope Delia will come to her senses soon and see what I see—and what everyone else in the world sees--that you're the sweetest, most adorable creature alive!"

Jen laughed in a loud, strident way to show the full force of her scorn and contempt for Delia. She felt hurt and betrayed by Colton's dropping her like a hot potato to run off for brunch with the Quinby women.

Grabbing her clothes, make-up, and assorted trinkets, she started tossing them haphazardly into her overnight bag. Ditto for Colton. Exiting the suite, they rode the elevator in silence to the lobby, then trekked outside to the Strip.

Rushed, and with a minimum of words, Colton plunked Jen in a cab. Handing the balding, big-bellied driver a fistful of 20s, he said, "please drive this lovely young lady to Summerlin and take good care of her."

Leaning into the cab, Colton quickly kissed Jen's cheek and purred, "bye, darling," before closing the door.

"Bye," she responded glumly, barely looking at him.

Turning abruptly, Colton started striding rapidly up the Strip to the Venetian.

Huddled in the back of the cab in her pretty red-and-white dress, a miserable Jen sat listening to stale tales of the driver's former life in the Bronx. She was crying softly and blotting her nose with a Kleenex. She felt dejected and humiliated. It hadn't been much of a weekend with Colton, just a dinner date and booty-call, followed by more Zane trauma.

Later that day, after Colton's long brunch and visit with Matt, he flew back to San Jose. Jen was hoping he'd call, just to check in, before he left, but he was too rushed and barely made his flight.

CHAPTER 19

H oney, what are you doing here?" Brandi asked when a forlorn-looking Jen wandered into the kitchen around noon. "I thought you were going to Lake Mead with Colton. Where is he?"

"Having brunch with Delia and Megan at Bouchon," Jen replied with a dismissive flick of the wrist. Then she told her mother about the morning she'd just experienced, including the Zane drama.

All Brandi heard was the Zane part. She was outraged, furious with Jen's psycho-ex, and the local cops.

"What are they waiting for?" she asked bitterly, "you or Colton to be killed? Will that finally get them off their asses and make them do something?"

"I don't know, Mom," Jen answered, "but Officer Nolan, the cop who came to our suite this morning, feels strongly that Zane is planning another attack. He said these less serious events are often a prelude to something bigger. If only they knew where to find him, or how to stop him.

"That disgusting threat he put under our door last

night is at the lab right now, being analyzed for fingerprints. Officer Nolan will call with the results. They have Zane's prints on file. I hope there's a match."

Sighing and shaking her head, Brandi pushed her cup of coffee aside.

"Every time he does something to you, it feels like I'm being attacked, too," she said in an anguished tone. "When will this torture end?"

"Mom, I'm sorry. Please don't get so upset."

Brandi was quiet for a moment. Putting the Zane issue on the back burner, she asked Jen about her date with Colton.

"We barely saw each other on this trip," she complained, "and then he ran off to be with Delia and Megan today. I wasn't even allowed to join them. Megan was okay with it, but Delia said no. Can you believe it? That horrid old bag told Megan I couldn't be at the brunch, or visit Matt with them.

"I felt humiliated in front of Colton. Things between us aren't good, Mom. We're losing each other," Jen said, her voice high, thin, and cracking a bit. "Last night was more like dinner with a booty call than a tender, romantic date."

"Honey, these are tough times," Brandi told her daughter. "You need to see things more realistically. Colton is dealing with a lot right now. Cut him some slack.

"If he doesn't want to come here because of Zane," Brandi went on, "maybe you could fly out to San Francisco sometime? You could meet his parents and younger sister. That would be nice for both of you, and it would get you out of Vegas. You two could have some fun without having to worry about your psycho-ex every minute."

"You know, Mom," Jen said, pouring them both a cup of coffee, "that's not a bad idea. I've always told Colton I want to come out to meet his parents and see the city. I'll talk to him about it the next time he calls."

"Good," Brandi said, "now sit down and have some eggs and toast with me. Who needs Bouchon?"

Jen gladly complied, and the Conover women savored a comfy, cozy breakfast in their cheery green-and-yellow kitchen.

A few days later, Officer Nolan called Jen with results of the fingerprint tests.

"We found prints on the paper and envelope, but they don't match the ones we have on file for Hollister. We have no idea whose prints those are."

Jen was disappointed, but she thanked him.

"Stay vigilant," he told her. "This guy is dangerous, a jealous rampage waiting to happen. Never allow yourself to be complacent. Look for little things that are out of the ordinary, any clues that he might be nearby, or trying to contact you.

"He's probably hiding out with one of his cohorts right here in Vegas, but we can't narrow it down at the moment. We'll call you the minute we have something more definite," he assured her.

Jen thanked Nolan again and let him go. Then she called Colton in San Jose to give him the latest.

"Um, I think it would be a good idea if I stayed away from Vegas for a while," he said somberly. "Our weekend was pretty tense and unpleasant. I don't want my life, or yours, to be in danger. I think my being there simply provokes this asshole more.

"There's so much work here anyway. The only thing is, I'll miss you, babe, and I'll miss seeing Matt, even though he's still in a coma."

Jen's heart sank.

"Maybe I could fly out there sometime?" she suggested, trying to sound upbeat. "We've always talked about it, and now would be the perfect time. To keep things proper, I'll stay at a hotel downtown. But if you play your cards right, I'll let you join me!" she added playfully.

"You can show me around San Francisco. We'll ride the cable cars, take a trip to Sausalito, eat clam chowder on Fisherman's Wharf. All those cutesy tourist things. What do you say, Colt? Are you with me on this?"

"Yes!" he replied, eagerly. "But not right away. I'm swamped. Maybe in the fall. It's gorgeous that time of year. We could take a side trip to Napa. It would be a blast. Great idea, babe."

After they hung up, Jen felt hopeful and happy about her relationship with Colton. But she couldn't help wondering how long it would last.

CHAPTER 20

All through the long, hot summer of 2017, Jen was beset with personal issues. There were problems with her mom, with Delia, with Colton, and the ongoing Zane saga was basically unbearable. Every time she left the house, she looked over her shoulder. Every time the phone rang, she jumped. And the sound of the doorbell made her run for cover.

To cope with the ongoing anxiety, she wanted to spend more time at home relaxing with Brandi. But the mother-daughter duo fought constantly about Zane, the DNA test, and Colton. Brandi would tell her, "You're going to lose Colton if you don't rev up your act. Show him you're independent, you don't need him, and everything's going well with your job. Then he'll want to be with you. If you act too fragile and needy, that will just bore him and drive him away."

"Oh, Mom," Jen would respond, throwing her hands up, "I'm just trying to stay alive. I don't need you to be a living, breathing Cosmo cover, with your silly, old-fashioned feminine advice.

"Telling me how to hold onto my man, blah, blah, blah. With Zane out there lurking around, I'm just trying to survive and keep Colton safe, too."

It was the same argument over and over. Brandi meant well, but she always said the very thing that would upset Jen the most. Same with Colton. Their phone calls would start out pleasantly, but then erupt into arguments about Zane or the DNA test. He felt strongly she should have it. She felt strongly she shouldn't because it would be disloyal to her mom.

Despite the ongoing stress, Jen was thriving at work. From June through September, prime convention season in Vegas, she worked two or three events a day, six to seven days a week.

Grateful for the work, and the distraction, Jen reveled in her pop-out gigs. Her enthusiasm and vibrant sex appeal brought a campy, Marilyn-Monroe-like warmth and humor to her performances. The customers ate it up. Jen's ratings were off the charts, five-stars all the way.

The hard work and dedication paid off. In October she landed a plum assignment at Stripper Grams. Concrete Universe, a global conglomerate specializing in all things cement, was going to stage its annual convention at Treasure Island on the center Strip. Only the crème de la crème of pop-out girls would be hired to emerge from the cakes at their events. That meant Jen of course.

The five-day gig was a sweet deal that all but guaranteed major exposure, huge tips, and a generous expense account. Comped rooms would be provided by Treasure Island for each girl so they could be available for events at any time of the day or night.

Jen was thrilled. Five days away from Brandi were just what she needed, and the money would help. God knows, both Conover women were always trying to rake in more. Yes, they had enough to get by, but there was no real security. They had to constantly hedge their bets merely to stay afloat, and go above and beyond to create a buffer, just in case.

When Jen told Brandi about the job, she was happy, but also concerned.

"Sweetheart, you've got to watch yourself on the Strip. What if Zane finds out you're staying in a room at Treasure Island by yourself and swoops in to hurt you or take you? Promise me you'll be careful at all times."

"I will, Mom," Jen nodded. "It will be fine, you'll see, and this is the perfect time for me to get away from everything, all the DNA stuff, and Colton, too. He's basically ignoring me, you know, and going workaholic.

"This is my career," she exulted, "and I've climbed to another rung on the ladder. Amber is coming along; we're doing a tandem act. She'll pop out of a cake at one end of the convention hall, I'll pop out of one at the other.

"It's very cool. Amber's a brunette, so the frosting on her cake will be buttercream. I'm blond, so mine will be chocolate. And we have these sexy new costumes. I'll wear a pink bustier with a black-lace bikini underneath. There's also a glittery-silver one trimmed with white lace.

"Amber will be in cobalt-blue or purple. The roses on the cakes will match the color of the bustier. Every detail has been thought out and coordinated by the stylists. I'm so excited!" Jen prattled on. "And someone will film the pop-outs, so I can use the videos for auditions. This will really help my career."

Pop-out girl Amber Dean, Jen's best friend, was from Kansas. Like Jen, she was in her early 20s and had started at Stripper Grams around the same time. Amber and her boyfriend, Dave Perkins, a lighting technician on the burlesque show, Fantasy, at Luxor, had been with Jen and Colton on SlotZilla when Colton had his bizarre accident. So she knew a lot about Jen's former life with Zane, her current life with Colton, and the whole stalking mess.

Brandi was relieved Amber would be working with Jen. Otherwise, she probably would have told her she couldn't stay at Treasure Island. Too risky, with Zane still on the loose.

In her sporty red Ford Focus, Amber picked Jen up, bright and early on a Monday morning in October 2017. The girls would rehearse that day and familiarize themselves with the ballroom venue. From Tuesday through Friday, they would work two events a day, and then check out of Treasure Island on Saturday.

Jen had packed a suitcase full of sundresses, work-out clothes, and lounge wear. Stripper Grams was transporting all the costumes, equipment, and props the girls would need.

As they drove to Treasure Island in their cut-offs, pastel-colored tees, and sandals, Amber and Jen were giddy with excitement. What an adventure for these two perky pop-out babes.

Amber was another all-American stunner, a young Priscilla-Presley-look-alike, with long, jet-black hair, blue eyes, pale skin, and a killer bod. Ideal pop-out material. And Jen, of course, was her blond counterpart, with long, golden locks, green eyes, and fair skin. They were both about 5'6", and slim but shapely.

As the girls checked into their rooms on the 14th floor, the excitement mounted. The digs were simple and basic, but first-class. King-size beds, large-screen TVs, spacious closets, bathrooms with well-lit make-up mirrors, and colorful paintings of birds and landscapes on the walls.

Giggling like school girls on holiday, Jen and Amber ran back and forth between their rooms, comparing their accommodations. Stripper Grams was spot-on with these two babes. They were both winners.

The rest of that day went well. In a cavernous, empty ballroom, Jen and Amber rehearsed for hours, learning their cues and familiarizing themselves with technical, sound, and lighting details.

That afternoon, while they were on break, their supervisor, a caustic, hot-mess, 40-something ex-stripper from Bayonne, New Jersey named Destiny Pellegrini, stopped by. She directed the girls, clad in shorts, tees, and sandals, to a large, round table for an impromptu meeting.

Destiny was dressed, as usual, in head-to-toe black: tights, tee-shirt, and a billowy blouse that concealed her pudgy body. Encircling her thick, butterfly-tattooed neck was a large, glittery, faux-diamond necklace that looked like a prop from the old Folies Bergere show at Tropicana.

As the three sat at a table in the empty ballroom sipping ice-cold Dr. Peppers, Destiny stressed the importance of the Concrete Universe gig.

"You girls are in the big leagues now, and you need to look the part," she said, gazing back and forth between Jen and Amber. "You're both hot, but lip injections and lash extensions would take things to the next level. Everything has to be super-sized, so the guys at the back tables are knocked out, too."

Turning to Amber, she noted, "Your boobs are a bit on the skimpy side. Some of these Concrete guys are flying in from halfway around the world, and they're not sitting on a plane 18 hours to see A and B cups. You need to get enhancements to a C or D down the road. Meanwhile, we can buff and stuff to pump you up.

"Jen, your boobs are okay. What cup size did you say they were?"

"C," Jen answered.

Doing a double thumb's up, Destiny went on, "But your ass could use some amping up. We'll pad for now, but you're going to need implants, like, yesterday."

Jen and Amber stared at Destiny and nodded like Stepford pop-out girls, as if they were on board with what she was saying. But of course, they weren't. They were both annoyed and totally turned off by the tacky, drill-sergeant attitude. They considered themselves adequate in every possible way.

"Any questions?" Destiny asked.

"Um, no," Jen and Amber murmured, shaking their heads.

"Awesome," Destiny replied before barreling on. "What you have to realize is, we're competing with bigger, higher-budget shows like Fantasy at Luxor, Crazy Girls at Planet Hollywood, and Girls of Glitter Gulch downtown. We have to go all out, kick ass and blow them away with every single pop-out. But it has to be tasteful. No nickel-and-dime stuff like Cupcake Dolls downtown, where they substitute cupcakes for costumes.

"Stripper Grams is a higher-class operation. We gotta have the hottest, sexiest, most virginal creatures popping out of these cakes. But it has to be classy. Am I making myself clear?"

Once again, Jen and Amber nodded and murmured yes.

"Awesome meeting. You girls need anything else?" Destiny asked.

"No, we're good," Jen said.

"Okay, then, I'm outta here. You two can get back to work. Call me if you need anything. I'll be around tomorrow for the pop-outs. Just remember, Concrete Universe has been with us from the get-go. They're a loyal customer that pays on time and minds their Ps and Qs. If they're not pleased, or we lose the account, my ass will be on the line with corporate. You gotta knock it out of the park with every single writhe and wriggle. Just sayin'."

Taking their final sips of Dr. Pepper, the trio concluded their meeting and got back to work.

As Jen and Amber trotted back to the sound and

lighting technicians waiting for them, they looked at each other and rolled their eyes.

"There's so much bullshit in this business," Amber said under her breath. "Destiny's a bitch-on-wheels, the supervisor from hell. If we weren't getting good money and lots of fringe bennys, I'd kick her ass."

Jen laughed and added, "And I'd help you!"

She was looking forward to the day when she got a gig in a high-class show on the Strip and didn't have to put up with this petty nonsense anymore.

Later that day, Brandi stopped in before work and joined Jen and Amber for a festive dinner at a Brazilian steakhouse. It was like three girlfriends who'd known each other for years, dishing about their jobs and the men in their lives over medium-well steaks with all the trimmings.

On Tuesday, Amber and Jen both worked an afternoon event attended by 2,000 concrete aficionados. The audience, 90% male, was wildly enthusiastic. What a treat for these concrete types: mixers, vendors, construction guys, a few architects, and retail pitchmen.

Jen's pop-out was killer, and on the other side of the convention center, Amber's rocked, too. There was a dinner break around 8 PM, and then a second show at midnight. They didn't get back to their rooms until 2:30 AM, or so, because of course there was "compulsory mingling" (Destiny's words) with the audience afterwards.

The men treated them like celebrities, which was very cool, a boost for their egos. But a few of the big guys got grabby, which was also typical. Jen and Amber both had long talks with Destiny, who gave them ridiculous, snarky pointers on how to deal with pushy customers who always want more. The bottom line was that you had to retain your hot, sexy, vulnerable aura while being assertive and firm, and then, at the right moment, get the hell out of there before anyone could grab your boob or ass, or talk you into going up to their room. Sweet and seductive, but assertive. Not the easiest mix to pull off.

Wednesday was a repeat of Tuesday. The convention was going gangbusters. Brandi met Jen for dinner that night, and all went well. Amber was dining with Dave, who would then spend the night in her room.

At 7:30 on Thursday morning, Amber called Jen to let her know she and Dave were going downstairs for breakfast at the coffee shop and they would be back shortly. Jen needed to know this because she and Amber were heading to Canyon Ranch SpaClub, across the Strip at the Venetian, for work-outs and facials at 10 AM.

Dressed in a purple-velour workout suit, Jen was lying on her bed watching a movie, when suddenly there was a knock at her door. What a pain, she thought, as she dragged herself up to answer it. The "Do Not Disturb" sign was off, so her room was fair game. Staring out the peep-hole, she saw a room-service waiter standing in the hall.

The dark-haired dude, wearing a tall chef's toque (hat), was dressed in a white coat and black pants. His cart, covered by a white linen cloth, held several covered dishes and a coffee-pot.

"Room service," he announced.

"I didn't order anything," Jen yelled through the door. "You have the wrong room."

The guy knocked again, this time louder and with more urgency. Jen felt flustered. Some of these hotel types could be so aggressive and disrespectful of your privacy, she thought. As soon as she was finished dealing with this pest, she would put the "Do Not Disturb" sign on, and leave it there for the rest of her stay.

A third time, the guy knocked and repeated, "room service, open up please."

Jen was getting more annoyed by the minute. What a pain-in-the-butt this guy was. He must have a hearing problem, she thought. Out of exasperation, she finally opened the door a couple of inches to peek out.

His dark-brown eyes stared in at her. His longish black hair was almost falling in his eyes under the hat. In a flash of horror, Jen suddenly realized she was looking at Zane!

He was standing outside her door, and she was totally alone. She instantly tried to push the door shut, but Zane pushed harder and barreled inside with the cart, kicking the door closed behind him.

Staring at him, Jen cried, "get out, get out, leave me alone! I don't want to see you, now or ever!"

"Playing hard to get again, babe?" Zane purred, gliding the cart down the carpet. "Why bother? You're looking hotter than ever." Edging closer, he nuzzled her neck and kissed it.

"Mmmm, sweeter than the frosting on one of those cakes you pop out of," he murmured.

Backing away, Jen snarled, "Zane, stop, you're delusional! We're not a couple anymore, and we haven't been since before you went to prison. What are you doing here? How did you find me?"

"Darlin', when you love someone as much as I love you, you just know where they are at all times. It's a built-in radar system," Zane said with a smart-ass smile. Moving closer again in his white coat, he caressed her cheek with the back of his hand.

Again, Jen pulled away. Pointing at the door, she warned, "You better get out of here before my friends come back. They'll check on me and know something's wrong. Get out now, or you'll wind up back in prison."

"Calm down, baby, and stop all this prison-talk. That's no way to turn a guy on. I don't want to hurt you. That's the last thing I want. If you just do what you're told, nobody will get hurt and we'll both have a real good time."

"You did that drive-by shooting at Piero's in March, didn't you?" Jen suddenly blurted.

"I don't know what you're talking about," Zane replied, with a dismissive flick of the wrist. "I don't do drive-bys, darlin'. That's gang shit, not my style."

"Colton's boss was shot and he's still in a coma," Jen retorted. "It's horrible for everyone who knows and loves him."

"Well, sorry to hear that," Zane replied sarcastically. "But what does that have to do with me?"

"Everything!" Jen said. "You did it. You were trying to shoot Colton and you hit him by mistake."

"Babe, I told you, I don't know what you're talking about. This is getting old, let's move on. You sound like a bad rerun of Law and Order. We haven't seen each other since last summer, and all you want to do is push me away and accuse me of shooting people. Come on, Jenny, I'm a lover, not a fighter, you know that," he said seductively, wrapping his arms around her.

Pulling away, Jen bristled, "Zane, I'm warning you, get out now. Take that cart and wheel it back into the hall. I won't say anything to anyone. It'll be our little secret."

"What is this, Let's Make A Deal?" he sneered. "There's a better prize behind door number two, babe. You come downstairs with me, we get in my car and get the hell out of here. Spend the day together, then the night, and see where it takes us."

Jen shrieked again, "No! Get out. Leave me alone. I have a job. I have to work today."

"Work? Is that what you call it?" he asked, throwing his hands up. "Popping out of a cake while all those slimy, concrete bastards get hard-ons staring at your tits and ass. Meanwhile, I get nothing, not even a kiss. That's not very cool, is it, Jenny? You're not going to that goddam job today—or ever again. Now, get your stuff. We're outta here!"

"Zane," Jen wailed, getting more desperate and panicky by the minute. "Please leave! Like I said, I have to work today. I can't spend the day with you. I don't even want to spend five minutes with you."

"There's a little something in my bag that might sweeten you up and change your mind," he said with a smarmy, sinister charm, bringing the room to silence.

Reaching inside a black leather bag hidden under a mound of linens on the cart, he extracted a small, silver handgun.

Jen's knees suddenly grew weak, her jaw was shaking. She knew Zane was more than capable of using the gun. She thought of Matt, lying comatose in a bed at Las Vegas General. She didn't want to end up like that. No matter how crazy things got, she didn't want to end up like that. She decided she would play along with him, for now, so that later she could break away and get out alive, functioning, and in one piece.

Zane tore his white kitchen coat off and tossed it on the bed. Underneath, he was wearing a grey shirt, black jeans, and boots.

"Babe, my meter's runnin'," he told her, "we need to go—now."

Standing in the middle of the room, wide-eyed and taut, Jen was watching every move he made.

After pushing the room service cart into the hall just outside the door, Zane squished his white coat into a ball and stuffed it in his black bag.

Then things started happening really fast.

CHAPTER 21

"G et your purse, darlin', it's show time," Zane ordered.

"No, I'm not going anywhere with you, leave me alone!" Jen wailed.

Taking her into his arms, Zane kissed her warm, soft mouth and neck, wet with tears. She jerked away, but he pulled her back, murmuring, "Don't cry, Jenny," as he covered her face with kisses. "The last thing I want is to hurt you," he said softly. "Now come on, let's go."

But Jen didn't want to go anywhere. Her legs were weak. She felt faint. Zane could see how pale she was, so he plopped her beige-leather satchel on her shoulder, and shoved her sandals on. Then he turned the volume on the TV up high and affixed the "Do Not Disturb" sign.

Leaving Jen's room, Zane gripped her arm tightly, pulling her along. On the way to the elevator, they passed a maid. Displaying tight little smiles, both of them nodded and bid good morning.

The halls at Treasure Island are endless, but eventually they made it to the elevator and hit the button. It took a minute or two, but the car finally came. When the steel doors opened, the first thing Jen saw was Amber and Dave. Behind them were a handful of other riders. As Amber stepped out, she stared at Jen.

"Who's he?" she asked, alarmed and curious, looking at Zane, "and where are you going? We have appointments at CanyonRanch in an hour."

Amber had barely spoken when Zane yanked Jen forward to enter the car. There was a strange, pale, scared-shitless look on her face. Zane was pulling her forward, but she wouldn't budge. Amber could instantly see what was happening.

It wasn't easy, but Jen jerked her arm away and yelled at Amber, "It's Zane, he has a gun!"

When they heard that word, everyone on the elevator panicked and started flailing about. People were screaming and hitting buttons frantically, but the car wouldn't budge because passengers were blocking the doors.

Reaching into his bag, Zane pulled his gun out. But he could see the situation was already out of control and he needed to get out of there fast!

Within seconds, he was racing for the exit stairs, with Amber's strapping, six-foot boyfriend in close pursuit.

"Dave, no," she screamed, standing outside the elevator, "come back here!"

"What's he doing?" Jen shrieked, throwing her hands up.

"I don't know, but I don't want him hurt!"

Amber then took off after Dave, and Jen chased after Amber. They all ended up in a nearby stairwell, galloping furiously down.

On the third landing, Zane suddenly halted and jerked around. Yanking a red fire extinguisher off the wall, he pulled the pin, squeezed the handle, and unleashed a stream of chemical foam at Dave. Blinded by the blast, the tall lighting technician throttled forward and tumbled hard down a bank of 20 concrete steps.

Amber and Jen heard him cry out, but couldn't see him in the cloud of chemical mist. Stopping cold, Amber screamed, "Dave, Dave, where are you? Are you alright?" But there was no response. She and Jen ran to him, lying sprawled and immobile on the 10th floor landing.

"Oh, my God!" Jen cried.

"What happened to him? He's bleeding like crazy," Amber yelled. "We've got to get the paramedics. My phone won't work in here. Can you go upstairs and call security?"

Staring down at Dave, both of them were horrified and nauseous. His head had been bashed hard. Blood was oozing out the back and also from a wide gash above his right eye. His nose looked bloody and broken.

A sickening mix of blood and foam was clinging to his light brown hair. Worst of all, he couldn't speak or respond to Amber's cries and questions.

Dropping to the floor, she carefully lifted Dave's bloody head onto her lap. Jen reached into her purse, grabbed some tissues, and handed them to her friend.

"Here," she said, "maybe these will help. Don't move him! Don't do anything till the paramedics get here."

"I have to put his head up or he'll choke on his own blood," a panicky Amber said. "It looks like his nose is broken and the blood is going down his throat. If I don't lift his head, he won't be able to breathe."

Staring down at Dave and Amber, Jen nodded, but she was terrified.

"Where's Zane?" she suddenly wailed, looking wildly around.

"Down there, somewhere," Amber said, pointing down the stairs. Then she added, "Quick, get the medics!"

"I'll go upstairs and call them," Jen told her. "You stay here with Dave."

"Please hurry!" Amber begged.

Turning abruptly, Jen leapt up the stairs. By the time she got to 14, her legs were weak and she was out of breath. Forging ahead anyway, she made it back to her room.

With trembling hands, she pulled the key out of her purse and opened the door. Inside, she staggered to the phone and called security. Her jaw was shaking so hard she could barely speak.

"A guy fell in the stairwell around the 10th floor," she blurted. "His head is bleeding, his nose looks broken, he can hardly breathe. Please send help!"

"What's his name?" the security guard asked.

"Why do you need that?" a flustered Jen answered. Then she sputtered, "Dave Perkins. He was running after a guy with a gun, my ex-boyfriend, Zane. He tried to kidnap me, but I got away."

"Where's the guy with the gun now?" the security guard asked, rushed and frazzled.

"I don't know," Jen shot back. "Maybe he's still in the stairwell, or the garage, or maybe he's gone. I don't know. Please hurry, you have to catch him!"

"What is your name, ma'am? Who am I speaking to?"

"Jen Conover, room 1482."

"We'll get someone to the stairwell right away," he said. "And we'll find the gunman ASAP!"

"Please, don't let him get away," Jen pleaded. "He's been making my life hell for over a year. Please get him!"

Within minutes, a team of EMTs raced to the stairwell to treat Dave's injuries. He was then carefully placed on a stretcher, taken down the service elevator, and rushed to Las Vegas General. A badly shaken Amber rode with him in the ambulance.

Meanwhile, a team of security people frantically combed the stairwell, garage, and entire hotel for Zane. But they got nowhere. It was too late. Somehow, he had made it down to the garage, out to his car, and away from Treasure Island.

CHAPTER 22

Back in her room, Jen was lying on the unmade bed, clutching pillows and blankets to steady herself. Her heart was racing. She was crying and numb at the same time. She wanted to call Brandi, but she knew her mom was working and had already missed so many days and been late so often. She was afraid that if Brandi left work to rush across the Strip to comfort her, she'd be fired, so Jen held off.

Then she thought of Colton. She wanted to call him and pour her heart out about how awful she felt: lost, sad, scared, and full of regrets about her past. Jen wanted to spill it all and have him console her and tell her everything would be okay. But she knew that was a fantasy. In reality, he would be aghast that the Zane saga was continuing, and more convinced than ever that he needed to stay the hell out of Vegas.

Jen couldn't call Amber either, because she was on the way to the hospital with Dave. Jen desperately hoped he would be okay. Amber seemed so scared. Why did he do it? Why did Dave run after Zane? Some kind of macho impulse, Jen figured. Wanting to protect Amber, and her, too.

So, who to call?

Reaching for her purse, Jen fished out her wallet and dug through it for Officer Bart Nolan's card. Steadying her hand, she dialed his number. She didn't think he would pick up in the middle of a busy weekday, but he answered on the second ring. When she heard his voice, she burst into tears.

"Officer Nolan, please come to see me at Treasure Island," she said, fighting to get the words out.

"Jen, is that you?" he asked.

"Yes, it's me. Please can you come to Treasure Island right away? I'm here for a few days working a job. Zane found out and came here this morning and tried to take me. I got away, but my friend's boyfriend got hurt. I'm in room 1482. Can you get here soon?"

"I'll get there as fast as I can," he told her. "Try to rest and don't let anyone in your room unless you know who they are."

"Please hurry," Jen told him.

Just hearing Nolan's voice made Jen feel better. Taking a deep breath, she lay back on a stack of pillows, trying to calm herself. Ten minutes later, the phone rang. Jen thought it might be Nolan so she picked up. But it was her bitch-goddess supervisor, Destiny.

"Jen, is that you? Your voice sounds weird," she blurted with typical bluntness.

"Yes, it's me, Destiny," Jen answered, her voice quivering a bit, "how are you?"

"Fine," she shot back, "The question is, how are you? I heard from security that your ex paid you a visit today, and Amber and her boyfriend got involved.

"Apparently, it was quite a double date, with EMTs joining the party. And the guest of honor got away. Are you okay?"

"I'm kind of shaky," Jen murmured.

"You're going to be able to work the retirement gig at three, right?"

Jen glanced at the clock. It was almost noon.

"I, uh, don't know. Maybe you should find a replacement for me. I need the day off, I think. If a sub could do the gig this afternoon and the one at midnight, that would be great. I'll come back tomorrow."

"Sorry, Jen. No can do," Destiny told her bluntly. "Every girl we have is out, doing parties and events. It's convention-central around here this week. We barely have enough girls to go around, and you and Amber are our top pop-out babes. You're the blond, she's the brunette. It's like salt and pepper. We need you guys.

"Concrete Universe is one of our biggest customers," she barreled on. "Special requests have been made. The old boys are panting for you and Amber. Must be awful to be so young and sexy that you drive men wild with lust, huh?"

"Um, I don't know what you're talking about," Jen replied softly, her voice trailing off.

"Yeah, whatever, Little Bo-Peep stripper Jen. So, where's your partner in crime?"

"Amber's at the hospital with her boyfriend. He

ran after my ex, who had a gun, in the stairwell. My ex ripped a fire extinguisher off the wall and turned it on him. Dave got blinded with chemical foam, and fell down a flight of concrete steps. It was horrible. There was blood everywhere. Amber was hysterical. We were both crying. His nose looked broken. I hope he doesn't have a concussion."

"Well, Jen, that all sucks, for sure, but I still need you and Amber to work the party three hours from now. Would you do me a favor? Get her on her cell and tell her she needs to be back here to work the gig."

"Oh, Destiny," Jen told her, "I really don't want to do that. She must be so upset. I think she should stay at the hospital with Dave till tomorrow."

"So, let me get this straight," Destiny replied, temper now boiling, "you're telling me that neither one of you can work today, right?"

"Right," Jen answered.

"Wrong!" Destiny fired back. "If you two don't work these parties, my boss will be all over me. My ass will be fired, and yours and Amber's, too. It's that big a deal, Jen. Either you two get your booties in gear and wriggle out of those cakes, or my ass is trash.

"I'll let you go now so you can call Amber. I don't care what shape the boyfriend's in. That's not my problem. I just need you both to work these events."

Closing her eyes for a minute, Jen tried to block it all out. Then she told Destiny she'd call Amber.

"Hi, it's me," she said softly when her bestie answered her cell on the third ring. "How's Dave?"

"Um, okay," Amber replied somberly. "The doctor said he has a concussion and his nose is broken. He'll need surgery in a few days, when the swelling goes down. He also has a couple of fractured ribs. He's on pain meds and antibiotics, but the doctor said he'll be back to normal in a few weeks.

"I've been on the phone with Dave's boss at Luxor. They're trying to find someone to fill in for him till he gets back. They'll hold his job for a month."

"Oh, God, Amber," Jen murmured, "I'm so sorry this happened to Dave, and to you, too. Why did he do it? Why did he run after Zane?"

"I don't know. That's just the way he is," Amber answered. "A good Samaritan, I guess. If he's in a crowd and something bad happens, he's the one who will jump in and do something. It's just his nature."

"Well, I hope he's going to be alright," Jen said. Then she got down to business and told Amber to come back to the Strip to do the parties. She made it clear that If she didn't, she could lose her job.

"Okay," Amber sighed. "But this is way beyond the pale, even for that sadistic bitch, Destiny. I'll try to hitch a ride in one of the emergency vans. How the hell am I going to do two pop-outs? I'm still shaking so bad, I can barely hold this phone. I need sedatives."

"Me too," Jen said, "but they might affect the energy of the act, so I think we should go in straight and sober."

"Goddamn it," Amber said, frustrated and upset.

"The minute the party's over, I'm going up to my room. No hanging out with grabby old geezers today. Destiny will be pissed, but that's tough. I'm doing her a favor just showing up." After agreeing to meet around 2:30 to go down to the convention center together, the pop-out girls hung up.

Fifteen minutes later, Jen's phone rang again. Officer Nolan had arrived and was on his way up. When she opened the door, he walked in, clad as usual in a crisp, sandy-beige uniform. Bursting into tears, Jen flung herself into his arms. He held her and comforted her for a few minutes. Then they talked.

"Zane was standing right here in this room--with a gun," she said, shaking her head in disbelief. "He pretended to be room service and tried to force me to leave with him. How did he know I was here?"

Reflecting on her question for a moment, Nolan responded, "Someone at Stripper Grams must be tipping him off for money or drugs. Same thing at Caesar's. Someone on the staff lets him know when you and Colton are there."

"Oh, my God, who could it be?" Jen asked, throwing her hands up. "How am I supposed to figure it out?"

"You're not," Nolan told her. "We're working on it, but any information you can provide will help."

"Isn't there a security camera in the hall?" Jen asked. "Wouldn't that have caught everything?"

"Yes," Nolan confirmed. "But what was there to see? Just Hollister in a white coat and hat pushing a cart to your door. Then him barging in when you opened it, and the two of you walking down the hall later, with him gripping your arm. That's it. I think he knew where the cameras were and positioned himself in such a way that there would be minimal exposure."

"Oh," Jen said, sighing. "So, the cameras don't really help a lot."

"Not in a situation like this, where someone knows how to get around them."

A familiar wave of despair washed over Jen. Would she ever be free from this menace? This was a guy she had loved at one time, and look what it had turned into. Something sad and sick, a sadomasochistic stalking game, with lots of people getting hurt.

Just then, Nolan got another call, and had to leave.

"Stay in touch," he told Jen on his way out. "Call if you need help, or if there's any contact with Hollister."

Jen felt better knowing he was a phone call away, and looking out for her. But she worried about him, too. Maybe Zane would do something awful to him if he found out he was helping her? What a sad thought, but a possibility in this horrid new Zane-centric reality.

CHAPTER 23

After the attempted kidnapping, Treasure Island offered to move Jen to a higher, more secure floor, and she took them up on it.

While she was popping out of a cake in the convention center, a few maintenance guys moved her things from the 14th floor to the more elite 22nd. The number of her swank new suite would not be listed on any guest register, nor would it be known to anyone on the hotel staff but a select few. And one guest would also know it: Amber.

On Friday morning, Jen invited her up to see her new digs. Perched on a pale-yellow silk-covered love-seat in Jen's pastel-hued living room, Amber plucked her phone out of her purse and dialed the hospital to check on Dave. A nurse told her he was stable, still on pain meds and antibiotics, and the swelling on his nose was going down. His surgery would take place in a few days, and, if all went well, he would be discharged the following week.

Switching off her phone, Amber took a deep breath and spilled the latest on Dave. Jen sympathized and tried to comfort her. She also thought of Matt, on the fourth floor in the same hospital, and hoped he was improving. She and Brandi were planning to visit him the following week, when obnoxious battle-axe Delia would be back in San Jose.

After their chat about Dave and a brief tour of Jen's suite, the pop-out girls went to breakfast in the lobby coffee shop. As they nibbled blueberry pancakes and bacon, some of the concrete guys from the night before ogled them from an adjacent booth.

When they finished eating, the guys ambled over to Jen and Amber's table and gushed about how wonderful the show had been. The half-dozen gawking, middle-aged contractors then asked the girls to autograph their Concrete Universe event planners for that day. It was a nice boost for both girls' egos. The pop-out life wasn't for everyone, but it certainly had its moments.

After breakfast, the besties trekked to Treasure Island's bustling lobby. While they hugged, Amber assured Jen she'd be back for their three o'clock pop-outs. Then she dashed out the revolving door and ducked into a cab that would take her to Las Vegas General.

As Jen rode the elevator back up to her suite, she felt anxious. Brandi was on her mind. Jen wanted to call her to tell her about the latest Zane incident, but she didn't want to alarm or upset her, so she put it off.

Meanwhile, back in Summerlin, Brandi was missing her daughter. Before starting her shift that day, she decided she would drop in on Jen at Treasure Island.

Clutching a bag of warm banana-nut muffins, Brandi, dressed in beige jeans and a pink blouse, knocked on the door of Jen's 14th floor room a few hours later. When a burly, big-bellied stranger opened it, a flustered, embarrassed Brandi quickly apologized and retreated to the hall, where she called Jen. A quick elevator ride later, she was on the 22nd floor.

"Hi Honey, surprise!" she said, hugging Jen, who was waiting for her. "I know how much you love these. I hope they're still warm. What are you doing on this floor? Where's Amber?"

Reaching for the bag, Jen smiled, opened it, and took a sniff.

"Mmm, these smell good, thanks, Mom. Amber's on 14, I'll explain later."

As they strode to Jen's suite, a wide-eyed Brandi gazed around at the crystal chandeliers, elegant wallpaper, and plush red carpet.

"I don't know what you're paying, sweetheart, but we can't afford it," she cracked.

"Don't worry, Mom, it's all being covered by the hotel."

Inside Jen's spacious suite, Brandi parked herself at the marble breakfast nook while Jen figured out how to use the coffeemaker. As they sipped and nibbled, Jen explained the grim reason she had been moved from the 14th floor. Brandi's jaw dropped. She was terrified for Jen, but also hurt and angry.

"And you didn't call me?" she asked. "I'm your mother. Don't you think I had a right to know that maniac tried to kidnap you yesterday?"

"Mom, I knew you were working. I didn't want to bother you. I was going to call you today, or tell you about it when I got home tomorrow. In the meantime, they moved me up here, and I love it. There's 24/7 security. I feel safe. I can finally sleep at night. Isn't it pretty?"

"Yes, it's very luxurious and nice," Brandi agreed. "But still, Jen, you should have called. Where's Zane now, and how are Amber and her boyfriend?"

"Mom, I have no idea where Zane is. Not a clue. And if I did, he'd be in jail right now, 'cause I'd tell the cops.

"Amber's doing okay, I guess," she went on. "Pretty shaken up, but no broken bones or bruises. And Dave's in Las Vegas General with a concussion, fractured ribs, and a broken nose. He's on pain meds and antibiotics and will need surgery to fix his nose."

"How awful," Brandi sighed, shaking her head. "So Dave's in the same hospital as Matt?"

"Yeah, Mom, isn't that bizarre?"

"I don't know how bizarre it is," she replied, "but if this Zane stuff continues, they're going to have to build a whole new wing just for his victims."

Jen did a double-take at her mom. Brandi sometimes said the strangest things and Jen didn't know how to take them. Usually, she just let it go. This was one of those times.

"And how are you doing, honey?" Brandi asked, taking a sip of coffee and breaking off a chunk of muffin. "You must have been scared to death."

"I was," Jen nodded. "And then we had to work two events, one yesterday afternoon, one last night. Destiny told us we'd be fired if we didn't show up."

"Oh, God," Brandi groaned, throwing her hands up. "When is this nightmare going to end?"

"You mean my job?" Jen asked.

"No!" Brandi shot back, "I mean the terrorizing and stalking by Zane."

Shaking her head, Jen took a deep breath. Then she mentioned Officer Nolan's visit and related his theory on how Zane had found her.

Brandi gasped.

"Someone at your job might be feeding him information on where your pop-outs are? Who could it be? How can you keep working there?" she asked.

"I told Destiny about it, and requested that my name be taken off the schedule for a few months," Jen replied. "She wasn't sure if the tech guys could do it or not. I don't know if I can believe anything she says. She's kind of a bitch, you know?"

"Yeah, I know," Brandi concurred. "I just hope she comes through for you. You shouldn't have to ask for something like that. How does it make you look? This whole stalking thing is wrong on so many levels.

"That piece of scum, Zane, has totally destroyed our lives since he got out of prison a year ago," Brandi continued, getting more upset by the minute. "Mark my words, honey, one or both of us will end up being kidnapped or killed by this lunatic."

"Oh, Mom," Jen groaned, clutching her head

with both hands and shaking it.

"Maybe we need to think about moving to another neighborhood," Brandi ranted on. "I don't feel safe in our house anymore. Or maybe we should move out of Vegas altogether."

"What?" Jen cried. "I've lived here all my life. I don't want to move!"

"But Jen, this is getting out of control and we have no one to protect us. Maybe we both need to learn how to use a gun. Nick told me he knows someone who owns a gun range. He said the guy could teach us all about firearms, and how to shoot to kill."

"Sounds grim," Jen said, leaning in. "I don't want to carry a gun in my purse. What if it went off by mistake? Someone could get hurt."

"That's a possibility, I guess," Brandi conceded. "I don't want to carry a gun either, but look at the way things are going. Zane won't stop till he gets you back, and we can't let that happen. But if he has a gun, what are we going to do? Grab a butcher knife off the kitchen counter?"

Setting her coffee cup down, Brandi buried her head in her hands and started to cry. Jen went to her, wrapped an arm around her, and nestled her head in her shoulder.

"Honey, I ran away from San Jose all those years ago with Lizard," the distraught mom said, her voice quivering as she dabbed her eyes with a Kleenex. "And then we got stranded with car trouble and I found out I was pregnant with you. It was tough, tough, tough. But Lizard married me, and you were born in Las Vegas General. Your first year of life, you slept in a dresser drawer at the Pink Swan Motel, where we were living, right near the Vegas sign.

"There was no money, no family, no help. It was a struggle, Jen, but I raised you right, despite the cocktail-waitress hours, three divorces, and lack of family ties. I raised you with love. I raised you to respect yourself and care about others. And then, at 17, you broke my heart when you took up with that low-life scum, Zane.

"Did you know his father died while trying to escape from a prison chain-gang?" Brandi asked, looking her daughter in the eye. "Billy Ray Hollister was a druggie who robbed convenience stores and dealt drugs. Like father, like son. Zane's a career-criminal, too.

"And who's going to protect us? Nobody, honey, nobody. Nick's a friend, but he can only do so much. We have no one. Maybe moving out of Vegas is the only answer. If the cops can't, or won't, help us, maybe moving to another city is our only hope."

"Mom, I don't want to leave Vegas!" Jen said again, gripping Brandi's arm and shaking it. "This is my home. I love it here. My friends are here. My job, my future as a showgirl, it's all here. I can't move anywhere else. Where are we going to go, Kansas City? Omaha? Salt Lake?"

"No," Brandi answered. "Maybe San Diego or Miami. Cities with good weather, lots of nightlife, and some pizzazz.

"We could move out of state and not tell anyone where we're going. Just disappear without a trace," she went on. "If we don't, Zane will come up with some way to track us down. What else does he have to live for? Nothing, Jen, nothing."

"Mom, please, you're scaring me. Don't be so grim. Just take it easy. Eat your muffin, drink your coffee. Relax. We'll figure something out."

"What about Colton?" Brandi asked. "Have you told him about this latest Zane thing?"

"No," Jen replied. "Between the pop-out gigs, all the problems with Amber and Dave, and the move up here, I haven't had time to call him. And God knows he's not going to call me. We used to talk every day, but not anymore.

"The weekend visits aren't happening either. Colton's too scared of something happening with Zane," she explained. "Another freak accident or shooting, more stalking and threats.

"Being terrorized by an ex-con-ex is not the sexiest thing in the world," Jen confided, shaking her head. "It's not much of a turn-on. If you want to destroy a couple's sex life fast, just put an ex-boyfriend stalker into the picture and let him scare the hell out of everyone. The sex will dwindle and die pretty fast, I guarantee. Goddamn bastard."

"Jen," Brandi said, leaning in. "I don't know about all that, but I do know this: you should not tell Colton what happened with Zane yesterday. If you do, he'll become even more distant."

"I don't know if that's such a good idea," Jen countered. "He'll find out somehow, and then he'll be furious that I kept it from him. That I deceived him or manipulated him into thinking he'd be safe here. And that's just not true. He's not safe here.

We're not even safe here."

"But Jen, how are you going to get closer to him and take your relationship to the next level if he's too scared to come here? I've made a lot of mistakes in my life, and I can tell you that saying anything about what happened yesterday will just drive Colton further away.

"Listen to me, baby girl," Brandi continued, setting her coffee cup down. "I blew my chance with Matt when I was 18 and could have married him, even though it probably would have been a disaster. Then I went through three marriages and divorces. One mistake led to the next. Now I'm over 40 and alone. I'm not happy about it, but I don't know how to change things. I think I'm too scared of getting hurt again.

"So, what I'm trying to say is, don't end up like me. This is not a good place to be."

Staring at her sad, beautiful mother, Jen took a deep breath and frowned.

"Mom, there's something else I need to tell you."

"More, there's more?" Brandi asked.

"Yeah, but not about Zane. It's about Colton. A couple of weeks ago, Amber told me she saw him walking through the Bellagio lobby on a Monday afternoon. I told her, no, he's not in town or he would have called me. But she insisted it was Colton and he was with two women that sounded a lot like Megan and Delia.

"So I called his office at QuInternet and asked to speak to him. And the receptionist told me he was out of town for a few days. So he was here. He probably flew in to see Matt, and spend time with

Delia and Megan.

"It broke my heart to think he came here and didn't call me. Further proof he's losing interest."

"Honey, I'm sorry," Brandi said, shaking her head. "That's pretty cold. I hope that nasty, bitter old hag, Delia, isn't poisoning him against you because of all this DNA-test stuff. Megan, Colton, and Delia all want you to have it. But I'm you mother, and I say no. And mark my words, when Matt comes out of the coma, he will confirm what I've said all along: that you're his daughter and no one else could possibly be your father. Then we can tell them all to go to hell!"

Taking a deep breath, Jen nodded and poured more coffee for herself and Brandi. They both reached for another muffin. It was one of those two-muffin kinds of days.

"So, Mom, where do we go from here? What should I do about Colton? I can't throw myself at him. I can't call him and be the pursuer. I don't want to look desperate or stupid or scared. I want to come across as strong, independent, and smart. Tell me, Mom, what would you do if you were me?"

Taking a sip of coffee, Brandi thought for a minute.

"What about the trip to San Francisco we talked about a couple of weeks ago? Maybe now would be the perfect time. The next time you talk to Colton, bring it up. Tell him you have a few days off and you'd like to get out of town. Remind him you haven't seen him in a while and you've always wanted to go to San Francisco.

"Just let it happen very naturally and casually.

While you're out there, you'll probably be invited to dinner with his family. That's the kind of thing that will move this to the next level.

"And if you end up going, be very careful about who you tell. We wouldn't want Zane to hear about this. He'd go ballistic and do something crazy."

Jen nodded.

"Okay, Mom. The next time Colton calls, I'll bring it up and see how he reacts."

CHAPTER 24

That fall of 2017, it was business as usual in Vegas. The Concrete Universe convention wrapped up on a Friday, and Jen was booked for two events a day from Saturday through Monday. That was a whole lot of popping out of cakes.

On Tuesday, she finally got a day off. Brandi was working an early shift for a sick co-worker, so Jen slept in. By eleven, she was propped at the kitchen table in a short, ice-blue satin romper, watching the local news while munching a toaster-waffle.

Oh no, Jen thought, when she heard the phone ringing: Destiny, or another pesky telemarketer? Too lazy to check the caller ID, she picked up without looking and said hello. A familiar voice on the other end said warmly and sweetly, "Hey sweetheart, it's me, how are you?"

"Colton!" Jen cried. "Is that you? Where are you?"

"Yes, of course it's me. Who were you expecting?" he cracked. "I'm at QuInternet, between meetings. Just wanted to check in with my best girl."

"Oh, that's sweet, but why haven't I heard from you?" Jen scolded.

"Sorry, babe, but it's been impossible here. I have to do my job, and then Matt's. One job was more than I could handle before, now I have two. Things are out of control. Delia tries to help, but she's in Vegas half the time looking after Matt. And when she's here, she's tied up with his kids. So, I'm on my own at big, sprawling-colossus QuInternet. I'm the man with the plan now, the one everyone turns to for answers."

"Well, man-with-the-plan, I need some answers," Jen teased.

"What are the questions, darling? I'll try to answer them to the best of my abilities," Colton said playfully.

"Here's one," Jen shot back. "My friend Amber, you remember her, don't you?"

"Yes, of course," Colton answered.

"Well, she told me she saw you at Bellagio on a Monday afternoon in August with two women who sounded a lot like Megan and Delia. Were you in town then, or was Amber seeing things?"

"It was no mirage," Colton replied. "I was in Vegas in August to discuss some business matters with Delia and to check on Matt. His condition has not changed a bit. It's just like the day he went into the coma. We don't know what will happen with him, which puts the company in a rather precarious position with stockholders, competitors, international clients, and everyone else.

"Anyway, Jen, I wanted to call you and have dinner or something, but it was so hectic, and I didn't want any weirdness from your ex. I figured that if I came to town and we spent time together, he'd find out from one of his spies and pull a crazy stunt. I wanted to protect you from further pain and agony."

"Oh, I see," Jen said, rolling her eyes. "That was nice. I guess I understand what you're saying."

"But it was sad to not see you," Colton added, "and I did miss you."

"I miss you too," Jen said softly, "always. Are you coming back to Vegas anytime soon?"

"Unfortunately, no. Too busy, and I'm helping my parents do some renovations on their house. For some insane reason, they trust my judgment and taste."

"I'm sure it will be awesome, they're in good hands," Jen said, her heart sinking a bit. "I guess we're not going to see each other anytime soon."

"Babe, it's just for the time being, with all that's going on. Don't get all sad and abandoned," Colton said.

"Well," Jen interjected, "here's a thought. Maybe I could come out there. Remember, we talked about this? I have some vacation time, and I've always wanted to see San Francisco. I'd love to meet your parents and sister. Plus, we could do some awesome things together. What do you say, Colt? It would be fun, and we're both overdue for some of that!"

"When would this be?" he asked.

"Early December," Jen replied.

"Oh, I think my parents are going to be in New

York for a convention then."

"Well, that might be even better," Jen giggled, "we'll have more time to ourselves."

"But, sweetheart, I'm so busy. Some guys from the UK and Switzerland are coming through around then, and they're going to need a lot of time and attention. My days will be one long meeting."

Jen felt terrible.

"Colton, if you don't want to see me, just say so, instead of coming up with all these excuses. You've always come here. I thought it would be nice if I flew out there for once. I'm capable of packing a suitcase and getting on a plane, too."

There was a brief silence.

"Okay, babe, I hear you," Colton said. "I'll make the time. Just tell me the dates and I'll make it happen. We both deserve a break. It would be nice to have you meet my parents and sister. They've heard so much about you. They would love it."

"It will be fabulous!" Jen gushed. "It's time, Colton. Life can't be all work, work, work. You need time off as much as I do. And I've always wanted to visit the Bay Area. Late fall would be the perfect time."

"You're right about that," Colton agreed. "Maybe we can go to wine country for a day-trip, and I'll take you to Sausalito. You'll love it."

"That would be so cool!" Jen said excitedly. She felt relieved and deliriously happy. Maybe she had imagined things to be worse than they actually were, and Colton had just been swamped with work? Maybe there was still hope for their relationship.

"Sweetheart, I'm so glad I called and that you want to come out here. It will be a terrific trip. Look, I've got to run to another meeting. I'll call you in a few days."

"Okay," Jen said. Then they both made some cutesy-kissing noises and exchanged intimacies as they hung up and returned to the mundaneness of their Tuesdays.

Jen couldn't wait to tell Brandi she had been right. The San Francisco trip would be just what she and Colton needed to get their relationship back on track.

But of course, after she hung up, she was beset with doubts and worries as she stared down at her cold waffle and coffee. Colton had been so charming, but was he lying about why he hadn't called her when he was in town? Was all that talk about wanting to protect her from another Zane incident bogus? Was the real reason he hadn't called because he didn't want to deal with all her baggage?

Of course, Jen had fibbed, too, by omission, not mentioning the attempted kidnapping by Zane at Treasure Island the week before.

Some relationship, she thought. We're both lying to cover up the bad stuff, while pretending everything's okay as we chatter on about this trip. Oh well, at least things are pleasant and civil on the surface. After all the trauma and turmoil of the past year, Jen thought, I'll take it.

PART THREE

San Francisco

CHAPTER 25

As he prepared for Jen's visit to San Francisco, Colton hoped and prayed his family would behave and not press her for too many details on her background and how they met. Over the past two years, he had been vague on all this because he knew they would frown on her lifestyle and job.

Another thing Colton had never mentioned: the nightmarish attacks and harassment by Zane. No, no, no. That would have set off all the alarm bells. His rich, conservative, Nob Hill parents would have gone ballistic and barred their 31-year-old son from returning to Vegas, or even seeing Jen again.

Colton's parents were aware of the car crash in December 2016 of course, because Colton had been hospitalized with his injuries. But they didn't know that Jen's lunatic-ex had most likely caused it. They also knew that Matt had been the victim of a drive-by shooting in Vegas in March 2017. But they had no idea Jen's ex had probably pulled the trigger and, more importantly, that their son was his intended target.

These dark, harrowing events were far removed from the pristine, privileged world inhabited by Colton's parents. Dr. Preston Barnes and his socialite wife, Trina, were attractive, highly intelligent go-getters, who believed that life revolved around three core concepts: getting a good education, working hard, and giving back.

Their own lives had been prime examples. Preston, who hailed from a wealthy East Coast family, had graduated near the top of his class at Princeton, and put in a long stint in the Peace Corps in West Africa. There he met Trina Walsh, a young, attractive Wellesley grad-student teaching English to disadvantaged girls in one of the poorest cities in Nigeria.

The couple married in a large, lavish San Francisco wedding. Two years later, Colton, their first child, was born. He was very much like his parents, brainy, hard-working, and ambitious. He made excellent grades all through school, learned mandarin, wrote for his high school and college papers, and became a star athlete in tennis and baseball.

He was a good-looking, upbeat California kid with an impressive background. But that didn't guarantee his getting into Stanford. Having deep-pocketed parents with the right social connections ultimately sealed the deal.

Similar to Colton in many ways was his 21-year-old sister, Courtney, a pretty, spoiled Nob Hill debutante in pre-med studies at UCLA. Like her parents, she was involved in various charity and community programs.

All the Barneses were well-known members of San Francisco society whose names often appeared in local newspapers and magazines. Needless to say, Jen Conover, a 24-year-old girl who had grown up in Las Vegas with a thrice-divorced cocktail-waitress mother, a run-away-dad named Lizard Moats, and an ex-convict ex-boyfriend who was now stalking the hell out of her, was not exactly the kind of companion they had in mind for their exceptional son. A girl who popped out of cakes while seductively singing and writhing, and then stripped down to a teensy bikini for a living, was not the sort of partner they wanted for straight-arrow systems analyst Colton. For these reasons, he had kept a great deal about Jen and their Vegas weekends to himself.

Jen had no idea what the Barneses knew or didn't know about her. She was just thrilled to be flying to San Francisco in December 2017 for a five-day stay. It had been tough, but she had gotten Destiny to find subs for all of her pop-outs. Destiny had come through, but reluctantly, because several huge conventions were scheduled for that weekend.

As Jen prepped for her trip, she was excited, but also a bit nervous. She wasn't sure if Colton's younger sister, Courtney, would join them for dinner or not. But either way, just "meeting the parents" was a huge step because it meant she and Colton were taking their relationship to the next level and getting a stamp of respectability.

On a cool, overcast Friday morning, Jen's heart was racing as she boarded a Frontier flight at McCarran International Airport. With her long, golden locks tumbling loosely over her shoulders, the green-eyed blonde with the million-dollar smile, looked like a newly crowned Miss America in her sleek red dress and black suede coat.

At the San Francisco airport, Colton greeted her with a kiss and a bunch of bubble-gum-pink roses. Into his shiny blue Jeep, he loaded his sweetheart and her luggage. They took off for the stately St. Francis Hotel, nestled on a busy plaza smack-dab in the middle of downtown. Colton, who owned a condo near QuInternet's headquarters in San Jose, had his heart set on spending the weekend at the iconic hotel with his Vegas honey.

Post check-in, a bellman whisked Jen's bags up to a 21st floor room with a stunning view. With their arms around each other, the deliriously happy couple savored it for a few minutes. Then Jen kicked off her heels, plopped on the bed, and stretched out her arms for Colton to join her.

"Hey, lover-dude," she purred. "It's been a while since we were together. I've missed you. This bed feels so soft and comfy. Wanna christen it?"

With a grin on his face, Colton gazed over at the stunning young pop-out girl lying seductively on the king-size bed. His heart melted. Walking over, he lay down beside her and started kissing her. Soon, they were rolling around the bed, ecstatic to finally be together again. They couldn't stop. Tearing each others' clothes off, they made love. All the pent-up passions, frustrations, and fears of the past few months came together to make their hot sex even hotter. It was ecstatic and tragic, all at the same time. Everything Jen and Colton were, hoped to be, and would become, fused together in this sublime act of love and passion.

With Jen's luggage, purse, and clothes strewn on the floor around the bed, it was a giddy fantasy-romp. Colton and Jen were overjoyed to be together in San Francisco, far from Zane and all the madness of the Strip.

Afterwards, with the clamorous sounds of the city percolating in the background, they lay beside each other for a long while, intertwined and content.

"I've missed you, babe," Colton murmured as Jen nestled close. "Last thing at night and first thing in the morning, all I think of is you. Kissing you, holding you, making love to you. You, you, you. You're all I see."

Jen smiled. She was filled with joy. "Me too," she whispered, reaching up to kiss his warm, soft neck.

A few moments later, Colton eased himself out of bed and brought things back to some semblance of reality.

"We're having dinner with my parents tonight," he announced, pulling his pants and shirt on, and buckling his belt. "I thought it would be Sunday, but they're leaving for New York tomorrow, so it has to be tonight. I've got to pick up wine and flowers. They just got back from Barcelona, so the food will have a Spanish theme. I hope that's okay with you. Mom is going all out. They're both excited about meeting you."

"Sounds amazing, I can't wait," Jen said, smiling brightly as she sat up in bed, gathering the sheets around her. "What about your sister? Do you think she'll be there? I'd love to meet her. She's only a couple of years younger than me. Maybe we can go shopping or have lunch tomorrow."

"I'm not sure about Courtney," Colton answered, looking a bit distracted as he hustled a brush through his mussed, dark-brown hair. "She's going through a rough time. When she went back to UCLA after summer break, her boyfriend dumped her out of the blue. He'd apparently gotten back together with his ex. He was Courtney's first serious boyfriend; they met at prep school in Santa Monica. Her heart is broken. I would love to kick his ass for doing that to her.

"So, about tonight, it's kind of up in the air. I think she was going to meet some friends for dinner. Who knows where she'll be, or what she'll be doing? I hope she makes an appearance. I'm sure she'll like you. Yeah, it would be cool if you two could go shopping or have lunch. You know, get a girlfriend-vibe going."

"That would be awesome," Jen said, shimmying off the bed in all her naked splendor, plucking her dress, bra, and panties off the floor, and tossing them on the bed. With Colton now re-dressed, she wrapped a pink-terry-cloth St. Francis robe around her, tied the belt, and started unpacking so she could get out to explore the city.

Before he left, Colton sidled over to her and whispered, "I'm so glad you're here, babe. Tonight's going to be perfect. You'll see, my parents will love you, just like I do. How could they not?" Jen smiled and felt reassured. With their arms linked around each other, they strolled to the door, where they kissed long and hard before he left on his errands.

CHAPTER 26

That night, Colton and Jen were greeted warmly at the Barneses' spacious townhome on Wellington Drive in Nob Hill. The three-story, red-brick colonial featured classic white columns and trim. Its front yard was a well-manicured lawn with lush trees and a thriving rose garden. Looming beyond all of it was a thrilling view of San Francisco Bay.

The elegant interior was a tasteful blend of whites, beiges, and taupes, with black accents. Mounted on the walls were a striking assemblage of modern art pieces in bold hues.

Jen was impressed by the house and Colton's attractive parents. Dr. Barnes radiated the image of a skilled surgeon, calm, precise, and detailed. And his wife seemed a real-life endorsement for his work. She was done up like a Fifth Avenue society matron or a Bergdorf mannequin, her flawless face the result of countless hours under the scalpel, and in the hands of the Bay Area's best skin doctors and cosmetologists. Trina's freshly blown-out, shoulder length light brown hair had recently been frosted with just the right amount of blond highlights.

She was rail thin from daily rounds of Pilates and yoga, and wore a taupe designer pants suit with a strand of marble-size, pastel-colored pearls.

The doctor himself stood about six-feet tall, like Colton, and was trim, bronzed, and handsome. His features were nicely chiseled, his dark brown hair flecked with just enough grey to give him a wise, authoritarian look. His charcoal pinstripe suit looked well creased and pricey, no doubt a custom-made creation from a Lombard Street tailor. The alligator shoes with bronze tassels also looked handmade.

After the polite, pleasant introductions, everyone settled in the living room for drinks and appetizers. As Dr. Barnes shook and stirred the cocktails, Mabel, the Barneses' plump, blond Scandinavian housekeeper, toted in trays of quiche and sushi.

And then, suddenly, there was a clatter in the hallway.

"Courtney, is that you?" Trina called out.

"Yes, Mom, I'm home, but I'm going out again later."

"Oh, what happened, Tiffany and Elyse couldn't join you?"

"No, they're both at the yacht-club dinner, but we're meeting later for drinks."

"Okay, sweetheart. So glad you could join us."

After tossing her coat, Chanel bag, and keys onto a marble table in the hall, lissome, sloe-eyed Courtney Barnes sauntered into the living room.

Trina introduced her to Jen; the two blondes shook hands and exchanged hellos. Jen had a big smile on her face, but Courtney's expression was more lukewarm and wary. Looking Jen up and down, she was obviously taken aback by her striking beauty. It was an appraising glance Jen had seen before. A pang of anxiety swept through her.

But why should Courtney be jealous, she thought? She was quite attractive, herself, fair, thin, and chicly dressed in a sleek black pants suit with a pale grey silk blouse.

In this sea of neutrals, Jen stood out in a low-cut, pale pink knit dress she had bought at an outlet mall in Vegas just for the occasion. It was feminine and sexy, but looked slightly jarring and banal in this zone of restraint. With its pastel hue and soft tailoring, it screamed "off-the-rack-discount." Looking around, she felt awkward and out of place, but she tried to rein in her insecurities and keep smiling.

With her lush blond locks flowing over her taut, young shoulders, there was a light dusting of make-up on Jen's flawless, pale skin. Despite the camouflage, her Sin City lineage stood out. She had the pallor of a girl who had spent too many hours under the lights in tacky casinos, smoky lounges, and over-lit convention halls. An exotic hot-house flower wilting among the staid, proper, garden-variety Barneses.

Perched on a cream-colored sofa in the Barneses' elegant living room, Jen was feeling a bit lost when Trina suddenly appeared in the doorway to announce that dinner was being served.

Taking Colton's arm, Jen and he ambled into the dining room. At the table, she couldn't take her eyes off the glorious centerpiece, a large crystal bowl stuffed with puffy, powder-blue hydrangeas and pink, long-stemmed roses similar to the ones Colton had given her at the airport.

The Barneses had just returned from an art-buying spree in Barcelona and were still very much in Spanish mode. A large, colorful clay pan of seafood paella and an artfully arranged green salad were brought in by Mabel. A basket of warm, freshly baked sourdough bread magically appeared, and Dr. Barnes poured glass after glass of Napa Valley chardonnay.

All five diners at the gleaming table seemed uneasy as the dinner progressed. The Barneses didn't have much in common with their lovely guest of honor. And things went from awkward to downright uncomfortable when Courtney began firing intrusive questions at Jen.

"So, do you have your own place or do you live with your parents?" she asked in a clipped, Bay-Area tone.

"I, uh, live with my mom," Jen answered softly, gazing across the table at her. "We have a ranch-style house outside Vegas In a suburb called Summerlin. We've been there 15 years, and we love it. It's a nice, rambling old place, with lots of families, kids, and dogs nearby."

"What about your father?" was Courtney's follow-up. "Where is he?"

"Um, my parents are divorced," Jen replied, a little defensively in this bubble of nuclear-family togetherness. "He lives in Chicago with his wife and kids. I talk to them all the time, but we don't see each other much."

And then Jen suddenly got the urge to reveal that she had found out recently who her real father was.

"Speaking of fathers," she said coyly, "I found out in March that Matt Quinby, Colton's boss, is…"

Across the table, a panicky Colton raced to intervene, suddenly finishing Jen's sentence for her, "uh, an amazing boss, and man, with three wonderful sons. Poor Matt. What a senseless tragedy his shooting was."

"Yes, what a shame for him and his kids," Jen agreed, nodding as she stared at Colton.

The room quieted ever so slightly. Then the conversation shifted to Europe and the artwork the Barneses had acquired on their recent trip. But Courtney couldn't resist prying further into Jen's fascinating life.

"So, I assume your mom works. What does she do?" she asked.

Feeling ill at ease, but determined to forge ahead, Jen answered, "she's been a cocktail waitress at the Venetian for 20 years. She got promoted a few years ago and now supervises the whole crew. She loves it. There's constant excitement, and the girls are so much fun. I know a lot of them. They're totally sweet, like daughters to mom and sisters to me."

That question was the deal breaker. Jen could feel a chill sweeping over the room. She definitely wasn't in Vegas anymore.

"Hmm, yes, I'm sure they are," Courtney responded a bit snidely. And then she added, with a burst of laughter. "I've never met a cocktail waitress I didn't like either."

Sensing how uncomfortable Jen was with his sister's questions, Colton dove in to distract Courtney by asking about her classes that semester. But this tactic worked only briefly. She then began bombarding Jen again, digging for more specifics on how she and Colton had met.

Giggling nervously, Jen explained that she had popped out of Matt's birthday cake at Caesar's. Glances of shock and confusion were exchanged by everyone at the table. Apparently, Preston, Trina, and Courtney were all under the impression that Jen and Colton had both been guests at Matt's party.

Jen was flustered by the way everyone was reacting. Colton had obviously not told them much about her family or job. Why? What was he afraid of? That they would automatically assume she was some kind of lost waif-woman, or slutty Vegas party girl?

While Jen wrestled with this, Courtney zeroed in for more details on her job. Keeping her head up, Jen explained.

"I work for a company called Stripper Grams. I do corporate events mostly, but also birthday and retirement parties. As a pop-out girl, I'm hidden away in the center of a six-foot, tiered cake. I wriggle out on a tiny platform and sing and dance, while removing bits of clothing that I toss to the crowd."

The Barneses were trying not to cringe as Jen went on. She was doing her best to reassure them, but all she was doing was digging the hole deeper. The crystal-chandeliered dining room was quickly becoming a snake pit of squirming and covert glances.

"I'm not totally nude or anything," Jen explained, setting her salad fork down and gazing around the table. "By the time I finish, I have a bikini on, like something you'd wear to the beach, but it's black lace. So it's not like I'm doing a real striptease. Total nudity isn't allowed on the Strip, anyway, you have to go downtown for that. It's topless only on the Strip, topless and bottomless downtown," Jen clarified.

Her hosts were hardly reassured. What kind of tacky creature had their son dragged home? Colton had obviously misled them about his Vegas girlfriend.

Sensing the darkening mood, Jen became upset and desperate for the evening to end. But she had to sit and endure the rest of the fiesta, making polite chit-chat while nibbling bits of paella and trying to pretend everything was okay.

It was one of the most humiliating nights of her life. She was made to feel ashamed of what she did for a living. She had never felt that way before. She loved her job. Stripper Grams was an exciting, dynamic company, one of the best in Vegas. The wait-list of girls trying to get in was a mile long. Jen felt lucky to have been hired, but that was obviously something these rich Nob Hill snobs couldn't understand.

Everyone at the table was rattled, especially poor Jen. After a dessert of warm flan with caramel sauce, coffee was served. Two sips in, Jen suddenly announced that she needed to get back to the hotel for an important phone call from her mom.

"Of course, of course, we understand," Trina said with faux sweetness as she fetched Jen's coat, and Colton grabbed his car key. A volley of good nights, swift and polite, were exchanged.

The minute they were in the car, a furious Jen was in Colton's face.

"How could you let me walk in there like that, after you misled them about everything? Do you have any idea how awkward tonight was for me? What is your sister, a detective or undercover cop? What do your parents think of me now? First impressions are so important. How could you do this to me?"

As Colton started up the car, he tried to reason and level with her.

"Okay, I'll admit that I didn't tell them much about your job. But I didn't deliberately lie or mislead them. I just didn't say much. I never dreamed Courtney would give you the third degree like that. What the hell was she thinking?"

"I have no idea, since I don't know her, and I don't think I want to either. What a bitch! Why couldn't she just let it go? Why did she have to keep pushing for more details?" Jen asked.

"I don't know," Colton answered, taken aback himself as they made their way back to the hotel. "And please don't call my sister names. It must be because of her recent break-up. She's hurting and wants everyone to be as miserable as she is."

"Well, it worked!" Jen cried, glaring at him from the passenger seat, her voice getting louder and more shrill. "Thanks to Miss Cotillion-bitch-on-wheels and you, I was the laughing-stock of the table. And you just sat there stuffing your face, not saying a word."

"Jen, I'm sorry. Believe me, I was so surprised by Courtney's questions that I didn't know what to say," Colton answered. "Embarrassing you was the last thing I wanted. I'm not ashamed of your job, but it's a little out of the ordinary to them. Being a pop-out girl is not exactly the kind of work they hear about every day, like being a corporate lawyer or event planner.

"Maybe you should have described it in more generic, less specific terms. You could have provided more details later on. Did you have to be quite so open and graphic the first time you met them?"

Throwing her hands up, Jen shouted, "Of course I had to be open and graphic. I'm not ashamed of my parents or my job, but I felt like you were tonight because you've never told them much about me. You didn't tell them because you thought they'd find it sleazy or low-class. But it's not, it's my life! Why should I pretend I'm something I'm not, just to make them like me?

"And then, I was about to tell them Matt is my father," Jen went on, "and that I found this out from my mom after he got shot. But you leapt in and shut me down."

"Jen, really, there's a time and a place for everything. Casually announcing to my family over dinner that Matt Quinby is your father, and that your mother was his high-school sweetheart and about to marry him when she bolted from San Jose

25 years ago, would have been highly inappropriate. Downright gauche, way beyond the boundaries of polite dinner-table conversation. It sounds more like the synopsis for tomorrow's Jerry Springer show."

"You bastard!" Jen shrieked. "My life story is no Jerry Springer show. Yes, it's a bit dramatic and unusual, but that's not my fault."

"No, it's not, it's your mother's," Colton shot back. "She's a hot-mess drama queen who refuses to let you take a DNA test to find out if you're really Matt's daughter or not. What the hell is that?"

"Stop putting my mom down!" Jen raged. "She feels the test would be demeaning and humiliating for both of us, since she knows Matt is my father.

"Mom did the best she could in very challenging, difficult circumstances. But why should I try to explain all that to you? What difference does it make? It's obvious we're from two different worlds, and this isn't going to work. Can't you see that?"

Colton was stunned.

"Jen, please don't talk like that! We get along great and really care for each other. You're the first girl I've wanted to have a relationship with in a long time. Usually it's just casual flings. But with you, it's different, more serious and emotional. We're going to keep seeing each other, right?"

"I don't know," she answered, shaking her head. "I just don't know. I've got some thinking to do, and so do you."

Jen was furious. This was their first real fight, and it was a category five.

Back at the St. Francis, Colton pulled the car into a parking space out front. He was all set to come in and spend the night.

"Babe, calm down, please," he said, turning to Jen. "Let me come in, and we can hold each other for a while and just relax. It's been a long, tough day."

"No booty call tonight, dude!" Jen snarled. "Go back to Snob Hill and spend the night with your precious parents and obnoxious sister. I don't want to be with you right now. You let me sit there, making a fool of myself. Why didn't you just tell me, before dinner, that they didn't know anything about my family or job?

"The only thing they knew about was the car crash because you ended up in the hospital, right?"

"Right," Colton admitted sheepishly. "They also know Matt was shot in a drive-by, but nothing else. It was just so unbelievable that you're his daughter with Brandi, his runaway-bride. How could I tell them that?

"And then there's the Zane stuff. They would never let me go to Vegas again, or even get near the place, if they knew what was going on. They would worry constantly and check up on me all the time. That's way too much for me to handle. So I tell them very little about what goes on with us. Essentially, what happens in Vegas stays in Vegas."

"That sucks!" a disgusted Jen said. "Just when are you going to tell them some things about me, and what's been going on with Zane? If you were serious about me, they'd know already. You don't really want me, do you? You're not telling them things because we have no future, do we?"

Staring at her from the driver's seat, Colton was

in agony and struggling to reply.

"I really like, I mean, love, you Jen," he finally said. "Honest. That's all I know. We've been dating three years, but with all that's happened since Zane came back, I feel blindsided and overwhelmed. I can't give you any answers about our future right now. I just can't."

"I never should have gotten on the plane this morning!" Jen wailed, in tears. "If you had wanted me here, you would have asked. But I needed to come because things in Vegas are so tense. So I made this happen, but it was a mistake."

"Don't say that, Jen," Colton said, reaching for her hand, which she promptly yanked away. "This morning was beautiful. We made love in your room and it was like old times. We were away from the nightmare of Zane's stalking, so we were able to relax and enjoy each other like we used to. The last time was at Caesar's, the night he called twice, and then left the threatening note under the door."

"Yeah, that's right," Jen shot back. "It was a booty call at Caesar's, and this morning was a booty call, too. You like having sex with me, but you don't actually want a relationship, do you?"

"Jen, that's not fair! After all that's happened, don't I have the right to be confused and uncertain about our future? Give me a break. Don't you think it's asking a lot to have me crystal clear on how I feel, when I don't even know if both of us would still be alive if I came to Vegas for a weekend?

"Don't forget, I stood in that parking lot and saw my boss, who's also one of my best friends, gunned down in cold blood by that goddam son-of-a-bitch you slept with for four years!"

"Don't throw that in my face now!" Jen shrieked. "So I made a mistake and got involved with Zane when I was 17. I was dazzled by him. What girl wouldn't be? I thought I loved him. So I'm a horrible, stupid slut because I fell in love seven years ago with a guy who ended up going to prison, and now he's stalking us. My relationship with him was a mistake, and now here I am with you. Maybe this is another relationship that's all wrong, and I'll end up regretting this one, too!"

"Jen, please try to see the good in what we have," Colton begged her. "Calm down and just be patient while I try to work through all this stuff."

"You don't want to work through this stuff!" Jen yelled. "You don't even want to see me. You've been coming to Vegas for months without even calling me. You spend all your time with Delia and Megan, and the three of you go visit Matt. Do you know how hurtful that is?"

"Why would I want to spend time with you in Vegas when I have to worry that one or both of us will end up in a hospital or the morgue?" Colton quickly countered. "Does that sound like a recipe for a fun, sexy weekend, or true happiness?"

"Go to hell!" Jen bristled as she opened the car door.

"Don't go," Colton begged. "Please, let's talk this through," he said, taking her arm.

Yanking it away, she said, "Leave me alone! Get out of here and leave me the hell alone!"

Jumping out of the car, she slammed the door and rushed into the hotel. For a while, a shaken

Colton sat there, trying to process everything that had just been said, and understand all the mistakes he'd made. How had he ended up hurting this sweet, beautiful girl he cared about so deeply? He wanted to run inside, pound on Jen's door, and demand that she see him. But she seemed so upset, and that sounded like something Zane would do. It would probably scare the poor girl, and that's the last thing he wanted.

Finally, when he felt like he could focus on the road, he started his car and slowly drove away from the St. Francis.

CHAPTER 27

Early the next morning, after a sleepless night, Jen repacked her bags, booked a seat on the first flight back to Vegas, and paid the hotel bill. Later, when Colton learned that she'd checked out, he was devastated. She had run off without even saying goodbye.

A few hours later, when Jen got home, Brandi was shuffling around the kitchen in a pink nightgown and floral-print robe, making scrambled eggs. She was surprised to see her lovely daughter, and alarmed by her red, puffy eyes.

"Honey, I thought you were coming back on Tuesday. What happened?" Brandi asked, concerned and staring at Jen.

In a strained, tearful voice, she recounted the entire dinner drama with Colton's family, and how it had been a total humiliation.

"Sweetie, they live in a different world from us," Brandi said, patting Jen's hand when she sat down at the table. "Colton knew they wouldn't understand your job, so he didn't say anything. He wanted them to accept you. Don't take it so hard. I'm sure his intentions were good."

"But Mom," Jen explained, "it was more than just my job. He's embarrassed by your life and three marriages. How you left Matt behind all those years ago, and now claim he's my father.

"It really was a disaster," Jen sighed, taking a sip of coffee. "I left San Francisco without even saying goodbye. The whole thing was so upsetting. I never want to see Colton, or his snobby family, again!"

"Jen, please," Brandi said, stroking her daughter's hand. "Let things cool down. I'm sorry my past is causing all this turmoil. It's a lot for someone like Colton to understand. So much has happened, with Matt's shooting and all. Give him some time to figure out how he feels. He's been so good to you. Don't write him off over this."

Then Brandi and a somewhat calmer Jen had breakfast. As they ate, Brandi thought back 25 years to her relationship with Matt. She was in love and about to marry him, but she was also an insecure, scared girl trying to cope with two dysfunctional parents. Plus, the powerful Quinbys didn't want her in their family. It was a bitter blow, similar to what Jen was going through now with Colton's parents and sister. All these years later, it still made Brandi sad. She thought of how she had panicked and run off with Lizard to escape the feelings of rejection and unworthiness, just like Jen had run that morning from San Francisco.

Like mother, like daughter.

A few hours later, while Jen slept, the doorbell rang. It was a delivery man with a huge bouquet of pink roses. The card read simply, "I'm sorry,

Colton." It was the first of many such bouquets that would arrive over the next few weeks.

Brandi was concerned with how sad and hopeless Jen seemed. She pleaded with her to give Colton another chance. She didn't want to see her daughter miss out on love and a secure financial future because of her pride. She was all too familiar with that scenario.

Mother and daughter argued each time another bunch of roses arrived or one more contrite phone message floated in. Jen adored her mom, and missed Colton, but she needed time to process what had gone down in San Francisco.

PART FOUR

Doughnuts on the Doorstep

CHAPTER 28

For Jen, the holiday season at Stripper Grams was always a blast, but 2017, not so much. Destiny was still being snarky about leaving her name off the Stripper Grams' schedule. She had asked repeatedly, but, to her horror and annoyance, her name and the details of where she'd be working were still being listed. For someone trying to avoid a crazy, unpredictable, dangerous stalker, it was one more thing to worry about.

Jen's fears about Zane's knowing her whereabouts were certainly justified. An inside source at Stripper Grams was bad news, for sure. But Zane had easier, more direct ways of getting information on Jen.

Like from his younger sister, Kacey. In December 2017, while he was visiting cousins in the California desert community of Barstow, Zane called her to check on his mom and kids. During the call, Kacey mentioned that Jen had recently traveled to San Francisco to visit her boyfriend.

How did she know this? Simple. The girl who baby-sat Kacey's kids, an aspiring showgirl named

Willow Divine, couldn't work one weekend because, as she explained to Kacey, she was subbing for Jen in a flurry of pop-outs at Caesar's and Mirage. Kacey asked where Jen was, and Willow told her about the San Francisco trip.

When Kacey relayed the news to Zane, he seemed to take it calmly and casually. But inside, he was going ballistic. Jen was the only girl he had ever truly loved, and he was obviously losing her. If she was going to California to visit the geek-prick, she was probably meeting his family, and that meant things were getting serious.

But the real killer was that Jen was spending her nights with that Silicon Valley loser. It enraged Zane that she was having sex, going to fancy restaurants, and doing other fun stuff with that candy-ass dickhead, while he was totally out in the cold.

If he didn't do something fast, she would be gone forever. Zane couldn't let that happen. Over the months, he had tried seeing other women, but none of them could hold a candle to Jen in terms of beauty or sweetness. And none of them meant a thing to him. She was the only one he wanted, the only one who had ever mattered.

He couldn't let this thing with the tech dude escalate into a permanent state, like marriage. That would be a direct hit on his ego, and he wouldn't allow it. No, he was the only man for Jen. Not this West Coast geek she had taken up with while he was in prison. It was wrong of this dude to steal his girl while he was in lock-up, and it was wrong of Jen to let him.

Zane felt like a total loser when it came to Jen. He had tried to get her back, but all of his heavy-handed tactics had failed. The three AM phone calls, zip line accident, car crash, drive-by, and attempted kidnapping at Treasure Island had all come to naught. And now Jen was going to sail off into the sunset with this dude she had met while he was in prison, missing her and dreaming of her every goddamn day and night.

After Zane's phone call with Kacey, he felt a certain panic, like he had to do something drastic, and do it right this time. Something big and important that couldn't be undone. He was in Barstow at the moment, but he would figure out the details and get his ass back to Vegas to do what he had to do. And this time he wouldn't fail.

CHAPTER 29

After San Francisco, Jen and Colton had remained on speaking terms, but barely. In mid-December, he called to say hello and see how she was doing. The call was polite, but strained.

And then there was a Christmas lunch at the elite, pricey Picasso in Bellagio. Colton had come to town to visit Matt, and had invited Brandi, Jen, and Megan to be his guests.

It was a pleasant, cordial outing. The lead topic was how each of them could do more to support and facilitate Matt's recovery. Afterwards, the four of them visited him at the Desert Oasis Rehabilitation Center, where he had been transferred to undergo intensive daily physical therapy. The goal was to stimulate various parts of his body, and get them all to reconnect and work in tandem with his brain. Hard to achieve with Matt still in a deep coma. As the months droned by, his future seemed increasingly bleak and uncertain.

At Picasso, Jen enjoyed her visit with Megan, but being around Colton made her edgy and uncomfortable. She was beginning to doubt they could ever relight the fire. Sitting across the festive lunch table from him in her pretty green-knit dress, she couldn't help wondering if their polite but distant relationship was the new normal.

Christmas 2017 came and went without incident. Grandma Paulina mercifully remained in Houston with her family. The Zane stalking nightmare now appeared to be in remission. Things had been quiet since the attempted kidnapping at Treasure Island in October. And Colton was in San Francisco, celebrating the holidays with QuInternet colleagues and his elite, accomplished family.

After all the withering drama of the past year, Jen was experiencing intermittent bouts of moroseness. But she had her job, classes, and friends to keep her going. Meanwhile, Brandi was frantically rushing about, meeting friends, and working extra hours for co-workers who needed time off for holiday plans. A real win-win, since it gave mother and daughter a break from each other, which meant less time to fight.

They both ended up working on Christmas day. Jen and Amber popped out of cakes at a huge Christmas dinner-reception at Luxor for an electronic dating service called FirstMoves.com. Afterwards, Brandi joined them, and all three were treated to comped holiday buffets by the Luxor concierge. It was a fun, festive dinner, and everyone walked away stuffed.

In early January 2018, life brightened for Jen when an invitation to a big blow-out wedding in Reno arrived in the mail. The bride would be her good friend, Carly Cassidy, a perky redhead and former pop-out queen.

Jen was thrilled at the thought of getting away for a long weekend, plus she loved weddings. From the time she was a little girl, she had daydreamed about her own, conjuring up elaborate fantasies about the dress, cake, and flowers. And so when she got Carly's invite, she immediately RSVP'd that she'd be there.

Getting out of Vegas for a fun-filled, relaxing few days was just what Jen needed. She and Brandi ran all over town trying to find the perfect dress. They finally chose a dove-gray silk-and-lace gown that would work well for a winter wedding. Matching four-inch heels would complete the look.

Jen was going to make the seven-hour drive to Reno with her friend, Brianna DiFalco, another pop-out doll and one of Carly's six bridesmaids. Jen was hoping Amber, who'd recently gotten engaged to Dave, would come along, too. But it looked doubtful since Amber and Dave were going to Kansas City to visit her sick grandmother.

On a cold, dreary Friday in mid-January 2018, an excited Jen waited to be picked up by Brianna at eight AM. Brandi, meanwhile, was pulling an all-nighter and wouldn't be home till ten or eleven.

Jen had packed a small suitcase and carry-on. She was flitting about the house, watering plants, and tending to other last-minute chores when the doorbell rang at the stroke of seven. For an instant, she wondered why Brianna had arrived an hour early. But she was psyched about the weekend and impatient to get on the road, so she flung open the door.

To her horror, it wasn't Brianna. There on the doorstep, in the flesh, stood Zane Hollister. Jen's heart dropped. Gasping "no!" in fright, she moved to close the door. Shoving his arm out, Zane quickly blocked her and charged inside.

Cowering in the hallway, Jen stared up at him, six feet of dark, brooding menace in black jeans and a worn leather biker jacket. His neck-length dark hair was ragged and disheveled, his brown eyes glassy and bloodshot. He was obviously high on pills, maybe uppers, maybe downers, maybe a combination of both.

"Hey darlin, what's goin on?" he said in a slightly slurred, faux-light voice. "Haven't seen you since Treasure Island. How've you been, beautiful?"

"Zane, you shouldn't be here. Get out!" Jen hissed, pointing at the door. "You're the last person I want to see, now or ever. The cops are looking for you."

"Let them look. As usual, they don't know jack!" he scoffed.

"It's seven o'clock in the morning," Jen shot back. "Why are you here? What do you want?"

"Just you, babe," he answered with a smarmy smile. "I heard you took a trip out west last month to see the boyfriend. Did you meet the folks? Sounds warm and fuzzy, but look out. A guy like me could get real jealous and do something crazy."

"How did you find out about my trip?" Jen asked. "Who told you, someone at Stripper Grams?"

"Babe, this is a small town," Zane retorted. "People talk all the time about all kinds of stuff."

"Well, I can't talk to you right now," Jen told him, "I'm leaving for Reno in a few minutes."

"I know," Zane said coyly. "I do business with Brianna's boyfriend, remember? He tipped me she was driving you, so I thought I'd swing by and grab you first. The early bird gets the worm, right? I'm taking you to Reno myself."

"No, you're not. I wouldn't go anywhere with you, not even if you were the last guy on earth," Jen said, getting in his face. "My life has been a nightmare since you came back. Phone calls In the middle of the night, weird accidents, a drive-by shooting, and then the Treasure Island thing. My friend's boyfriend ended up in the hospital with a concussion and broken nose. It was horrible.

"I know you did it all. Please, it's got to stop! If you keep doing this crazy stuff," she warned, "someone's going to get killed, and you're going to wind up back in prison."

"What crazy stuff, sweetheart? I don't know what you're talking about," Zane replied with faux innocence. "The cops talked to me after the crash. I wasn't even here that week. They can't prove a thing, and neither can you. There's no evidence.

"And I heard about that zip line thing with the broken cable. Sounds like a freak accident, or some badass karma. The drive-by thing, too. Some dude in the wrong place at the wrong time got plugged. It's got nothin' to do with me. You're barkin' up the wrong tree, babe.

"Besides, that was then and this is now. Come

on," he added, grabbing her arm, "time's a wastin'. We need to get on the road."

"No!" Jen cried, digging in her heels. "I'm not going anywhere with you. Brianna will be here soon. Please let me go. I have stuff to do before she gets here."

"Sorry, sweetheart, this is non-negotiable," he told her, moving closer, his tall, muscular frame crowding her slender, five-foot-six one against a wall. "I'm driving you to Reno. We were there a few times, remember? We had a blast in that king-size rack at the Silver Legacy, didn't we, Jenny? It will be even sweeter this time around. Come on, quit stalling, where's your cell?"

"What do you mean, this time around?" Jen asked.

"I mean it's time we got back together, and this time forever. The dickhead-computer-geek is history. It's you and me against the world, babe!"

Jen's green eyes grew wide with fear and panic.

"We can't be together, Zane. I have a boyfriend," she told him firmly, even though she and Colton were on the outs. There was no way she was going to level with Zane about that.

"He's history, Jenny," Zane went on in his cocky way, "lucky to be alive after taking you from me while I was in lock-up. I can't help the way the law works in this state. I got busted and had to do time. He's a piece of scum for moving in on my girl. Now where's your cell?" he demanded.

"In my purse," she answered, her voice trembling a bit.

"Well, get it out," he snapped.

Reaching into her crammed, black leather satchel, Jen fished out her smartphone.

"Call Brianna and tell her you decided to drive yourself to Reno, that you need your car up there so you can go places. Go ahead, call her, quick."

"No!" Jen shouted, staring up at Zane defiantly.

He grabbed her arm.

"I'm warning you, don't make this any harder," he growled, reaching in his pocket to extract a shiny, pearl-handled pistol. Caressing it in his hand, he added, "This isn't the time to argue. Get her— now."

Numb with fear, Jen stared at the gun and then up at Zane. For an instant, her mind went blank. Then, with fingers cold and shaking, she somehow dialed her friend's cell. Brianna picked up right away and Jen told her not to come, that she would take her own car.

Brianna seemed puzzled for an instant, but she was too frazzled to give it much thought. After working a party the night before that ran late, she had overslept and was rushing to finish packing and last-minute chores before leaving her house. As they hung up, the two pop-out girls agreed to meet in Reno later that night, or maybe the next morning, before the wedding.

Jen tucked her cell back in her purse. Clutching his revolver, Zane ordered her to get ready. She yanked on her boots and pulled a beige, suede fringe-jacket over her pink sweater and jeans. Then she gathered her suitcase, a garment-bag holding her dress, and her make-up case, and moved them into the front hall.

Outside in the windswept driveway, Jen climbed into the cushy, leather passenger seat of Zane's Chevy Tahoe. After locking her door, he piled her stuff in back. As she buckled the seat belt, her heart sank. Scanning the nearby houses, she desperately hoped someone walking their dog or going to work would catch a glimpse of her in the strange, black car. But no such luck. It was seven-thirty on a cold, drizzly, mid-winter morning, and all was quiet on Rosita Way.

A shivering Jen pulled the collar of her jacket closer as Zane revved the engine. Backing out the driveway, a feeling of doom swept over her. Now she was totally in Zane's hands.

CHAPTER 30

Through the quiet, winding streets of Summerlin, they cruised. After slipping in a Guns N' Roses tape, Zane reached over to caress Jen's thigh. She cringed.

He maneuvered the SUV onto U.S. 95, on Nevada's western edge, and up the freeway they zoomed. Huddled in the passenger seat, a feeling of hopelessness engulfed the 24-year-old beauty. Since Zane had gotten out of prison in July 2016, he had been making her life hell. It was now January 2018, and the long trail of horrid and harrowing incidents had led to this god-awful kidnapping at gunpoint. Jen was shell-shocked by this latest brazen act. Her mind was reeling with thoughts of escape. How, when, and where were the only details she needed to figure out.

Outside Vegas, grayish-brown flatlands dotted with scrubby cactus and diehard acacias suffused the landscape. In the distant horizon loomed an endless range of cocoa-colored mountains. The skies above were vibrant blue, with vast stretches of stringy white clouds. It was a dramatic vista, worthy of a vintage postcard or movie backdrop. But all of it was lost on Jen, who stared blankly ahead, woeful and berating herself for opening the door so fast that morning.

At one point, in tears, she turned to Zane and asked plaintively, "What are you going to do with me?"

With his steely dark eyes glued to the road, he answered in a patronizing tone, "Don't worry, babe, I'm going to take good care of you. Reno's always been our town. Just relax and enjoy the ride. Everything's cool."

Desperate and depressed, Jen stared back at him.

Their first stop was a quiet hamlet called Beatty, some 80 miles up the pike. They filled up on gas and Zane bought snacks. As Jen climbed out of the car to stretch her legs, he stashed her purse and cell under his seat. Eyeing a white-haired old dude in denim overalls two pumps down, filling his creaky pickup, she weighed her odds. But not fast enough. Before she could make a move, the elderly gent got in his truck and drove off.

As the sun grew brighter and temperatures edged into the mid-50s, they burrowed deeper into the vast, desolate netherworld of the Mojave. Every time they slowed, even for an instant, Jen fantasized about hurling herself out the car door, even though it was locked, and making a run for it. But, really, where would she have gone? There was little but sand, cactus, desert rats, and the occasional coyote for the next 400 miles.

In Tonopah, another sleepy burg, they got more gas and ate burritos at a dingy roadside hut called

Cisco's.

It was 210 more miles to Reno. As the shiny black SUV pounded north on the ribbon of concrete, Jen's mind drifted to thoughts of Brandi. Surely her mom would try to call her later and find it odd that Jen didn't pick up. But on a weekend away, she and Brianna might be too busy gabbing to even hear the phone. So maybe Brandi wouldn't find it so strange?

At their final stop, in Hawthorne, Zane filled the tank again. Then he revealed to Jen what he had in mind in Reno. As they meandered around a patch of dried-out grass at a rest stop, he broke the news that she would still be going to a wedding the next day. But it wasn't going to be Carly's. It would be her own. Yes, he announced boastfully that on the following day he, Zane Hollister, would enter into holy matrimony with Jen Conover.

"Oh, no, no, this is totally insane, I can't marry you. I'm sorry, there's no way!" Jen wailed, stopping dead in her tracks, frozen in shock and staring up at him.

Gripping her forearms tightly, Zane replied with a callous smile, "Babe, take it easy, you'll get used to the idea. And just to help you along, remember that bright, shiny piece in my pocket. There's a reason it's there. Don't make me use it on either one of us."

The panicky look in Jen's eyes was starting to get to him, so Zane tried another approach. After a brief pause, he declared intensely, "I'm a desperate man, Jen, a desperado crazy in love with you. Like I told you after I got out, all I thought about in lock-up was you. The two of us together and how good it was going to be. But you wouldn't give me the time of day when I got back. Even after I told you how much I loved and wanted you, you blew me off. I wrote you all those letters, but you never got them because your psycho-bitch mom grabbed them first.

"The way you treated me pushed me over the edge. If you had just given an inch and agreed to see me, talk to me. But, no, you got all high and mighty with your nerd-ass new boyfriend, so I had to take matters into my own hands."

"Zane, what are you talking about?" Jen yelled above the roar of rushing cars on the nearby freeway. "I'm not marrying you, tomorrow or ever. I love Colton," she insisted. "Don't you get that?"

"Jen, stop it. You're confused. You don't know what you want. But I do. I'm a better man for you than that candy-ass prick from California. I'm the right dude for you. He's a weak pussy. I've had to fight for everything since the day I was born, just like you. We're two of a kind, don't you see?

"There's a lot of history between us, babe, and tomorrow we're taking it to the next level. We're going to make it official at the Chapel of the Bells."

"What?" Jen yelled, throwing her hands up. "There's a chapel in Reno that will actually marry us tomorrow? Oh my God! What are you talking about?"

"A guy I knew in the slammer got hitched at this place called 'The Bells.' He just showed up one day with his girl and they did the rest. It will cost a few hundred, but that's okay. I brought a suit and you can wear the dress you were going to wear to that chick's wedding. I want it to be a real cool celebration. I'll get you flowers. We'll buy rings at a pawn shop. We're going to do it up right!"

"Zane, stop talking like this," Jen broke in, grabbing his arm. "You're high and acting crazy. You're not a bad person. You just have a drug problem that's out of control. But you can get help for that. Come on, we can go back to Vegas right now. You can walk away from this and I'll forget it ever happened. Just please turn the car around and drive us back!"

"Jen, you're still not listening," Zane replied with a certainty that made her shudder. "We're tying the knot tomorrow. You and me in a private ceremony in 'The Biggest Little City in the World.' First class all the way. No more talking. Let's get in the car and keep truckin', darlin'. We're almost there."

With a deep breath and a groan, Jen trudged back to the hulking Tahoe. The groom-to-be was tightly gripping her arm. There were a few bystanders at a nearby picnic table eating sandwiches, drinking coffee from thermoses, and talking loudly. For an instant, Jen thought of jerking away and running to them for help. But Zane spotted her staring and instantly knew the score.

Pulling her to a secluded spot, he leaned in and whispered menacingly, "Don't even think about making a run for it, babe. I have the gun to back me up. But if you do get away, remember this. I have friends in Vegas riding the meth train and real itchy to break into your house, grab a few things, and rough up your precious mother. Think about it,

Jenny, she's all alone in that house. Do you really want to see her hurt because of some stupid mistake you made?"

Zane's threat shook his horrified ex to the core.

"Okay, okay, just leave my mom alone," she stammered between sobs. "Tell me nothing bad will happen to her."

"Don't worry your pretty little head," he said smugly. "Mama Brandi will be safe as long as you do what you're told. My future mother-in-law is totally chill at the moment."

As they got back in the car, Jen was still crying. With the tears flowing, she hunched against the door, her thin frame shaking with pent-up tension from an ordeal that had now stretched into hours.

Smiling cruelly, Zane turned to her and asked, "Pre-wedding jitters?" as he dialed up the Guns N' Roses and focused on the open road. "No worries, sweetheart, you're with big daddy now."

CHAPTER 31

W hen they rolled into Reno that afternoon, the skies were dark and menacing, with storm clouds closing in.

Down Virginia Street they cruised to the Silver Legacy hotel. While Zane checked in, Jen gazed around at the sprawling lobby, quiet and dingy in the depths of winter.

An elevator ride away, their eighth-floor room was neat and compact, with a queen-size, four-poster bed dominating it. The minute they entered, Zane ordered Jen to call Brianna and tell her she was in town, but felt tired and like she was getting a cold, so she wouldn't make the pre-wedding dinner that night. Zane then told Jen to ring up Brandi and leave a message that she had arrived, was feeling sick, and would call again when she felt better.

"Your voice needs to sound normal," he warned. "No crying or whimpering."

After Jen made the calls, Zane put her cell back in his leather bag. Then he unplugged the hotel phone, which he later stashed in a closet while Jen was in the bathroom.

He demanded that they go everywhere together and gripped his bride-to-be's arm tightly while they roamed around town to stretch their legs after the long drive.

Just south of the Truckee River, they strolled under the brightly lit arch proclaiming Reno, The Biggest Little City in the World. Farther down Virginia Street, and just beyond a filthy, noisy underpass, they wandered into a gritty outlet called Planet Pawn. The retail dive billed itself as a smart jewelry house, but the staleness in the air, threadbare carpets, and scuffed counters marked it as something else.

In seconds, Zane's eyes caught an assortment of wedding bands glistening under a glass case. Jen stared at them, dazed and wondering if the previous owners of these 14-karat rings could possibly have been more miserable than she was at that moment.

The bogus couple tried on some gold bands. When they found a matching pair that fit, Zane pulled out a wad of cash and laid three crisp $100 bills on the grimy counter. Whooping "biggest sale of the day," the shrewish clerk eagerly scooped up the Benjamin Franklins and tucked them into a brass, antique cash register.

Across from the hotel, dinner passed without incident at a seedy, overheated Chinese hash house that reeked of rancid grease. Jen and Zane then passed time in the Legacy's labyrinthine casino, working the one-armed bandits and dabbling at the blackjack and Pai-Gow tables. Jen went through the motions, but with a heavy heart. She was queasy from the half-cooked Kung Pao chicken and long hours of tension, on the road and off.

That night, the "newly engaged" couple lay nestled in each other's arms on the fluffy, queen-size bed. In a long, magenta nightgown, Jen tried to sleep as best she could, curled alongside Zane, who promptly fell into a deep, drug-induced slumber. But not before pulling Jen close, wrapping his arms around her, and kissing her deeply.

While Zane slept, Jen cried softly. He had handcuffed her left foot and arm to the bedposts so she couldn't run. All night long she lay awake, her mind spinning with ideas of how she might break loose before the wedding tomorrow. But then she remembered Zane's threats against her mom and her hopes faded.

Jen's cellphone lay tantalizingly close, inside Zane's leather bag on the bedside table near him. If only she could get to the bag, Jen thought over and over, she could call Brandi's cell and leave a message about where she was, and what had happened. But the steel cuffs left her powerless to reach the bag, and Zane had her locked in his muscular arms. To Jen, the forced confinement felt like a jailhouse or a straitjacket in an insane asylum.

Bright and early on Saturday morning, Zane had Jen call Brianna and report that she wouldn't be at the wedding because her cold was worse, and probably contagious. She then called her mom, left a similar message, and told her not to worry and that she'd be resting all day in her hotel room with her phone turned off. Then Jen and Zane took a shower together.

"Sorry, sweetheart," he muttered as he removed

her nightgown in the chilly, white-tile stall, "but I've got to keep my eye on you or you'll be a runaway bride. That wouldn't be very romantic, would it? Besides, we can wash each other's backs."

Under the rushing streams, he pulled her close and kissed her. Jen was limp and unresponsive. She gazed at his naked body, which she hadn't seen in over four years, and realized how much more muscled and filled out it was. More manly and powerful than ever.

She remembered loving Zane and their first time in bed together at his house in Vegas. She was a 17-year-old virgin at the time, and he was a hot, 25-year-old stud, very experienced with women, and a tender, affectionate lover. She had craved his body after that, and every time they were together it just got sweeter. And now here they were, seven years later, sharing this hideous shower at the Silver Legacy and she was totally turned off by the sight of his bare skin and dark hair. It looked alien and scary, like the body of a dangerous stranger. She endured his deep kisses as best she could and prayed that some miracle would save her from marrying him that afternoon.

Post-shower, Jen dried her long, golden locks while Zane stood beside her, shaving. Then, with a cold, shaky hand, she dabbed some make-up on her pale skin and puffy green eyes. Dressed in jeans and sweaters, the couple trooped to breakfast in the diner downstairs. As they ate, he kept a protective grip on her. Then they blew more time on the slots and somehow managed to clear a few hundred dollars. A bountiful haul, but hardly the omen she was looking for.

By two P.M., they were back in their room, where Zane ordered Jen to put on the dress she had planned to wear to Carly's wedding. It was a floor-length, pale-gray lace creation with a silk underlay, low-cut sweetheart neckline, and long, lacy sleeves with pearl buttons. Jen cried as she smoothed the size-eight gown over her slim waist, full breasts, and firm hips. She didn't know exactly what was going to happen, but she abhorred the thought of going through with a wedding she desperately didn't want.

Zane put on the black suit, lavender shirt, and purple silk tie he had brought in a garment bag from Vegas. Slung over his shoulder was the small leather satchel holding his gun and Jen's cell.

Dressed to the nines, the couple climbed in a cab on Virginia Street and headed to the Chapel of the Bells, a tidy, clapboard bungalow on Fourth Street with an ivory and gold wedding chapel nestled inside. Greeting them on the other side of the front door were two mangy white doves fluttering quietly in a tarnished cage.

After check-in, they were directed to a cream-colored limousine driven by a man named Duane, who ferried them to the Washoe County Marriage License Office. There they presented drivers licenses and social security cards and laid out $60. No blood test was required, and no waiting period either.

The anxiety was building as Duane ferried the couple back to the chapel. There they were met by a bald, portly justice of the peace and an elderly, silver-haired gent named Clifford, who would serve as their witness. Zane handed the gold bands to the JP's chubby, plaid pant-suited wife. He had coughed up another $300 for the Tonight's The Night wedding package, which included an eight-inch bouquet of white silk flowers for Jen and a matching boutonniere for him.

Even before the ceremony began, Jen was in tears. Soon she was crying openly in the foyer while hunched on a white antique bench festooned with pink velvet ribbons. To ease any suspicions, Zane calmly explained to the dreary group, "weddings have a way of turning on the waterworks, don't they? My wife-to-be is upset because her mom is sick and couldn't be here. After the ceremony, those will be happy tears."

There were nods of sympathy and kindness for Jen all around.

"Let's get this show on the road!" an excited Zane proclaimed. "We've been waiting a long time for this day."

With all the participants gathered, the candles were lit and the taped wedding march began wafting through the chapel. Jen felt weak-kneed and nauseous. This was an unfolding nightmare come true. How could this disaster possibly be happening? And how could it be stopped? Was she actually going to become Mrs. Zane Hollister? What would he do if she turned around and ran screaming from the chapel? Chase after her with his gun, shoot her right there on Virginia Avenue, and then kill himself?

From all she had seen over the past year and a half, she absolutely believed this ghastly scenario could happen. She thought Zane was that desperate and depraved.

Events were now moving too fast to stop. The ceremony consumed barely seven minutes, and then, in an instant, it was over. Zane kissed his new wife as the flash bulbs popped. The bride's smile was strained. She couldn't seem to help herself. She looked pale, tense, and out of sorts. There were dark circles under her bloodshot eyes. Zane tried to explain her pallor and sickly demeanor by saying they had just driven up from Vegas and she was bone-tired.

With Jen's bridal bouquet, and a dozen 5" x 7" photos, plus a silver memory card holding more images of the frightful ceremony, Jen and Zane spilled out of the chapel.

Back to the Silver Legacy they were driven in the white limo. In the lobby, several strangers congratulated the handsome couple and wished them luck. While Zane beamed and thanked them, Jen nodded politely and stared down at her white, silk bouquet.

By the time they got to their room, the twin furies of exhaustion and depression had battered Jen into a state of numb detachment. From the long months of harassment, threats, and scary accidents, to Matt's shooting and her own kidnapping and forced marriage, she had now become a mental basket case. After the traumatic wedding, she felt barely able to comprehend events swirling around her or threats in her midst. She was finally succumbing to the greater forces of confusion and despair that had overtaken her. But her single, fervent hope remained: to escape with her life, and her sanity, intact.

CHAPTER 32

Back in their room, Jen was too exhausted and drained to feel much of anything. Zane, on the other hand, was over the moon and ordered champagne from room service to celebrate their nuptials. When the bottle of bubbly arrived nestled in a silver ice bucket on a linen-covered cart, he craftily slid the two chilled champagne flutes aside. While Jen stared blankly out the eighth-floor window, wishing she could jump, Zane quickly emptied the contents of a Quaalude capsule into one of the glasses and poured champagne over it.

Jen took a few small sips and then downed the rest, unaware that the frothy liquid was laced with an illegal date-rape drug Zane had scored from one of his dealers. Within a few minutes, she grew groggy and very, very tired. She was soon sprawled on the bed in a semi-conscious state with her muscles weak and wobbly. In this drug-induced trance Jen would have no memory of what followed, and that was just as well. While in this altered state, Zane undressed her and proceeded to have sex with her.

It was a desperate, depraved, delusional act. Seven years before he had been her first lover, and now he had sunk to this level. Jen was an innocent, naïve girl who at one time had been wildly in love with him. But then he had gone to prison and she had met and fallen for Colton.

Zane couldn't handle the rejection. While he was behind bars he had dreamed of her 24/7 and jerked off to her photo every day. The image of Jen's flawless young body had been burned into his mind. He had memorized every exquisite detail and remembered her passion and excitement for him. And now he was drugging her in a feeble attempt to recreate these passionate moments after forcing her to marry him in a hideous farce of a wedding.

Jen's body was limp and malleable. She moaned softly a few times, but uttered no other sound. Zane did what he wanted with her and felt a huge surge of relief and release when he finally came. But really, what kind of pleasure or satisfaction could he have gotten from this horrid act of dominance and perversion? In his warped, sicko mind, it was an act of love and passion, but it was more like a violent invasion and conquest. He might as well have been back in his cell jerking off.

Jen woke up a few hours later, naked and barely covered by a sheet, with her right leg cuffed to the bed. She was still groggy and suspected right off that she had been drugged. And then, seeing that her clothes were on the floor, she instantly knew there had been something more. When she realized she had been raped, she started crying and flailing on the bed, and then screaming at the top of her lungs with fury.

"You did something to me, didn't you?" she howled. "You drugged me and raped me. You gave me a pill—it was in the champagne, wasn't it? You filthy lowlife bastard, how could you do this to me?"

Zane ran to the bathroom, grabbed a washcloth, and stuffed it in Jen's mouth so violently that she thought her teeth would be knocked out. When she tried to pull it out, he jumped on top of her and held her arms down. She could barely breathe and finally had to stop struggling.

Zane removed the cloth, laid down beside her, and took her in his arms. He was crying now, too, and she was too weak and drained to resist as he held her and kissed her. They stayed in that crude, awkward embrace for endless minutes, the just-married Mr. and Mrs. Zane Hollister in Room 812 of the Silver Legacy.

"Jen, I'm sorry our honeymoon got off to such a rocky start," Zane finally whispered. "Yeah, I gave you a muscle relaxant to help you unwind because you seemed so uptight. Honeymoon jitters, I guess. We were lovers for four years, so I didn't think it was such a big deal to have sex with my new wife. This is our honeymoon, right? Get a grip, babe, we're Mr. and Mrs. now."

"Married, yeah, but it was the last thing I wanted!" Jen replied bitterly. "You threatened me with a gun. You said one of your friends would hurt my mom. I had no choice. It was against my will."

"Why do you have to be such a romance

wrecker?" Zane asked, smiling slightly, trying to lighten the mood. "Just give it a chance, baby girl. It's me, Zane, the guy you used to love having sex with. Remember all those hot nights at my place? You might learn to love it again."

Shaking her head, Jen stared hard at him. She realized at that point that trying to reason with him was useless. Zane was living in his own warped version of reality. She would have to play along as best she could until she could somehow break away.

An hour later, Zane and a still dizzy, limp Jen took another shower together. Afterwards, Zane told her to put her wedding dress back on so they could go out for dinner and dancing. Taking a deep breath, Jen picked her dress up off the floor, pulled it on, and Zane zipped it up. Then, as if in a trance, she brushed her long, golden locks and touched up her make-up.

CHAPTER 33

That chilly January night, Jen and Zane made their way to a dark, intimate steakhouse a few blocks from the hotel called Longhorn. Over shrimp cocktail appetizers, the gleeful groom announced another big surprise for his bride.

"I'm taking you to Hawaii for our honeymoon, babe. The flight leaves at eight tomorrow morning. We're going to a quiet, hidden beach on the remote island of Kauai. I'll have you all to myself there. We'll have a hot honeymoon and then find a place to start a new life."

A wave of panic swept over Jen.

"Hawaii, Zane? This is crazy!" she cried. "I can't go over there with you. I have a job and my mom is back in Vegas. She needs me. What about your kids?"

"Don't worry about them," he said, shaking his head while scarfing down another forkful of shrimp. "They're with my mom, just like when I was in lock-up. They'll be fine with her. You're my wife now, a stepmom of two. We're one big, happy family. It's all good.

"Just forget about your mom and job," he went on with a dismissive flick of the wrist. "This is our honeymoon. I know things haven't been too romantic so far, but it'll get better. Once we're on Kauai, everything will be cool. I know a guy over there from the Strip. I saved his ass from being busted, so he owes me big time. He owns a big estate; he'll let us crash in his guest cottage. When the kids get out of school, my mom can send them over. They'll love it."

Jen stared at Zane, stunned that he had their future, however delusional, all planned out. She was still half-zonked from the Quaalude, but she had to play nice. She couldn't argue with him. Somehow, she had to pretend she was going along with the program till the right moment came.

"Okay, that all sounds great," she murmured, forcing herself to smile and nod as she stared into his dark, glistening eyes. "But I didn't pack any bikinis or sun dresses. We'll have to pick up some new stuff over there."

"No problem, I have mucho dinero, babe," Zane told her with a grin. "Once we get to Kauai, I'll buy you all the bikinis and sundresses you want. You'll turn into my own personal mermaid. It will be paradise for us, away from all the bullshit in Vegas and all the assholes who tried to break us up. Just the two of us on a far-off island on Cloud Nine, living a dream."

Zane rambled on some more about Pork Pie, his pal on Kauai, as he tucked into his rib-eye steak and gravy-drenched mashed potatoes. Across the table, Jen grew more panicked, but also more determined.

There was no way she was getting on that plane. This nightmare had gone on long enough. She had to find some way to escape, and the sooner the better.

She knew Zane wouldn't let her out of his sight, but there was one place she could grab a few minutes of privacy: the ladies room. He was a bit startled when she suddenly got up, announced she had to go, and dashed off so quickly that he couldn't react.

A few seconds later, inside the pale-pink powder room, Jen took a fast look around and saw that a wood-framed, cobweb-streaked window leading to the alley was her best chance. It was small, just two feet by two, and high up. A long shot, but she figured she could worm her way through. She was deathly afraid of what Zane would do if he burst in and caught her, but she had to take that chance.

Her leg muscles were weak, but she managed to heave herself onto a small, wobbly table beneath the glass and balance shakily on the old, cracked wood. Then she tugged on the chain to ease the window open and hoisted herself up and onto the filthy, splintered sill.

It was a long, tough squeeze. She tore the sleeve of her dress and cut her arm on an exposed nail, but she managed to worm her way through. Seconds seemed to turn to minutes. She was petrified Zane would barge in, but she finally made it through the window and onto the outer ledge.

Perched perilously, she gazed down at a hulking dumpster, full of food trash, directly below her. Gripping the window ledge, she somehow lowered herself onto the rim of the huge metal bin. Balancing on it with her toes for a harrowing instant, she tumbled to the ground, a full 12-foot drop. The rough asphalt gashed her knee and the four-inch heel on one of her pumps broke. But that didn't stop her.

Still in one piece, with blood trickling from her arm and knee, a dazed Jen hobbled as best she could down the dark alley until she reached an intersection. Then she turned left and headed towards a cluster of neon lights.

It was 35 degrees, dark, and the winds were howling. Jen was cold and shivering, but at least she had gotten away. Despite the wobbliness in her legs, she made it to nearby Fourth Street, and through the glass doors of the sprawling, neon-blazing Desert Rose Inn. Stumbling into the casino, she collapsed in front of a slot machine. With her head in her hands, she leaned forward and started to sob.

The loud, raucous noise of drunken revelers and ringing slots all around drowned out her mournful weeping. But eventually, the white-haired woman at the next machine noticed she was acting strangely and her arm was bleeding, so she jumped up to find a security guard.

"Miss, are you all right? What happened to your arm?" the grizzled, snow-haired guard inquired when he finally got to Jen. She struggled to put him in focus.

"Please help me," she whimpered, her glassy, red eyes staring up at him.

"I'm from Las Vegas," she murmured as he leaned down to listen. Then, in a trembling voice, she laid out the basics of her plight, ending with a few broken words she labored to repeat.

"He made me marry him...he had a gun...I couldn't get away."

"Where is he now?" the guard asked. In all his years in security, he had never heard such a bizarre story.

"I don't know, back at the steakhouse, I guess," Jen replied weakly.

A small crowd had gathered and was relishing the drama. Hoisting herself up from the chair, Jen collapsed in the guard's arms. He comforted her for a few seconds as the crowd watched. Then he wrapped an arm around Jen and half-carried her through the thicket of one-armed bandits to the dimly lit security office. There she tumbled onto a lumpy couch. Dazed and swaddled in blankets, she lay there until the police arrived.

CHAPTER 34

Back at the steakhouse, Zane had figured out pretty fast that Jen was no longer in the ladies room. When he charged inside and saw that his new bride had escaped through an open window, he kicked a stall door in rage, ran back to the table, and threw a fistful of twenties down. Then he ran outside and began frantically searching the streets for her. But except for the glare of neon, he could barely see in front of him in the misty darkness. He couldn't waste any more time looking and raced back to the hotel.

Without bothering to check out, he took the elevator to the eighth floor, crammed all his stuff and Jen's in plastic bags, and rode back down to the parking garage. After loading everything in his car, he jumped in, gunned the engine, and blasted the hell out of there.

It was his wedding night and Zane should have been back at the Silver Legacy, making love to his beautiful bride. Instead, he was tearing along Interstate 5 heading north, running from the law. He was still wearing his wedding suit, with a black leather jacket thrown over it. Checking out his left hand, Zane saw the gold band Jen had placed on it a few hours earlier, and punched the steering wheel.

Cursing, he asked himself, why did she do it? Why did she leave me like that? He was outraged. Couldn't she understand he meant her no harm? So he had brought her up to Reno against her will, forced her to marry him, and then drugged her and had sex with her. He only did all those things because he loved her and wanted them to be together. He knew it was crazy logic, and no doubt against the law. But to him, it made perfect sense.

Why didn't Jen get it? Why did she overreact like that, climbing out of a bathroom window like a drama queen in some cheesy music video? He had told her he was taking her to Hawaii for their honeymoon, and to start a new life, and she seemed happy about it. So why did she run?

He was hurt and furious, but he refused to take the ring off. He considered himself married to Jen. Till death do we part, the couple had vowed to each other in front of the justice of the peace that afternoon, and Zane had meant every word.

In a plastic bag on the back seat of the hulking SUV were the Washoe County wedding license, a receipt from the chapel, Jen's silk bouquet, some wedding photos, and a memory card holding more images. And stashed in the inner pocket of his leather jacket were a couple more 5" X 7"s. Solid proof, all the way, that they had gotten married that day. Jen could sneak out a restroom window, report him to the cops, and run home to mama, but they were still hitched, a legal entity, Mr. and Mrs. Zane

Hollister.

The Interstate was starting to get icy and wet. It was damn cold that night. Luckily, the car had snow tires, plenty of gas, and a good heater and radio. Driving straight through from Reno to Seattle would take a good 14 hours in these slick conditions. Zane was heading for the Emerald City because he had a pal up there, a guy he had met in the Big House.

Benny Gumba had drawn a one-year sentence after getting busted, along with three other dudes, in a bizarre gambling scam at Binion's in downtown Vegas. In the pen, he was assigned to the same cell block as Zane, who quickly took the sallow, pudgy, downtrodden Fish (new inmate) under his wing. Zane pulled Benny out of a few tough jams, and Benny was the type who never forgot a favor. When he left the slammer, he told Zane to get in touch if he was ever in Seattle. Zane decided that now was the time to cash in his chits.

Meanwhile, back in Reno, Jen was still lying limp on a sofa in the security office of the Desert Rose. She was groggy and crying when two cops from the Reno Police Department arrived. After questioning her briefly, they dispatched two officers to Room 812 of the Silver Legacy. But Zane was already gone.

The cops finally calmed Jen down, cleaned and bandaged the cuts on her arm and knee as best they could, and gave her hot coffee and a fleece jacket to warm her. They also called Brandi at work and left a message on her cell. At midnight, she called them back and promptly went into a panic when they told her what had happened. She pleaded with them to let her talk to her daughter, but they didn't want to upset Jen again, so they put her off. The cops advised Brandi to spend the night at a friend's house, or have someone stay with her, because of Zane's threats. She called Nick, and ended up staying at his place that night.

Jen burst into tears of relief and joy when she learned her mom was okay. She had been worried Zane would send one of his scummy cohorts to hurt Brandi after she escaped. But so far, that hadn't happened. Still anxious and distraught, Jen climbed into the back of a Reno P.D. squad car. After being driven to the station, she spent a cold, restless night thrashing around a lumpy cot in an empty office.

Early the next morning, she was taken to the Reno Rape Treatment Center for a forensic medical exam that would be used as evidence against Zane, if and when he was charged and the case went to trial.

Jen still had no phone, purse, or wallet, since Zane had taken everything. The lack of ID made the testing process more difficult and complicated, but somehow she got through it.

While Jen tried to pull herself together in Reno, Zane was barreling down the open road towards Seattle. The cold temperatures and night-time snow had made the drive longer and harder. He popped some Dexedrine to stay awake and washed the pills down with swigs of Jack Daniels or the high-octane coffee he picked up at truck stops in Oregon.

As the sun was coming up that Sunday morning, Zane crossed the Washington state line. In Olympia, he slipped into a tiny truck stop for bacon and eggs and to get the car fueled up. After he ate, he darted into a cold, dark men's room to change from his wedding suit into dark jeans and a heavy knit shirt.

Back on I-5, he kept speeding northwest. By noon he was standing at a pay phone in downtown Seattle, ringing up Benny, whose number was in the phone book.

The two ex-cons met for a bite at a hash house out on a country road. It was 50 degrees and sunny, so they sat outside at an old wooden picnic table. Majestic, snow-covered Mount Rainier loomed in the distance, as did the towering Space Needle downtown.

This innocuous setting was a stark contrast to the dank, overcrowded chow hall back in Carson City, where they struggled daily to choke down runny scrambled eggs, spam sandwiches, and half-cooked Jello with rock-hard marshmallows. They both laughed just thinking of it as they chowed down on juicy burgers, crisp fries, and thick shakes. Then they chatted about the bad old days, and what had become of some of their buddies.

After a long spell of guy talk, Zane leaned in and confided to Benny that he had gotten himself into a jam with a babe back in Vegas and needed a place to lay low for a while. Balding, pudgy Benny glanced across the table at suave, buff Zane and smiled. He was burning with envy, but he totally understood and quickly volunteered that his former bro-in-law had a place for rent at the rear of his property.

That afternoon, Zane met tall, sandy-haired nerd,

Fred Norbert. After making a quick tour of a sparsely furnished one-bedroom apartment in a rambling stone house in the Highland Park area, Zane plunked down $800 cash for the first month's rent.

The ground-floor apartment with its own entrance was more than adequate for Zane's needs. There was a small kitchen with a dining area that seated four; a nice-size, fully-carpeted living room with a dark green sofa and chairs; and a fairly large bedroom with a queen-size bed. The apartment also offered a stunning view of 14,000-foot Mt. Rainier, towering majestically in the distant, snow-covered Cascade mountains.

Highland Park was a sedate, middle-class neighborhood that Zane could easily blend into. And more good news: he would be able to park his SUV in Fred's two-car garage to get it off the street, where a cop might spot it.

CHAPTER 35

Back in Reno, Jen was still dealing with the aftermath of the kidnapping, forced marriage, and rape. On Sunday morning, Brandi flew up from Vegas with her on-again, off-again boyfriend, Nick. The divorced, 52-year-old father of three was the man she turned to in any crisis. And he was crazy about her. They had been romantically involved at one point, but when she found out he was seeing other women, she hit the reset button, and gave him the "let's be friends" speech. Nick's male pride was hurt, but he understood where she was coming from, and they were able to remain friends.

Though Brandi didn't trust Nick with her heart, she leaned on him completely in legal and police matters. At the Reno airport, they rented a car and drove straight to the police station. At first glance, Jen's appearance shocked them both. Pale, nervous, and dazed, she was slumped on a steel chair in a barren room.

"Honey, what happened? Are you alright?" Brandi asked, engulfing her daughter in a hug. Jen, who was still wearing her grey lace wedding gown with the ripped, bloody sleeve, poured everything out as best she could.

"Mom, I opened the door on Friday morning at seven, thinking it would be Brianna," she said in a rush of words, "but it was Zane. He found out I went to San Francisco last month to see Colton, and that set him off. Everything's been a nightmare since. He had a gun and made me go with him. He made me marry him, and then he gave me drugs and…and…forced himself on me. I had to have a rape medical exam today."

"That goddam son of a bitch! With God as my witness, he'll pay for this," Brandi raged, tears streaming down her cheeks. "He'll spend the rest of his life behind bars if I have anything to say about it."

"It was horrible," Jen went on. "After a nightmare wedding at a chapel near the hotel, we went back to our room. He put sedatives in my champagne and had sex with me while I was groggy and barely able to move."

By then Jen was in tears too. Brandi handed her some tissues and held her for a while.

"I'm not really married to him, am I?" Jen asked plaintively, looking at Brandi and Nick when she finally calmed down. "I keep asking everyone, but they won't give me a straight answer. Can Nick find out?"

"Sure, honey," Brandi replied, stroking Jen's long blond hair, which was matted and streaked with blood. "Nick will find out everything he can from the officers. Don't worry, you're safe now. I'll get you some tea. You're so pale, and your dress is torn. Why is your sleeve bloody? What happened to your arm?"

"I cut it on a nail when I climbed out the bathroom window to get away," Jen explained breathlessly. "As I pushed through, it got gashed all the way down. I didn't feel anything, but after I jumped off the dumpster and started walking, I could see blood dripping down my hand. It looks horrible, but it's okay now. The officers cleaned it last night."

Jen was talking fast and seemed to still be in a state of shock and totally exhausted.

"You don't need to answer everything now," Brandi told her, looking more closely at her arm. "We can talk later. Nick and I need to ask the officers when we can get you out of here."

Disheveled himself, Nick had barely slept the night before. His lean, taut face was looking craggier than usual from the ongoing tension. He was wearing a beige trench coat over grey pants and a light blue shirt. In a long talk with the officers, he provided more details and background on Zane's extensive history of trouble with the law in Vegas. He also provided details on all the stalking incidents involving Jen and Colton over the past year and a half.

Nick was trying to get Jen out of the police station, but it was complicated because she had no ID, and the cops had more questions. They needed the name of the limo service, wedding chapel, and justice of the peace that performed the ceremony. They also wanted more information on Zane's car and the drive from Vegas.

Jen gave them the gold band on her ring finger and the name of the pawn shop where she and Zane had purchased it. She told them Zane had two tickets for a flight to Kauai at eight that morning. When they checked with the airline, they found out the tickets hadn't been used.

From what the cops could glean, Zane had disappeared into thin air. If and when he was found, Jen agreed to press charges against him for armed kidnapping, coercion, false imprisonment, and sexual assault. If convicted, he would spend a lot longer than two years behind bars this time. But of course, the cops had to find him first. And they seemed to be drawing a blank.

After Jen endured another long interview, Brandi and Nick signed release papers and they were all able to clear out of there.

From the station, Brandi, Nick, and Jen went to Harrah's-Reno, where they checked into adjoining rooms for a couple of days. Jen needed to calm down and get some rest, food, and a change of clothes. Because she was too anxious and agitated to be left alone, Nick watched over her while she slept. Brandi, meanwhile, went to a boutique in Harrah's lobby and bought jeans and sweaters, as well as personal grooming items at the drug store.

Later, as Jen gradually opened up about the whole ordeal, Brandi was struck again by what her daughter had been through. Nick did his best to comfort both of them, while promising over and over that the "animal" would be brought to justice.

Jen couldn't fly back to Vegas because she

didn't have ID, so they ended up spending two nights in Reno, then driving home. While Nick and Brandi sat in the front seat of Nick's rental car, Jen sat quietly in back gazing out at the relentless blur of rocks, gnarly cactus, and clay-colored soil. Her mind was on Zane. She was wondering where he was, and despising him for what he had done. What would happen if they caught him, she wondered. How long would he be in prison this time? What if there was a long trial and she had to face him every day in the courtroom? How would she handle that?

She was also thinking about Colton, of course. She felt sorry for him for being dragged into this whole mess with her. But she also remembered that, before Zane had come back from prison, the two of them had enjoyed a blissful, nine-month love affair.

She wondered how Colton would react to the nightmare she had been through over the past few days. Would he somehow be able to process it and move beyond it? Or would he be so turned off and appalled by what had happened that he would want to dump her and wash his hands of all involvement?

Jen also had a slew of doubts and fears about her job. After the forced marriage and rape, how would she ever go back to being the cute, perky pop-out girl she had been before?

CHAPTER 36

Back in Vegas, Jen tried to rest and recover from the nightmare In Reno. Her arm healed, but the gash left a nasty scar. Her doctor prescribed sleeping pills and tranquilizers to get her through the days and nights. She was on an unpaid leave from Stripper Grams, so she had some time to pull herself together.

To deal with her many fears, Jen started seeing a therapist. She was terrified of being alone in the house, wouldn't answer the phone or door, and refused to go anywhere by herself. She feared Zane would come swooping in from wherever, remind her they were married, and try to abduct her again at gunpoint.

After Reno, Officer Nolan and the Metro cops reopened their investigations into Matt's shooting, the zip line accident, and car crash. They planned to throw the book at Zane if and when he was found.

Jen had to get a new cell phone, driver's license, and address book to replace the ones taken by Zane. It was an inconvenience, but at least she was alive and okay, and she hadn't heard a word from her alleged husband, which was the best news of all.

Jen was stunned to learn their marriage had been valid. Having it dissolved was a more complicated process than she had imagined. But the Reno cops assisted, and six weeks after the grim wedding, a Washoe County judge declared the union null and void.

Though she was single again, nothing could take away the trauma Jen and her mom had endured. Brandi lived in constant fear that Zane would carry through with the threats he had made to Jen about harming her if she ran away.

A week after Brandi returned from Reno, Megan called just to check in, and Brandi told her about the latest Zane nightmare. As soon as Jen found out that Megan knew, she called Colton and relayed to him, in a soft monotone, the entire grisly drama. The San Francisco dinner disaster instantly got put on the back burner. Stunned and outraged, Colton asked, "What do the cops say? How can this Zane stuff still be going on?"

"Um, they're trying to find him, but he disappeared in Reno," Jen replied, flustered and embarrassed. "No one knows where he is, so they can't question him or throw him in jail."

"They sound like total incompetents," Colton retorted. "That lunatic should have been arrested after the zip line thing. What the hell's wrong with the legal system?"

"There was no evidence," Jen sighed, "and then he disappeared. Hiding out is Zane's specialty. He's been doing it for years."

"Enough about that asshole," Colton shot back.

"How are you doing? If I ever get my hands on that son-of-a-bitch, I'll rip him apart!" he swore.

This was the last thing Jen wanted to hear. She just wanted Colton to be loving and supportive of her, not vengeful and violent towards Zane. But of course, she didn't have the words to convey this to him, so the macho-dude behavior continued, which meant less compassion for her, and more rage for Zane.

Two weeks after their phone call, Colton flew to Vegas on a Friday night, as usual, and rented a car for the weekend. Jen was happy about the visit, and he was looking forward to seeing her, too. But it didn't go well.

Over dinner at Rendezvous, the conversation grew tense when Colton pressed Jen for details on the kidnapping and her escape. He was appalled by the incident, and wondered why she hadn't tried harder to break away before the wedding.

"How could you go through with it? Why didn't you escape the night before?" he asked.

"My arm and leg were handcuffed to the bed that whole night," Jen explained awkwardly. "Zane told me over and over that if I ran away, he would have one of his scummy associates go to our house, rob it, and beat Mom up. Just thinking about that scared me more than anything else."

"But still, you actually married the guy. Couldn't you have broken away at the chapel? Wouldn't someone have helped you there?"

"I don't know, I just don't know," a confused Jen murmured, shaking her head. "I did the best I could. After everything that happened over the months, I knew he was capable of following through with his threats against Mom and me. He had a gun in his bag. If I had run from the chapel, I was terrified he'd shoot me, and then maybe himself, too.

"I only got up the nerve to escape when he told me at the steakhouse we were going to Hawaii the next morning for our honeymoon. The thought of that pushed me over the edge," Jen went on.

"What if he got me over there and I was never heard from again? I had visions of being held captive in some remote beach hideaway with bars on the windows, no phone, and no place to run. So I somehow squeezed through that ladies' room window and got to the Desert Rose."

Colton heard every word Jen said, and it made sense. But he also knew about her long, storied past with Zane, and he couldn't help wondering if, beneath it all, she still had feelings for him and that was why she had gone through with the wedding.

When Colton tried to bring this up, Jen grew hurt and angry. He tried to backtrack, but she sensed he was blaming her for what had happened. It was the first of many long, agonizing exchanges in the months to come that ate away at the intense feelings the couple had once had for each other.

Jen already felt shame over the fact that she'd had an earlier, teenage relationship with Zane for four years. She deeply regretted her poor judgment and how it had come back to haunt her. It was almost a confirmation that she had some inherent flaw that would always lead her to make the wrong choices when it came to men.

Colton believed that the roots of Jen's attraction to Zane came from a simpler, more basic place. He thought back to all the pretty girls he'd known in high school who were irresistibly drawn to bad boys for the glamour, excitement, and danger. Jen, he now believed, was one of those.

That Friday night, when the couple returned to Colton's suite at Caesar's, they didn't make love. He mumbled something about a back problem, and she said something about the whole trauma with Zane, and how she wasn't ready for sex or any type of physical intimacy.

It was a very lonely, awkward night, and the rest of that weekend was pretty much the same. Colton spent most of his time with Delia and Megan, and saw Jen only once more, for a quick lunch on Sunday.

The simple truth was that he no longer wanted her in a sexual, or emotional, way. The San Francisco dinner fiasco, and now the kidnapping and forced marriage, had totally turned him off. He was beginning to wonder if maybe his parents had been right about Jen all along, and that she truly was from a different world and the two of them could never really know or understand each other. They were both sad and confused. There was a sense of relief, but also foreboding about the future, when they parted ways on Sunday and Colton flew back to San Jose.

CHAPTER 37

A few days after his arrival in Seattle, Zane had his jet-black Tahoe painted a bland, "old-lady" beige. Stashed under the driver's seat were a pair of "souvenir" license plates from his days in the pen, where they manufactured them. Once the car had been re-painted, he removed the old Nevada plates and replaced them with these shiny new ones.

With his wheels now disguised, Zane had a new lease on life. He felt safe driving around Seattle, and even kicked back with Benny for some fly-fishing and sea-duck hunting on the Olympic Peninsula.

Of course, Jen was on his mind, day and night. Zane never took his wedding band off. As far as he was concerned, they were married. No ifs, ands, or buts. He didn't know if Jen had taken legal action to end their union or not, but he hadn't signed anything, so, as far as he was concerned, it was still on.

Though he was outraged that Jen had run away, he never regretted taking her from Vegas and marrying her in Reno. In fact, he considered it the best thing he'd ever done in his life. Jen may have run back to her mom in Vegas, but he knew it wasn't over. He would never let her go. They were soul mates, destined to be together forever.

But none of that meant he had to live like a hermit in Seattle. Benny had a bartending gig at a dimly lit hole-in-the-wall called the Feral Pig, and Zane would drop by for a burger and fries a few nights a week. Parking himself at the bar, he would throw back some Blue Moons, watch basketball, and flirt with the waitresses.

Zane also maintained a cordial relationship with his landlord, Fred, a laid-back, easy-going dude whose fish-monger gig at the Pike Place Market downtown kept him hopping. He was in and out at all hours, too busy to ask a lot of nosy questions. As long as Zane paid his rent on time and put the trash out on Tuesday, everything was peachy.

For a couple of months, all was cool in Seattle, with Zane staying well under the radar. Of course, he didn't have Jen, and that hurt. He was still furious and stunned that she'd bolted on their wedding night. He sometimes thought about payback, like having her mom's house robbed, with her getting roughed up in the process. But after mulling it over, he realized he didn't really want to hurt Brandi. He also didn't want to get the Vegas cops all jacked up, so he decided against it.

Meanwhile, Colton continued to distance himself from Jen. With all the assorted traumas that had befallen them over the months, he felt it best to keep things distant but polite. There was just too much baggage for anything closer or more intimate.

Unaware of this, a lovesick Zane remained in agony, imagining Jen and Colton in bed together, or just kicking back on the Strip. It killed him that his wife was sleeping with another guy. As time went by, it became more and more unbearable. At some point, he knew something would have to be done. This situation couldn't go on forever.

Despite Seattle's dreary weather, Zane was settling into some semblance of a life on the rainy coast. So what if it was sort of boring and empty? At least he was out of lock-up, on his own, and not looking over his shoulder every minute for the Vegas cops.

His plan was to stick around through the summer of 2018, and maybe have his kids come up when they got out of school. It would be a fun adventure for them all. There weren't too many good times to look back on with his own dad, and that was a pain he didn't want to inflict on his son and daughter.

But then, in March 2018, events took a sharp turn when Zane got an unexpected call from his 25-year-old sister, Kacey, back in Vegas. The sibs had always been close. She had a steady job as a stripper at Girls of Glitter Gulch, a nudie dive on Fremont Street downtown.

Little sis was one of the few people back home who knew where Zane was. They talked every other week or so, mostly about his mom and two kids, who were living with Grandma. But the tone of this call was different.

"Zaney, you okay?" were Kacey's first words, uttered in a tight, whiney voice.

"Yeah, I'm cool, why wouldn't I be?" Zane shot back.

"Um, I wanted to let you know right away," she said in a rush of words. "A cop came into the club last night. He couldn't get ahold of me at home. I never answer the phone, so he showed up at work. He asked if I knew where you were. I said I haven't heard a word.

"I just wanted to give you a heads-up. He asked if you were somewhere in the Northwest. I said I didn't have a clue, but he kept saying they had reason to believe you were in Oregon or Washington."

"How the hell could they know that?" Zane interrupted her. "That asshole was just faking you out. They don't know jack. It was just a fishing trip."

"No, Zaney, it's more than fishing. He pulled a wedding photo of you and Jen out of his pocket. He said a janitor at a truck stop in Olympia found it on the men's john floor. He saw pictures of you on TV, and recognized you as the dude the cops were looking for.

"I just sat there playing dumb, like none of it was registering. Then he asked if the groom in the picture was you. I looked at it real close and said no. He asked if I ever saw the bride before. I said no again, I have never seen this dude, or this chick, before in my life. But it was you and Jen at the wedding chapel in Reno."

"Goddamn!" Zane erupted. "I had a couple wedding photos stashed in my pocket the night I left Reno. When I changed clothes at the truck stop in

Olympia the next morning, I was in a hurry. It was a tiny hole in the wall, filthy, dark, and colder than a witch's tit. I was rushing to get the hell out of there. I guess one of the photos fell out of my pocket. There were other papers on the floor, so I never saw it.

"Did he say anything about Seattle?" Zane asked.

"No," Kacey answered. "But they're getting warmer. Metro talked to some of the prison guards in Carson City to find out if there were other ex-cons you might hook up with on the outside. They found out you had a couple of pals in the Northwest that have also been released."

"I gotta get the hell out of here, like yesterday!" Zane exploded. "Those Metro fucks are closing in on me. If they find me, I'm a dead man walking. They'll throw more charges at me than Bonnie and Clyde. I'll be in lock-up for the next 30 years. I can't handle that. Two years was a fuckin' nightmare."

"I know," Kacey agreed. "I remember how messed up that whole scene was, and how much you hated it. Every time I went to see you, I thought about Dad and how he died in prison, shot in the back while trying to escape from a chain gang. I was always scared the same thing would happen to you."

"Me too," Zane said. "I made it through two years, but if I ever got sent up again, I'd never last. I'd hang myself any way I could, with shoe laces, sheets, anything I could get my hands on. Or they'd take me out, just like they did Dad, trying to escape.

"What phone are you calling from?" Zane suddenly asked.

"Mack's cell. He's at work and the babies are sleeping."

"You better not call here again," he warned her. "They're watching you, Kace. They could be tracing your calls. I'll get in touch when I can."

"Cool," Kacey shot back. "You'll let me know where you are, right?"

"For sure, I'll call you," Zane answered.

"You're scaring the shit out of me," Kacey said. "I feel like something terrible's gonna happen to you."

"Nothing terrible's gonna to happen to big-bro, unless they put me back in lock-up," he told her. "As long as I stay on the outside, I'm cool. Just help Mom out with the kids, okay?"

"Yeah, sure, but they're a handful," Kacey told him. And then, in a more urgent, upset tone, she asked, "Where are you going? South America? Mexico? Canada? Where? I'm your sister, you can tell me."

"I'll call you when the time is right. I gotta run, Kace. It's Plan B time. Bye."

"But Zaney, wait!" Kacey screeched as she heard the click on the other end.

CHAPTER 38

After the call from Kacey, Zane never had another peaceful minute in Seattle. In short order, he mentioned to Fred that he'd be moseying on down the road soon.

"Time to move on," he explained vaguely, as if he were some kind of singing minstrel or rolling stone. "I'll pay my rent through the end of the month and send you a postcard."

"Cool," Fred replied with a laid-back shrug. "We're gonna miss you around here, dude, you've become part of the landscape."

Zane nodded. It was an amicable parting, and he hadn't experienced many of those.

Later, at the Feral Pig, he waited for Benny to go on break, then they had a beer.

"Ben, my friend from the pen, my stay is sadly coming to an end. I'm going to be heading out on the road again. Seattle's been good to me. I plan on coming back. Can I leave my car and a couple guns in your spare garage while I'm gone?"

"Yeah, dude, whatever, there's plenty of room," Benny offered. "I hate to see you go, man, but you'll be back, or you wouldn't be leaving the car and guns, right?"

"Right," Zane nodded.

"Where you headin'?" Benny asked.

"Maybe Southern California. Some place back in the desert would be cool. The weather up here's a bitch. But first things first. I gotta drive back to Vegas to do a quick pick-up. My wife's down there, you know. After I get her, we'll drive back up here. Then we'll take off in a day or two for an extended honeymoon."

"Sounds like a plan," Benny said, taking a sip of Blue Moon and gazing across the table at his dark-eyed, leather-jacketed buddy. Since their earliest days in the slammer, he'd harbored a kind of hero-worship for suave mystery man, Zane. A totally cool dude. Coolness beyond anything Benny could ever hope to achieve.

"If any cop-types come around asking questions after I'm gone," Zane added, "don't say shit. Fred, too. Say nothing and get rid of them, fast. Goddamn cops. Never know when to mind their own business."

Benny nodded.

Zane then made plans to go to Vegas to "pick Jen up." Of course that wasn't what it would be like at all. It would be a kidnapping at gunpoint. He would find out where she was working, and then wait for her in the middle of the night in her driveway. Then he would force her into his car, lock her in, and drive her back to Seattle.

They would spend a day or two getting reacquainted in the apartment, then take off for their delayed honeymoon in Kauai, and to start a new life there. That was the plan: a permanent honeymoon on the beach for Mr. and Mrs. Zane Hollister.

Of course, Zane knew Jen would fight the idea at first. But he would convince her that this was the only way either one of them would ever truly be happy. They were soul mates, after all, meant to be together forever. That was his obsessive dream. Zane would make Jen believe it. He could be very persuasive, and a loaded gun in his hand would get the idea across even faster.

CHAPTER 39

My the third week of March 2018, one year after Matt's shooting, Zane was ready to drive from Seattle to Vegas to reclaim the wife he had married two months before in Reno. Step one was finding out her work schedule, so he would know when to surprise her in the driveway. He knew Brandi liked to work on Saturday night, so that would be the ideal time to strike.

On a Monday morning, Zane called Stripper Grams' corporate office on Dean Martin Drive, right off the Strip. Kelsey Davis, the new receptionist, answered. The bouncy brunette, a recent graduate of Valley Vista High, aspired to become a pop-out girl the minute she turned 21. Meanwhile, she was 'manning' the phones.

Making an effort to sound nice, normal, and casual, Zane told Kelsey he was coming to that weekend's WrestleMania Awards' Dinner on Saturday night at Caesar's. He asked if Stripper Grams was handling the entertainment, and Kelsey chirped "yes."

"Well, I've seen a few of your pop-out acts,"

Zane followed up. "And my hands-down favorite is a hot blonde named Jen Conover. I was wondering if she'll be working the dinner show this Saturday night?"

"One moment, sir, I'll check the schedule," Kelsey answered.

Lucky for him, Jen's name and the events she'd be working continued to be listed. Destiny still hadn't been able to get the computer people to stop posting them.

Perky Kelsey got back on the line and answered, "Jen will be working that event, and so will her tandem partner, Amber. Both of them will be popping out at 11 PM after the WrestleMania dinner. Does that work for you, sir?"

"Let me check my calendar," Zane answered, very nerdy and proper. "Yes, that works fine," he told her. "We're all looking forward to the show."

"I'm sure the girls will be awesome; they're both rated five-star," Kelsey added.

"Great. Thanks for your help, young lady. Have a nice day," a delighted Zane said before hanging up.

A big smile was on his face. The drive would take 17 hours; he would leave Seattle on Friday morning around seven and arrive in Vegas at midnight.

He planned to stay at Palace Station on Sahara Avenue because it was a good distance from the Strip, which he wanted to avoid. Too many cops buzzing around, and too many people who might recognize him. He was a local, after all, with a wide network of friends, acquaintances, and associates.

Zane reserved a room at Palace Station under the name, Joey Redd. He owned a fake ID with that name. In Seattle, he had gotten a similar ID made for Jen under the name, Kristin Redd. From Seattle, the couple would travel to Kauai as the just-married Redds.

At Palace Station, Zane would get some food and a good night's sleep. He would hang out in the casino all day Saturday and check out of the hotel that evening, before driving to Jen's.

After her 11 PM show, he figured she'd get home around 1:30 or 2 AM. Then he would grab her in the middle of the night, and hope she didn't struggle too much or make too much noise. That would be a big problem because, if any of the neighbors called the cops and Zane got busted, he knew his ass would be in the can for a long time, maybe even the rest of his life.

But for the moment, thoughts of prison were far from Zane's mind. Planning this trip excited him beyond belief. For as long as he could remember, Zane had been chasing his elusive love, and each time his hopes had been cruelly dashed. Now, finally, he and Jen would be together, with nothing, and no one, to stop them.

Zane felt like he was on the last leg of a long, hard journey. With any luck, he and his bride would be back in Seattle on Sunday night, and fly off to the islands on Tuesday as the Redds. On Kauai, there would be just the two of them to think about. No over-protective mothers, sadistic bosses, nosy cops, or dickhead boyfriends.

Zane would live in paradise forever with the love

of his life. Could it get any better than that?

CHAPTER 40

O pening his front door to the early morning chill, the first thing Zane saw was a box of Krispy Kreme doughnuts Benny had left on his doorstep. Inside were three sprinkle and three glazed, Zane's favorites. Benny always stopped for these warm, chewy treats on his way home from work. He got a lot of pleasure out of sharing them with Zane. Sort of a sweet reminder they were now free men, and no longer in that hellhole down in Carson City.

Picking up the box, Zane smiled as he headed for the garage. It was 7:30 on a Friday morning in March 2018. He was about to leave Seattle and drive to Vegas, via Salt Lake City. It was 40 degrees, and a cold, light rain was falling. The doughnuts would warm him up, though he had dressed appropriately enough in jeans, a plaid flannel shirt with a grey hoodie, and a black leather jacket. He couldn't wait to get to Kauai, away from this constant cold-and-rain shit, and lay on the beach every day with Jen.

In his beige Tahoe, Zane was soon throttling

down I-84 towards Salt Lake. It would be a long day, but he was prepared and slipped in a Guns N' Roses tape, which he blasted.

In Salt Lake, he fueled up and grabbed a quick burger at a truck-stop diner. The weather remained cold and damp, but he was heading back to the desert, so that made it all bearable.

Picking up I-15 in Salt Lake, Zane drove straight through to Vegas. There were a few pit stops along the way, including one in St. George, Utah, for gas, and chicken-pot pie at the very cool Black Bear Diner.

Eighteen long hours after he'd left Seattle, Zane was pulling into the sprawling parking lot of the Palace Station Hotel-Casino at I-15 and Sahara. It was just this side of two on a Saturday morning, but he was elated to have made it back to Vegas. As he pulled his bag from the back of the car, he noticed the air was warmer and dryer, even in the middle of the night.

Inside Palace Station, scores of Friday-night revelers were spilling into the lobby from the casino, restaurants, and bars. But there was no line at the registration desk, so Zane checked in, lickety-split, as Joey Redd, with his fake ID. There was no way he would have used his real name. Zane Hollister was a wanted man in Vegas, for stalking and harassment, Matt's shooting, Jen's kidnapping, and assorted other charges. He would have to have been a complete idiot, or have some kind of death wish, to even think about using his real name.

After a quick elevator ride, Zane entered his 8th floor room. It was clean and spacious, with a king-size bed, wide-screen TV, walk-in-tile-shower, pictures of sunflowers on the walls, and a decent view of the parking lot and strip-mall next door.

Zane was exhausted; it had been a long day. After hanging the "Do Not Disturb" sign on the door, he dropped his bag on the floor, flopped on the bed, and, within seconds, was off to dreamland.

Ten hours later, he woke up hungry and horny. Funnel-Cake French Toast at the Brass Fork downstairs took care of the hunger. But only one thing could get rid of the horniness: Jen.

Zane spent the day main-lining on slots. Normally, poker and blackjack were more his style, but he didn't want to interact with other players because someone might remember him later. So he dressed in a dark-blue pullover knit shirt, black jeans and boots, and pulled a black baseball cap over his shiny dark locks. Inside the hotel, his quick, alert brown eyes were mostly concealed by the cap. Outside, in the bright sun, he wore shades.

It was a Saturday, and as Zane lingered in the casino, pummeling the Repeat Bet buttons on the slots, he noticed a flurry of wedding parties drifting by. The brides wore fluffy white gowns, carried elaborate bouquets, and tenderly held the arms of tuxedoed dudes with slicked-back hair.

As he watched them, Zane thought back on his wedding to Jen two months earlier. She had been upset that day, but now he vowed to make it up to her big time in Kauai. She would have a happy, easy life there, and never want for anything.

In his pre-prison days, Zane had boasted of "mucho dinero," as he always put it, stashed in bank accounts nobody could trace. The money was still there, and only he could access it. Jen would be taken care of in style. It would be like the old days, when all was sunshine and roses, glitz and glam. Only this time, all of it would be accompanied by Hawaiian sunsets, luaus on the beach, and the smell of white-orchid leis encircling Jen's swan-like neck.

Zane had to restrain himself from calling his mom and kids, or sister, that day, just to say hey. After what Kacey had told him on their last call, he knew it wasn't a good idea. They were probably all being watched by the cops. It would put them in danger, and him, too, so he needed to lay low and not contact anyone.

He did call the Venetian, though, and ask for Brandi, just to make sure she was working that night. The switchboard operator told him she wasn't in, but would be later. Bingo! Confirmation that mama bear was working that Saturday night, as usual. That meant she wouldn't be home till three or four AM.

Back in his room, before checking out, Zane cleaned and loaded his Glock-19 handgun. Afterwards, he reloaded the magazine so it would be ready if he needed it.

Around 10 PM, dressed in black, from his baseball cap to his leather boots, Zane checked out of Palace Station and loaded his gym bag into the back of his car.

Jen's pop-out act was on from 11 to 11:30. She'd be invited to the party afterwards for a meet-and-greet with the WrestleMania crowd. Then she'd change back into jeans and a sweater and drive home. By 1:30 or 2 AM, she'd be cruising down her driveway on Rosita Way. Zane would be there by 1 AM, just in case she made it back early.

From the moment he woke up that day, Zane felt nervous and excited. He couldn't wait to be reunited with his bride and whisk her off to Kauai for a sexy, romantic honeymoon. In his mind, he had been a model of patience, waiting two whole months. But now the jig was up.

Around 12:30 AM, Zane drove to Summerlin. One block from Jen's house, he parked his beige Tahoe in a secluded bank parking lot. After walking to Jen's red-brick ranch-style-house, he positioned himself behind a large hedge just off the driveway. Stashed in the pocket of his black leather jacket was the loaded Glock-19.

Rosita Way was a small, suburban street, and not very well lit. Above Jen's front door, a single-bulb porch light flickered dimly, but, aside from that, the surroundings were pitch-black. Few cars were backing in or out of driveways that quiet Saturday night. Perfect conditions, Zane thought, for reconnecting with his honey and whisking her away. But first he had to accost her when she got out of her car, and then move her, with or without her cooperation, to his SUV a block away. That would be the tough part.

Like clockwork, Jen's silver Honda Accord appeared at 1:45 AM. Do I know my girl or what, Zane thought, when he saw her car gliding down the driveway and coming to a stop. The minute gorgeous, blond Jen slid out of the driver's seat, Zane ran up to her.

"Hey babe, guess who?" he teased, putting his hands on her arms and pulling her close. "Your number one fan. How was the pop-out gig?"

"Zane, what are you doing here?" Jen bristled, flinging her hands up and jerking back from him. "Get away from me! Get out of here. Leave me alone!"

Grabbing her forearms, Zane pulled her towards him.

"Take it easy, sweetheart. I'm giving the orders around here. Do as you're told and no one will get hurt. That's what they always told us back in Carson City."

Jen's legs turned to jelly. It was just like two months before, when Zane showed up at her door at 7 AM and forced her to go to Reno with him. It was happening all over again, the same goddamn thing!

Jen was terrified, furious, and totally blindsided. Her mind went blank. She tried to scream, but Zane pulled a washcloth he'd lifted from the hotel out of his pocket, balled it up, and shoved it in her mouth.

She was flailing around in his arms, shaking her head no, no, no, and trying to yell. But it was getting her nowhere because of the gag. They were standing outside her car, with the door wide open. Early on, she had dropped the key.

Pulling and pushing her, Zane was trying to force her to leave with him and go to his car. But she wouldn't budge, and continued punching and kicking.

Taking the gun from his pocket, Zane poked it hard into Jen's ribs on the left, while somehow getting a grip on her neck with his right arm. In a tight chokehold, he started dragging her backwards down the driveway and out to the street, while she continued kicking and elbowing him.

He warned, "Stop wriggling or I'll shoot. This gun is loaded!"

Suddenly Jen heard a volley of loud barks barreling their way. Clyde, the bulldog-German Shepard mix who lived across the street and had known and loved Jen for years, had become alarmed by the sounds of a struggle and was charging over to help.

In an instant, the big, strong mutt leapt on Zane's back, growling, biting, and tearing away at him like an unhinged grizzly. Zane was totally caught off guard. Dropping the gun, he crashed to the ground.

Clyde and Zane were wrestling and struggling. Then Zane managed to grab the pistol and shoot the 90-pound, frizzle-haired beast. The bullet entered his shoulder, but didn't kill him. The dog winced in pain as a pool of blood formed. But to his credit, he stayed on the attack and continued to struggle with, and tear at Zane.

Beside them, a panicky, scared Jen snatched her key off the ground and tried to get back in her car. She almost made it. Reaching up, an unhinged Zane grabbed her ankle and pulled her to the ground. Now Jen, Zane, and the bloody Clyde were thrashing around, just beyond the open car door.

Somehow, some way, in the confusion and chaos, Jen's fingers located the gun, coated now with warm, sticky canine blood. Gripping the Glock with her right hand, she found the trigger. As she and Zane tore away at each other, she blindly squeezed it towards what she thought was him. It was. After a single shot, he cried out in agony and lunged upward, gripping his mid-section, then falling back down with a hard thud.

He was writhing around, groaning incoherently. Blood was spurting everywhere: Zane's and Clyde's. Still holding the gun, a blood-drenched Jen somehow managed to stagger back to her feet. For an instant, Zane stared up at her, his brown eyes filled with pain, rage, and betrayal. It was a look she would never forget, the look that launched a thousand nightmares.

Struggling to raise his bloody hand, he reached for Jen. In a raspy, broken whisper, he mouthed the words, "Jenny, Kauai, Jenny," as she leaned down and took his hand. Seconds later, it went slack and dropped to the ground.

Jen was stunned. Was Zane dead? She thought so, but she wasn't sure and she was too scared to find out.

Staring down in horror at her right hand, she dropped Zane's bloody gun on the lawn.

"Somebody help me, please, somebody help me," she whimpered over and over.

CHAPTER 41

For some reason, Tilman and Patsy Landry, the retired couple who owned Clyde, had awakened, looked out their bedroom window, and seen the craziness unfolding in the Conovers' driveway. Tearing out of their house in their pajamas, they ran across the street to help Jen.

Patsy gasped when she saw the wounded, immobile Zane, and burst into tears at the sight of her bloody dog. Plopping on the ground in a pool of blood, she gently placed Clyde's head in her lap and did her best to soothe and stroke him.

"He's not going to die, is he?" Jen asked in a soft, trembling voice.

"I don't think so," Patsy whispered as she cradled Clyde's head in her lap. Then, looking up at Jen, she added, "we'll get him to the emergency vet in a few minutes."

Standing near Patsy, Jen stared down at her bloody hands and then at Zane, sprawled on the ground with his abdomen ripped open and raw. She was horrified, but also strangely relieved. She couldn't believe the siege of stalking and terror was finally over, and that he would never again appear on her doorstep with a gun, threatening her and demanding that she go with him.

Alarmed by the bloody, chaotic scene in the Conovers' driveway, a wide-eyed Tilman asked Jen, "what happened here tonight?"

"Um, he was an ex-boyfriend who was stalking me," she replied, trying to speak despite her shaking jaw. "The police know who he is. He tried to force me to go with him. We were fighting when Clyde ran over and jumped on him. If it wasn't for Clyde, I'd be in his car right now, on the way to God-knows-where."

In his dark plaid pajamas, Tilman nodded, walked over to Jen, and wrapped his arm around her.

"Well, he looks pretty torn up," the retired bricklayer said gently, shaking his head. "Take it easy, honey, he can't hurt you now.

"I called 911," he added after a brief pause. "It's a Saturday night, so it may take a while, but they'll be here."

When the EMTs finally arrived, they took Zane's vitals and pronounced him dead at the scene. Glancing down at his left hand, Jen was startled to see the gold band she had placed on his ring finger just two months before. While the medical technicians loaded Zane onto a stretcher, the Landrys gently approached Jen.

"We hate to do this," they said sheepishly, "but we've got to get Clyde to the emergency room. He's losing blood and getting weaker. The cops are on the way. Will you be okay here by yourself?"

"Um, yes, I think so," Jen nodded weakly, glancing down at Zane.

After running over to their house to get jackets, Tilman and Patsy loaded the heroic but bloody Clyde into the back of their SUV. Off they sped to Vegas Valley Pet Hospital, where surgeons promptly removed the bullet lodged in his shoulder. A few days later, the Landrys brought their beloved canine home. Clyde did recover, but he limped for the rest of his life.

CHAPTER 42

When the police arrived at the Conovers' driveway, they picked up Zane's gun, with latex-gloved hands, and placed it in a plastic evidence-bag. They also urged Jen to go to the hospital to be checked out, but she refused. She was a bloody mess, dazed and shaken, but she was not actually injured, aside from some cuts and bruises. She did not want to endure the bright lights and intrusiveness of a hospital visit. She just wanted to go inside and rest until Brandi got home.

No one had been able to reach the frantically busy cocktail waitress. Four conventions were running that weekend at the Venetian, so the casino was packed. Plus, Brandi was working a private party in a massive ballroom, and didn't have access to her phone.

Inside the Conover home, a couple of officers remained with Jen and questioned her about what had happened. She mentioned Officer Bart Nolan, and they called him. He came right over.

Jen and he hadn't seen each other since the attempted kidnapping at Treasure Island five months earlier. Collapsing in his arms, she burst into tears. He comforted her and then assisted the other officers in interviewing her and filing the necessary reports.

"The gun will go to the lab," Officer Vince Rayman explained to Jen. "They'll check for fingerprints. If yours are found, we'll have to question you as a possible murder suspect. That's standard procedure."

"What?" Jen asked, almost fainting with shock.

Officer Nolan sprang to her defense.

"Zane Hollister was a two-bit thug with a rap sheet a mile long," he explained. "He's been stalking and harassing her for a year and a half.

"Two months ago, he kidnapped her at gun point, forced her to marry him in Reno, and sexually assaulted her. Somehow she got away. Tonight, he tried to kidnap her again. Clearly, Jen shot Hollister in self-defense. No charges should be filed against her by anyone."

Rayman responded with a mere shrug. Grabbing his jacket on the way out, he told Nolan, "I'll run all this by the captain. He'll have the final word on the charges."

"Don't worry about that hothead," Nolan assured a dazed Jen after he left. "He's just another macho rookie trying to score points with the captain to advance himself."

Gazing at Nolan, Jen nodded weakly. Sinking onto the sofa, she tried to rest, while Nolan and another cop asked more questions and filed more reports.

By 5 AM, an exhausted Brandi was cruising

down Rosita Way in her white Ford Fiesta. She tried to park in her driveway, until she spotted the flurry of yellow crime-scene tape and dried blood stains. Crying out in panic, she parked her car, jumped out, and sprinted into the house.

"What happened? Who are you?" she barked at Nolan the minute she got inside. "Where's Jen? Is she alright?"

"Mom, I'm right here," Jen said, bursting into tears as she sat up on the couch.

"You're all covered with blood!" Brandi gasped, dropping down beside her and inspecting her blood-stained hair, sweater, and jeans.

"What happened to your clothes, honey? Why do you look like this?" she asked.

"Mom, where were you?" Jen cried, staring at Brandi. "We tried to call you. It's Zane," she said, between sobs. "He tried to take me again. He had a gun." Then in terrifying spasms, she recounted the nightmare she had miraculously survived.

As she finished, an incredulous Brandi's eyes widened.

"You shot Zane with his own gun?" she asked.

"Yes," Jen replied, nodding slowly, still trying to take it in herself.

"That goddam son of a bitch!" Brandi raged, throwing her hands up. "Where is he now?"

Stepping forward, Nolan introduced himself and informed Brandi that Zane had been pronounced dead a few hours earlier in the driveway.

"He's probably at the morgue by now, transported by EMTs a few hours ago. The coroner will take it from here."

Staring at Jen, Brandi buried her head in her hands and started crying. The thought that her daughter had killed someone, even the reprehensible Zane, completely unhinged her. It would take some getting used to. Jen, meanwhile, had crumpled back into a fetal-ball position on the couch.

Nolan suddenly felt like he was intruding. Checking his watch, he announced, "My shift's over, ladies, and my wife's waiting. I'll check in with you later today to see how you're doing."

CHAPTER 43

The death of Zane Hollister had been unnerving and messy, and so was its aftermath. Once the shock wore off, Brandi was relieved, but still furious that her daughter had been subjected to yet another gut-wrenching trauma.

"If the cops had done their job in the first place," she fumed to Nick days later, over coffee at the kitchen table, "Zane would have been behind bars and none of this would have happened.

"Then Jen was questioned like she was the criminal. Those cops were so concerned about the way Zane died. It was all about his rights. Who was holding the gun, who pulled the trigger, who was on the ground, whose fingerprints were where.

"Just look at Zane's record of crimes and abuses against Jen," she went on, "and it's plain as day she shot him in self-defense. Any idiot could see that."

"Brandi," Nick tried to explain, setting his coffee cup down and patting her hand. "This is all about department procedures. When you're a cop, you have to do things by the book, or the captain comes down on you. Those are the rules. Jen's in a good position. Thanks to Bart Nolan, there won't be any charges. The questioning is just a formality. Everyone has to go through it."

Despite Nick's kind words, Brandi was still outraged. The papers and TV news had all covered Zane's death, and Jen's name was blasted around town. She was being described everywhere as "the pop-out-girl femme-fatale who works at Stripper Grams."

"What happened is awful, for you and your ex," Destiny conceded when she called Jen the week after Zane's death. "But on the other hand, our phones have been ringing off the hook. Everyone and their mother wants you to pop out of their next cake. It's great publicity for the company."

Then she added, "you're going to have to watch the other girls when you come back. They're jealous of all the attention you're getting. Your pictures have been all over the papers, and you look really hot."

Taking a deep breath, Jen rolled her eyes.

"Um, Destiny, that's nice," she murmured. "It will be good to return to work and get my life back on track."

Jen then asked for a couple of weeks off. Destiny agreed, reluctantly, and made it clear that the general manager of Stripper Grams wanted her back as soon as possible.

Not everyone was so impressed by Jen's newfound notoriety. Kacey Hollister was devastated that her big brother had been killed by his "alleged wife and trampy obsession." In a drunken rage, she called Jen one night and unloaded on her.

"You murdered my brother in cold blood!" she shrieked, boozed-up and in tears. "My mom had a stroke a few days later. We didn't even know Zane was in town. Now his kids have no one. They're in the custody of child protective services, and they'll end up in separate foster homes. Just know this, bitch: you destroyed their lives."

Jen returned fire, yelling, "Zane is the one who ruined my life. He forced me into a marriage I didn't want, and drugged and raped me in a Reno hotel room. My boyfriend ended up dumping me. He couldn't take the stalking and terrorizing any more. Zane's toxic jealousy made my life a living hell!"

Then she added, "He's the one who caused all the problems in your family, not me. Don't call me again. My lawyer told me not to speak to you!"

Slamming the phone down, Jen burst into tears. She had deeply conflicted feelings about killing Zane. There was a sense of relief, of course, but also revulsion that she had taken the life of another human being, even though he was a threat to hers.

The day after Zane's shocking death, Megan Quinby, in town for the week from Atlanta, heard the latest on Vegas's local news. From her hotel suite at Bellagio, she tried to call Brandi to offer help. But Brandi's cell was turned off and her message queue full. Then Megan dialed Colton in San Jose to relay the traumatic developments.

"Oh my God," he exclaimed, trying to process the news, "at least the ongoing nightmare is over. I'll send Jen flowers. I feel sorry for her. Maybe if she'd had a different kind of childhood, with fewer stepfathers and someone steady and reliable like Matt steering her in the right direction, her life would have turned out differently and we wouldn't be having this conversation."

"Yes," Megan agreed, sighing. "Things have gone in that same troubling way for Brandi, too. She's got that same fey, lost quality, the ultimate waif-woman. Beautiful but doomed. Kind of like her mom, Paulina, the Waffle-House waitress who ran off with the minister. It's those green-eyed Putnam women. Mom always says they're cursed."

"Well, cursed or not," Colton retorted, "look where Matt ended up. Zane Hollister is supposedly the one who shot him, but he was really aiming for me. Now Zane's dead, shot by Jen. It's just a senseless, hopelessly tangled mess."

"I agree," Megan said. "The worst part of all of this is that Matt's in a coma, and has been for over a year. If only that night at Piero's hadn't happened. If only Matt had been spared those bullets. If only he would come out of the coma and just be the same great guy he's always been," Megan went on, her voice trembling a bit and then trailing off.

"Hang in there, Megan," Colton said, feeling her pain. "We all love Matt and need him. On some level he knows it, and he'll come back to us. He'll come back."

CHAPTER 44

Megan believed strongly in celebrating Matt's birthday. It was a way of reminding herself and everyone else, including the staff at Desert Oasis, that he was still an important part of their lives and very much loved. And so, when her brother turned 45 in October 2018, Megan flew to Vegas and invited both Conover ladies to a special dinner at Cornucopia in Bellagio.

That Tuesday night, Brandi and Jen arrived at the elite eatery at 6 PM for an early dinner. Both looked chic in silk pants outfits with brightly colored tank tops. Megan showed up in a Kelly-green shirt-waist dress, accessorized with classic pearls and pumps.

After warm hugs, the ladies were shown to a quiet corner table elegantly set with fine China and silver.

"So, how's your mother doing?" Jen asked, looking around warily after the trio ordered drinks and appetizers. "She's not in town this week, is she?"

"No, no," Megan assured her. "She's back in San

Jose, taking care of her grandsons and running QuInternet with, um, um..."

"Relax, Megan," Jen told her, patting her arm. "You can say Colton's name. I won't fall apart or anything. How's he doing?"

"He's doing great," she replied. "Very busy with work. He just got back from Hong Kong, where he's putting together a mega-deal for the company. Mom is beyond thrilled."

"Oh, that's nice," Jen said. "Is he, uh, dating anyone? Sorry to get into the personal stuff, but he doesn't call me anymore. I haven't seen Colton in months, even though I know he's been here to visit Matt."

"It's okay, Jen," Megan replied. "Colton is dating someone. She's a systems analyst from the UK, who's working at QuInternet on a two-year assignment. She's attractive, dynamic, and smart as a whip. Top of her class at Oxford."

Brandi and Jen looked at each other and sighed as Megan went on.

"Mom got them together after she hired Daphne at a tech conference in London, and moved her over here. They've been dating a few months. Mom says it's going well, but I can tell you, Jen, that Colton still asks about you all the time. It's not like he's forgotten you or anything."

"Oh, that's nice," Jen murmured, looking down sadly as she tried to absorb the shocking but Inevitable news about her former boyfriend.

"What a jerk!" Brandi bristled, as she spread pate on a slice of French bread. "The way he dumped Jen over the Zane stuff was disgraceful. And, guess what? Zane is no longer with us, thank God. He has moved on big time, and hopefully will burn in hell for all the people he hurt.

"Can you believe it? After all Jen went through with that psycho-loser, Colton dropped her like a hot potato. Classy, huh? It was like a double heartbreak."

"Mom, please, you're embarrassing me," Jen said.

"Sorry, honey," Brandi told her, "I'm just telling it like it is."

"So, Jen, what about you?" Megan asked. "How's everything at work? Are you dating anyone?"

"Everything at Stripper Grams is cool," Jen replied. "There were so many conventions this summer, it was like one long pop-out!

"On the dating front, there's not much to report. After all that happened with Zane and Colton, I'm taking things slow."

"Oh, don't listen to her!" Brandi retorted. "She has so many men chasing after her. The owner of Stripper Grams, Chuck Tyson, is trying to date her. But she won't give him the time of day."

"Mom, he's in his forties, and has been divorced three times," Jen said, rolling her eyes.

"So, what's wrong with that?" Brandi cracked. "I'm in my forties, I've been divorced three times, and I'm still sane, fun to be with, and desirable. People make mistakes, honey. They learn from them and move on. You should give him a chance, Jen. He's richer than hell, with a mansion in Santa Barbara and a big estate in Henderson. You're crazy to not go out with him."

"Mom, I'm considering it, okay?"

Brandi took a deep breath.

"Meanwhile, she insists on seeing a guy named Todd Rome, who's in the Thunder From Down Under show at Excalibur," Brandi barreled on. "Not only is he a male stripper and former porn star, but he's married to a woman in Australia, and has a second wife in San Diego. And he's the one Jen chooses to go out with. Why, honey, why?" an exasperated Brandi asked, throwing her hands up.

"We're not dating," Jen said, shaking her head and turning to Megan. "Todd knows my friend, Amber, and her fiancé, Dave. We all go out for pizza sometimes. That's it, really. There's no big romance, Mom! Why don't you let me run my own love life already, okay?"

"We tried that, sweetheart, and it didn't go so well, did it?" Brandi shot back. "I came home from work at 5 AM one Sunday to crime-scene tape in my driveway, blood all over the place, and cops in my living room questioning you about Zane.

"And then, look at what happened with Colton. The way he danced away and moved on to someone else. I'm sure she's not as beautiful, sweet, or talented as you, Jen. But bottom line, he's with her, not you.

"You've made some really bad life-choices, starting with Zane. And now his sister is threatening to have you charged with murder. When will it end?"

"Is that true, Jen?" an alarmed Megan asked, turning to her.

"No, it's not," Jen answered. "I've checked with Metro, and they say I'm in the clear, for now.

"I can't worry about the crazy stuff coming out of Kacey Hollister's mouth," she added. "My job is to get up every day, look in the mirror, and like the person I see. Sometimes it's not so easy. I'm still trying to deal with the fact that I shot Zane in our driveway, and then Colton dumped me.

"I need some time to process all that. Years, maybe. In the meantime, if I want to have pizza with Amber and Todd, I will, okay, Mom? Give me a break!"

"Sorry, Megan," Brandi said, shaking her head. "You see how it is with us. We go round and round in circles. We don't mean to air our dirty laundry over the dinner table."

"It's okay," Megan said. "Typical mother-daughter stuff. Mom and I get into our share of arguments, too.

"So, Brandi, what about you?" she asked. "What's going on in your life? How's the job? Are you dating anyone?"

"My job is fine," she replied. "I'm busier than ever, but I'm not dating. After all these years, and so many disappointments and failures in the love department, I'm hoping for a do-over with Matt, if and when he comes out of the coma.

"We were happy as kids," she went on wistfully. "If we can just get together again, recapture those feelings, and somehow make it work, that would be my idea of happily-ever-after-a-la-mode!"

All three ladies nodded and smiled.

Over many glasses of pricey Sauvignon Blanc

and soothing entrees of creamy lemon-chicken with rice, the drama queen dinner rolled on. As the plates were being cleared, Megan suddenly announced, "No dessert for anyone. I ordered a chocolate birthday cake from the bakery. We'll take it to Desert Oasis. It's Matt's favorite. After we sing happy birthday to him, we'll cut a few slices and give the rest to the staff."

"Works for us," Brandi said, glancing over at Jen.

The ladies sauntered into Desert Oasis around 9 PM. They were all a bit tipsy and feeling celebratory as they approached Matt's room. For 19 long months, he'd been in a coma. It was very discouraging for the three of them. They all loved and needed him, and had stood by him, reading, talking, playing his favorite music, and even singing to him through the endless days and nights. But so far, their efforts had all fallen short. Nothing, it seemed, could rouse Matt from the deep, sleep-like-state that shielded him from consciousness. Even the doctors were helpless. They could do nothing, nor could they explain his agonizing plight.

And then at long last, with hope wavering, the miracle that everyone was praying for finally happened. Matt Quinby, amazingly, showed signs of awakening on his 45th birthday.

Around his bed the three ladies gathered. Megan was holding the cake as they all sang the birthday song. Then, without warning or provocation, his eyelids began fluttering, ever so gently. The ladies all stopped singing, stared hard, and moved closer.

Their cries of joy were muted by astonishment,

as if they were witnessing a miracle. Slowly, Matt's eyes opened and he started to look around. On one side of his bed, his sister was leaning towards him, smiling broadly and calling his name. Brandi and Jen were on the other side, jumping for joy and doing the same.

Matt smiled back and gazed at them all, his blue eyes lingering on each. It was the best birthday of his life. He was finally home again.

ABOUT THE AUTHOR

Luckily for all you fans of romantic fiction, Irene Woodbury knows that what happens in Las Vegas doesn't have to stay there. The Denver-based author has captured the heart and soul of Sin City in her colorful, suspenseful novel, Romeo Stalker (2021). Irene, a successful travel writer whose favorite destinations are London and Las Vegas, is currently working on another novel.